Bubba and the Dead Woman

By

C.L. Bevill

Table of Contents

Chapter One

Bubba and the Dead Woman

Thursday through Friday

The eleven hours and twenty-odd minutes immediately preceding Bubba Snoddy's discovery of a dead woman in his backyard had been disagreeable. Disagreeable was a somewhat mild term that Bubba's mother would have used instead of the foul and blasphemous string of words that Bubba actually used.

At approximately eight PM on Thursday, Bubba stopped in to see if the day mechanic needed a hand with a malfunctioning Chevy Camaro. Bubba found out that he had become the head mechanic in charge of Bufford's Gas and Groceries at the bottom of the exit ramp from Interstate 38. The day mechanic's abrupt departure was due to greener pastures at the Walmart Supercenter fifteen miles up the road, and what that really meant was Bubba had become the *only* mechanic in charge of Bufford's Gas and Grocery. More precisely and adding to no little part of Bubba's general irritation, he was the *only employee* there that night.

Upon Bubba's arrival, a clerk named Billie Jo hauled butt from the store to play bingo at the local Methodist church, peeling out of the parking lot in an old clunker that didn't appear capable of being able to go from 0 – 60 mph in a week. She was in a hurry because money was to be had at Super Bingo in the amount of $500 per game and up. She didn't care to wait for the swing shift clerk, thinking incorrectly that Bubba could handle the store for a few minutes. However, the swing shift clerk, a boy named Mark Evans who was a nineteen-year-old college student from Pegramville Community College, called in to quit about five minutes after Billie Jo's departure. Mr. Evans ranted and railed at Bubba, as if Bubba were George Bufford, the not-so-kindly owner of the Bufford Gas and Grocery. There was a significant amount of profanity involved from the telephone end of the student who invited Bubba to inform George Bufford to place portions of his body inside other portions of his body that Bubba didn't rightly think would fit. There were also references to George's ancestry in general and his possible relationship to the canine family.

Bubba took the call in good humor until his calm demeanor obviously upset Mark Evans even more. The young man was keenly intent on a monumental exit from the prodigious gas and grocery sector. Then Mark grew angry and proceeded to recount his opinions on Bubba's own ancestry.

Bubba was a big man in life, standing six feet four inches and weighing close to two hundred and fifty pounds. He was quite positive that the absent Mark would not have been so vociferous in his telephonic epithet calling if he had been standing directly in front of that particular man. On the contrary, he would have been running swiftly away from the dark look that formed on Bubba's face when the subject of Bubba's mother was mentioned.

There was one witness to this sordid affair. She was a little old lady on her way to commit various nefarious acts of misdemeanors with great glee in her

6

heart. Mary Jean Holmgreen was going to a midnight rendezvous involving an illegal gambling circle organized by none other than Bubba Snoddy's own not-so-sainted mother, Demetrice Snoddy. Mary Jean stopped at the Bufford Gas and Grocery to pick up Cheetos when she had caught the so-very-interesting, if one-sided, conversation.

Bubba held the phone up to one ear while he tried to stuff the large bag of Cheetos into a grocery store bag too small to hold it. Mary Jean was one year shy of her eightieth birthday and was not so old that she couldn't appreciate the fine specimen of a man who stood before her, even if he was demolishing her Cheetos. Besides his portentous size, Bubba had the dark brown hair and cornflower blue eyes of his mother with the fine, well-favored features of his father.

The older woman briefly said a prayer thinking of Elgin Snoddy who was dead many years. He, himself, had been a superlative figure of a man, the proverbial tall, dark, and handsome of mysterious gothic novels. He had died long before his time, not even thirty-five years old. And there were all kinds of juicy whispers about his life and especially about his death. However, Mary Jean focused back on his son before her brain dissolved into silly memories and damned innuendo.

Bubba said forebodingly into the phone in his slow, Texan drawl, "I don't think that it's quite right for you to be talking about a woman behind her back."

Mary Jean stood up straight. *Gossip*, she thought. It was hard to be a prim and proper Texan lady with all the gossip to be had in such a small, east Texas town as Pegramville. It was a trial for her each and every day. The Lord Himself surely did not approve of gossips, and Mary Jean's own mother had held that there was a special place in Hell for gossips where they burned as though sixteen fires had been lit under their behinds and people they could not quite hear whispered things about them that they ached to hear but never would. So she leaned closer so that she might hear what the person on the other end of the telephone was saying.

Bubba finally successfully jammed the bag of Cheetos in the too-small grocery bag with a loud crunching noise that denoted the demise of hapless snack-foods. While he was staring down at the top of the compacted bag of Cheetos, the reply over the phone came clearly to Mary Jean as if her dainty ears, with hearing aids inserted, were pressed up against the phone themselves. The hysterical, high-pitched tones of a young man came through, loudly inviting Bubba to kiss his...

"Oh, dear," muttered Mary Jean. Then, by muttering something she missed the remainder of what was said. But then Mary Jean muttered again as Bubba's face grew positively black with anger. She took a step backward and felt one of her support hose slip precariously down her knee. She clearly recalled what a terrible temper Elgin Snoddy had possessed and the rumors about Bubba's mother, Demetrice, having to wear long-sleeved dresses and scarves about for extended periods of time after one of his drunken fits. Although a good-looking man, the deceased Elgin Snoddy had not been the best tempered of men. Mary Jean recalled many a time when Elgin had come to town stinking of rum and covered with dirt from head to toe as if he had been digging a hole to China. *More rumors*, she thought, and then hastily brought her attention back to Bubba to hear the remainder of succulent tidbits.

"Now why would I want to kiss that?" Bubba asked, clearly perplexed, the flagitious look evaporating from his face. He finally made eye contact with Mary Jean and shrugged apologetically. He reached for a container of chocolate-chocolate fudge flavored ice cream and laboriously entered numbers into the cash register; his large fingers were too big for the keys. The cash register made a strangled noise as if it were genuinely confused or dying and abruptly stopped.

Bubba peered closely at the cash register and asked to the person on the other end of the phone, "Don't suppose you know how to make the cash register unstick?"

There was a burst of indignant sound from the phone and then an abrupt dial tone. Bubba took the receiver away from his ear, gave it an uncertain look, and hung it up. Then he found a bag that fit properly over the ice cream and stuck it in. "Sorry about that, Miz Mary Jean." Then he put the bottle of Thunderbird in beside the ice cream.

Mary Jean stepped to the counter again and primly supervised Bubba's loading of her groceries. "That is not a problem. But Bubba..."

"Yes, Ma'am."

"I wouldn't be associating with a young person who would repeat such profanity to one such as yourself."

Bubba's fine features clouded up for a moment. "I wasn't exactly associating with him." One large fist came crashing down on the cash register forcefully. Mary Jean almost squealed until she realized the

Bubba was merely trying to get the cash register to work. On the other hand, Bubba knew exactly what kind of big mouth Mary Jean was and did not care to explain away the anger of one Mark Evans, late an employee of Bufford Gas and Grocery. Since Bubba had not an earthly clue as to why Mark was so infuriated with George Bufford, he wasn't about to pass that information on so that half the town of Pegramville would be yakking on the subject at their morning constitutions. Bubba did suppose that George wasn't inclined to work out mutually convenient hours for college students such as the inimitable Mark Evans, and thus, that individual did not feel kindly toward the former. But that was none of Mary Jean's business. None of his own as well, except that that young man had seen fit to make it so.

Bubba smiled with a blinding amount of white teeth when the register came to life again, clicking and whirring loudly. He ruefully glanced up at Mary Jean. "Damn, new-fangled, computerized gadgets, Miz Holmgreen. This place is going to be in an awfully lot of trouble if we ever get nuked by some damn other country we riled all up."

"Bubba Snoddy," Mary Jean admonished, "Pegramville will undoubtedly survive, as will the remainder of these lesser 48 states." Her voice lowered a bit, "I cain't honestly say about Hawaii and Alaska. You never know when those Russians will get their moxies up again and take back that land they sold us." She nodded firmly. Then she added in a low, conspiratorial whisper indicating the terrible meaning of thing she uttered, "Communists."

Bubba glanced at the cash register, not concerned with any communist not immediately in front of him waving a hammer, a sickle, and an AK-47. "Believe it's about ten dollars and fifty cents, Miz Holmgreen," he told the older woman amicably. Briefly, he wondered just what was going on at these damned poker parties his mother organized that required Cheetos, cheap wine, and ice cream. Then he decided he didn't really want to know.

"That sounds about right," Mary Jean ascertained, regally regaining her composure, and handed Bubba a ten dollar bill. She extracted a change purse from the cavernous bag hanging at her side and meticulously counted out fifty cents in three dimes, three nickels, and five pennies. Bubba took the whole lot and threw it haphazardly in the register.

"Let me carry those out for you, Miz Holmgreen," Bubba offered, picking up bags and walking around the counter. There wasn't another customer to be had in the small shop on a warm, moist night in this late spring.

Mary Jean's mind was a-ponder on gossip that could be passed along to the next large-eared individual she met. She knew that the big, handsome Bubba was dating the beautiful Miss Lurlene Grady, the waitress down at the Pegramville Café. But somehow, she didn't think that the phone call had anything to do with Miss Lurlene. *Too bad*, she considered. Gossip was much more lurid when it involved sex, drugs, and illicit affairs. She brightened. Of course, her retelling of the incident might include such things. Then there was the oddest thing about Miss Lurlene. Damned if the cute blonde didn't remind Mary Jean of someone, but she couldn't think of whom. *Oh, well.*

11

Bubba held the glass doors open for her and cast a look back over his shoulders at something. "Now, Precious," he began in a pained voice.

"I beg your pardon," enthused Mary Jean, cutting him off. Had Bubba just called her precious? Just wait until she told Mabel Jean down at the hardware store. Almost eighty years old and she still had a little pizzazz.

"My dog, Miz Holmgreen," he explained, jerking a thumb back at the door that he had shut firmly behind them, "her name is Precious." A big Basset hound suddenly appeared and pressed its nose against the glass like a moth drawn to a flame. Ears flew up and everywhere as the dog went left and right trying to faithfully follow her owner out of the store but was hindered by the closed doors. Finally, she sat down and proceeded to slobber over the glass as she watched the two humans just outside her dogly reach. Her large brown eyes were intent on every move that Bubba made. A moment after that, she apparently decided that this was an unacceptable situation and began to howl, baying in a way that only hounds can. "My dog don't go nowhere without me. She's of a mind to think I'm gonna up and leave her in the store every time I go out to pump gas and such."

A few minutes later, Mary Jean was on her way to a wild and raucous game of poker, as Bubba was well aware, leaving him by himself. Billie Jo was undoubtedly punching bingo cards galore with large neon orange markers and George Bufford was off on a vacation to the Bahamas with his secretary. Everyone knew that except for Shirlee Bufford, George's wife, who thought he had gone to a business convention in Minnesota. So Bubba was on his own. The more he was by himself, the more irritated he got because he knew he could be completing the work on the awaiting vehicles that were sitting only feet away from him in various car comas from which they might never awake.

His evening had started with an angry teenager screaming epithets at him over the phone and only got worse. Fifteen minutes after Mary Jean had left, two teenagers he didn't know came in and tried to use a fake identification to buy beer. They wanted to argue with him until he shifted the stool behind the counter and stood up. One of them looked up at Bubba with an awestruck expression on his face, indicating something along the line of holy-crap-it-blocked-out-the-sun. He said, "Uh, we'll buy it someplace else, mister."

"Hey!" Bubba yelled when they were halfway out the door. Both teenage boys looked back at Bubba, wincing. "Don't you drink and drive, y'hear?"

"Shithead," commented one of the boys. The other one hauled ass for their beat-up Mustang parked at one of the gas pumps. The first one followed at light speed when Bubba warningly rose up off the stool again. Neither one saw the quick smile that passed over his lips.

Bubba had better things to do than to mind the cash register. He had old Mr. Smith's transmission to rebuild and some kind of clanking problem with Bryan McGee's Ford truck. He drove it; it made a noise akin to an old, liquor still about to explode. I.e., something was wrong with the truck. And Bubba didn't even want to mention the broken down Camaro. But no one was at the register, and Bufford Gas and Grocery stayed open twenty-four hours a day, seven days a week, three hundred and sixty-five days a year. Even the garage side of the business was supposed to be open, not that most decent folks brought their broken cars into the place at three AM.

Looking around for a calling list of other Bufford employees, Bubba had finally found one. He considered calling Mrs. Shirlee Bufford. But he knew he couldn't look her in the face without thinking of old George doing the wild thing in the Bahamas with his secretary, Rosa Granado, a woman some twenty years younger and twenty inches smaller in the waist than the missus. Bubba sure hoped that George's insurance was paid up because Rosa was going to kill him one way or another.

In any case, Bubba called the relief cashier only to listen to a nonstop ringing on the other end. He finally decided that he would tend the damned register, even if he didn't have a clue of how it worked and let the clerk in the morning clear up any mess he made. He would make up the work on Bryan McGee's truck and Mr. Smith's Mercury the following night. To hell with the Camaro.

At half past ten, Lloyd Goshorn came rambling in for smokes. He was the town jack-of-all-trades and not one to keep to banker's hours. He leaned his rickety frame over the counter after purchasing two packs of Marlboros and discussed the humidity as related to his fifty-year old bones. Bubba nodded once or twice, said, "Uh-huh," once, and even once asked, "Is that right?" Old Lloyd wasn't a bad sort. He looked for honest work, did a trustworthy job, and didn't pass out drunk on the town square like the town mayor had done the previous Fourth of July. Lloyd even did a chore or two for Bubba's mother, Miz Demetrice, when Bubba was too busy to take care of the housely business.

14

Whilst Lloyd was talking about possibly having gout and the agony of an ingrown toe nail, a car pulled up to a gas pump on the outermost islands. Bubba half stood up to peer over Lloyd's gangly shoulder. Lloyd didn't budge, but merely shifted his smokes around between his hands, and continued to speak about various home remedies for relief of various ailments. "...Favor taking coffee grounds at least five days old, mind you, combined with boiled dandelion juice, then..."

The driver got out of the car and fiddled with the pump some. Bubba glanced over at the computerized do-hickey and saw that the driver had used the pay-at-the-pump option with a credit card. But he stared over Lloyd's shoulder until the other man finally noticed.

"That's a rental," he said thoughtfully.

Bubba glanced at Lloyd with surprise. "How'd you know that, Lloyd?"

"Stickers on the bumper from the company. Hertz," he said genially.

It wasn't the car that Bubba was intent on but the driver. For a second, in the fluorescent lights that lit up the islands out on the asphalt, he had thought that she was someone he had known from awhile back. Her hair was blonde in the dim light, no doubt about that, a light honey blonde, and there was something about the way she moved. It put a knot deep down in the pit of Bubba's stomach that threatened to grow like a cancerous tumor.

The other man was saying, "...You know her?"

Lloyd finally determined that the younger man's concentration was fully lost in the customer outside. A few seconds later Bubba figured out that Lloyd had asked if he knew the woman.

15

Staring at the lonely shape by the gas pumps, Bubba finally shook his head. There was no point in dredging up memories of three years past. He didn't know that woman. Nope. He didn't want to know her. "Naw, Lloyd," he drawled.

Lloyd knew of every woman under the age of forty in Pegram County. His purely male mind spent a significant amount of time categorizing women. And he most certainly knew of all the blondes. He glanced over his shoulder and then back at Bubba Snoddy, positive that he didn't know that particular one. "Someone you knew from the Army?"

Bubba shrugged. It didn't matter now.

Not one for long farewells and intent on catching the middle half of The Tonight Show, Lloyd took the opportunity to grab his smokes and slide out the door before Bubba even said goodbye. Bubba watched as the woman approached Lloyd on the far side of the asphalt, and they talked for a moment. She was standing in the shadows, and Bubba couldn't rightly get a good look at her face. Lloyd motioned eagerly left and right, pointing as they spoke. It dawned on Bubba that Lloyd was giving the woman driving directions. She thanked him with a wave of her hand and went back to her car. Lloyd watched and then shuffled off toward his ramble-shack home a mile down the freeway.

On the floor beside the stool that Bubba sat on, Precious snored away, her paws twitching as she dreamed of all things canine. The rental car's lights came on, and the woman drove off, leaving Bubba to think of things in the past. These were things he didn't care to be thinking of, but there wasn't a damn thing he could do to prevent the thoughts from trickling into his mind as he sat in the silent and lonely gas and grocery store.

As it turned out, he didn't have a single customer until well after midnight, and that one, Martha Lyles, an elementary school teacher, had awoken from a dream about winning the lottery. She had felt compelled to come down to the store in her bunny slippers to immediately purchase the numbers of which she had dreamt. It had taken Bubba a good twenty minutes and a lot of help from Martha to figure out how to work the machine that dispensed lottery tickets.

Bubba lost any good humor he had left when a couple of drunks drove into Bufford's Gas and Grocery around two AM, intent on purchasing cheap beer and pretzels. Bubba didn't care to let these two on the road and wouldn't let them leave until they had called a cab to pick them up, leaving their Dodge truck in one of Bufford's undersized parking places. After that, there hadn't been another customer until five AM, when the earliest working folks began to trickle in to buy coffee and donuts that they didn't have to make themselves.

Coffee, Bubba felt sure, was the one thing he could do, after he spent about thirty minutes looking for filters and coffee grounds. Unfortunately, when the coffee began to percolate it smelled as though something had died in the coffee pot, rather than redolent from the fresh aroma of coffee beans.

Only an hour late, Leelah Wagonner wandered in at seven AM sharp to relieve the night shift, finding a grumpy Bubba behind the counter, money sticking haphazardly out of the cash register, and Precious snoring to Kingdom Come underneath Bubba's feet.

Bubba had a look on his face that indicated that not only was he unhappy, but that he was also not pleased.

Leelah, a married woman of five years with two toddlers causing havoc back at her mama's house while Leelah's husband, Mike, worked at the manure factory, deduced correctly that Bubba Snoddy was highly irate and agitated. She was late because of her kids deciding that tennis shoes made dandy containers for mud pies, and Bubba did not look thrilled to hear her hastily muttered explanation.

"Where's Mark Evans?" she asked carefully, studying burns on Bubba's arms that could only come from the hot dog machine. She knew because she had gotten some herself when she had first started working at Bufford's. And she was uncertain why Bubba Snoddy had thought to fill that machine up so early in the day when it would most probably go to waste.

If Leelah had asked, Bubba would have said he had put the hot dogs in because of some low-carb-minded idiot who demanded one of the all-beef weenies for his breakfast, sans bun. Bubba thought that was the culmination of his day because he determined that the hot dog machine was a diabolical machine invented by satanic hands in order to ruin mankind. It had finally become obvious to even Bubba that one was not supposed to insert one's arms into the innards of the devilish device. His dark eyebrows drew together in a fierce frown, and he finally answered Leelah's question. "He quit."

"Why didn't you call Mary Bradley?"

"I did."

"So she didn't come in?" she said cautiously.

"Mary didn't answer the phone," Bubba said softly. Precious woke up and began to bay softly, sensitive occasionally to her master's moods.

"Uh, Bubba," Leelah felt compelled to observe, "If the Health Department comes in and sees that dog in here, we're going to hell in a hand basket."

Bubba gave Precious a nudge toward the door. "As far as I'm concerned," he called back over his shoulder, "we're already there."

Leelah, in all of her twenty-three years on the planet Earth, had never seen such a mess as what Bubba Snoddy had left in Bufford's Gas and Grocery. The cash register was awry. There was a hot dog stuck in the self-propelled mechanism of the hot dog display. Coffee was strewn on the floor from the cash register to the back store room. Furthermore, the coffee smelled like an unholy cauldron from a witch's circle. She shrugged and began to clean things up before the big morning crowd came in. She only briefly looked out the large, glass windows when Bubba revved up the engine in his old truck and peeled out onto the highway, leaving a trail of rubber ten feet long. Neither he nor Precious ever looked back at Bufford's.

Twenty minutes later he pulled into the Snoddy family estate. It consisted of an antebellum mansion, replete with columns, flaking paint, and the odd termite, and a caretaker's house out back. The caretaker's house used to be a stable but was converted just after World War II. Elgin Snoddy's father, Lionel, had wanted to rent it out to soldiers stationed at nearby Fort Dimson and make a few bucks in the process. All he really accomplished was to convert a perfectly good stable into an oddball residence, which most normal folks didn't care to rent anyway.

The grounds were still inundated with the last century's plush gardening and landscaping. There was even a koi pond out back with koi that had grown into the size of trout and a whole mess of water lilies that threatened to take over the entire pond. It was all Bubba could do to keep up with trimming the yard and gardens out of complete wilderness. He noticed with dismay that if he didn't get his weed whacker out soon the weeds were going to take over the front veranda of the Snoddy mansion, and a machete would be necessary to make one's way to the front door.

When Bubba parked his truck, he noticed with dismay that Miz Demetrice had a visitor whose car was parked on the side of the mansion. A visitor whose blue Honda sedan had Hertz stickers on the sides, he observed with a growing sense of something he couldn't quite identify. No, wait, he could identify it. Anger. It had been her.

Obviously, Miz Demetrice had taken her right in, probably even dragged her over to the poker game too, he thought. But there was a hesitation. It was after ten PM when he had seen the young woman at Bufford's. Miz Demetrice should have been long gone from the Snoddy residence and probably wouldn't come back until every woman over the age of fifty in Pegram County had lost their sewing monies and most likely some welfare cash as well. Certainly, Bubba hadn't seen Miz Demetrice crawl back into the mansion before noon after most poker nights.

Bubba got out of the truck and let Precious clamber down as well. Almost instantly, the dog began to howl again, snorting at the ground and shuffling

20

around. She began to sniff around a pair of boots sticking out of the tall weeds at the side of the caretaker's house. Then she fixed her master with a look that fully indicated that he should also come and take a sniff.

Bubba took a step over toward the boots and realized that they were attached to legs. Then the legs were attached to a torso. And the torso was attached to a...

A man appeared beside Bubba and looked down at what had Bubba dumbstruck. Precious barked at the man and backed off a ways, variously baying and barking as she saw fit. Bubba glanced up and saw Neal Ledbetter, the real estate agent who had been pestering Miz Demetrice for months about selling the Snoddy lands, or at least what was left of the Snoddy lands. Neal had walked from the front of the property where he had parked his Lincoln Continental after following Bubba's truck down the road a bit. Neal never was one to let it be said that he didn't take every opportunity to talk a potential client into a sale.

That man gazed down at the woman at their feet with an expression akin to pure befuddlement. Finally, Neal, not the most smart and congenial of fellas, looked back at Bubba and stated, "Bubba, that woman is as dead as road kill."

Chapter Two

Bubba and the Sheriff

Friday

While Bubba Snoddy was standing wordlessly over the dead woman, Neal Ledbetter extracted a compact, cellular phone, and made a call to 911. Bubba barely heard the real estate agent saying to the emergency operator, "Yep, Mary Lou, this is Neal Ledbetter down at the Snoddy's place. Yes, I am still trying to get them to sell their house. Well, you wouldn't believe how stubborn and obstinate that Miz Demetrice can be. You would? You remember the time that she chained herself to the cannon in the town square? You know the one the mayor passed out next to? Yeah. That was...oh, yeah, there's a dead woman out here at the Snoddys' place."

Bubba took a half-stumbling step backward, suddenly discomfited in his realization of how short life was and how the past had come back to bite him on his proverbial white cheeks. Precious stopped her baying and approached her master with doglike concern. He hunkered down and put his hand on Precious's head. The dog butted his hand in order to promote the proper human-dog social interaction of petting. He absently scratched behind one of her large, floppy ears and then behind the other. One of her hind legs scratched air in gleeful assistance.

In the background, Neal was saying, "It's the damnedest thing. She looks like she's been shot in the back...Because she is on her stomach lying down, Mary Lou. I can see where she's been shot. I was in the Marines for four years. I know what a gunshot looks like...no, I never shot anyone when I was in the service. So the sheriff's on his way, hmm? Good, what else has been happening? Someone broke into the library last week? Well, damn, what fer? Scattered around some of the old records? That sounds pretty stupid. Damned kids. Did you hear about George Bufford and his secretary, Hot Rosa?"

Bubba might have listened but his mind was in another world altogether. There was a dead woman lying in the tall grass in front of his house. But not only that, he knew this dead woman. He had known her for years, although he hadn't seen her for the last three.

Her name had been Melissa Dearman. When he had first met her it had been Melissa Connor. Now she lay in the grass like a discarded toy. Her face was turned toward him, long honey-blonde hair spilling over her face and shoulders. What was truly disturbing was that her sky blue eyes were still open and staring just above her open mouth, a perfect 'O' of surprise. She seemed as though she had lain down in the grass a few minutes before and would bounce up any second now. Clad in blue jeans, a blue chambray shirt, and leather boots, she seemed as willowy and attractive as she had ever been.

Melissa hadn't changed. He reconsidered. *Except for being dead.* Death changed everything, no doubt about that.

Bubba's eyes went down her slim figure to that which had killed her. A bullet hole was prominent on her body, in the middle of her back, right between the shoulder blades, only a little blood staining the blue of

23

her clothing directly around the injury. He wasn't about to turn her over to see if there was an exit wound, but he expected there would be. It looked to be a large caliber weapon that had been used.

Bubba turned his head toward her neatly parked rental car. Melissa had gotten out of the vehicle, and then for some reason, the reason probably being some person with a large gun, had run toward the smaller house in the back. Long before she had reached what she might have thought was sanctuary, she had been ruthlessly shot in the back and died immediately. The tiny amount of blood about the wound told him that.

One of Bubba's large hands was still and leaden on Precious's head. She whimpered and retreated to a nearby tree to watch her master with an indignant look on her dogly face.

Finally, he stood up, and glanced over at Neal who finished his prolonged conversation with Mary Lou of the emergency line on how today's society was quickly descending into the seventh level of hell. Neal clicked the 'end' button on the cell phone and said, "Sheriff will be here P.D.Q., Bubba."

Bubba, Neal knew, was not a real talkative man, especially after he had returned from military service some three years before. It was Neal's personal opinion that the Snoddys, especially the matriarch, Miz Demetrice, were mostly a bunch of snobs who thought that their kaka didn't stink. Of course, this opinion was tainted by the fact that Demetrice had three times refused to sell any of the Snoddy lands to Neal's corporation, so that a Walmart Supercenter might be built here. The nearest one was fifteen miles away and Pegramville needed one, by God. It was, after all, the best location in the town, with plenty of room for a huge parking lot and a gardening section. It was dying, no pun intended, to be a Walmart, if only Neal could convince the Snoddys of that. There was also the additional advantage of this particular venue being legal unlike other suggestions that Neal had received lately.

However, Miz Demetrice had chased Neal off the front veranda with a shotgun over her arm the last time he had dared step on the property and threatened to give the realtor a 'shotgun enema' if he ever returned. *Where did a tiny old woman learn a phrase like that?* he wondered, awestricken.

But Neal wasn't the type to give up, and having noticed Bubba this morning driving in front of him in his old, battered truck with Precious slobbering in the wind, halfway out the passenger window, he had decided to give it the old college try. Certainly, Miz Demetrice wasn't getting any younger, and Bubba might inherit the properties any time, given the fact that enormous jet-liners were falling out of the sky each and every blessed day. An individual never knew when one might fall on Miz Demetrice's little, stuck-up head. So he parked his Lincoln Conny just in front of the big house and ambulated around the building to have an influencing word with the younger Snoddy.

Even so, there had come this other problem. A dead woman was lying in the grass in the garden of the Snoddy mansion with Bubba staring down at her as if he had never seen a woman before. Just as sure as anything Neal had ever seen.

Bubba took another long look at Melissa, stepped forward, leaned, and closed her eyes with the thumb and forefinger of his left hand. He didn't say a word.

Neal commented, "I don't think you should touch her, Bubba."

Quite frankly, Bubba didn't care what Neal Ledbetter thought. He snapped to his dog, "Precious! Heel!"

Precious's ears flopped as she obeyed. She recognized the tone of voice that her master had and wasn't about to disobey. She scampered up to Bubba and placed herself accordingly, just behind his feet.

Neal watched as Bubba and dog tromped off in the direction of the caretaker's house. Bubba entered the house and slammed the door with a resounding bang. The realtor looked around, surprised to be by himself. *Well*, he amended to himself, *me and a dead woman.* A little chill ran down his spine. He sure hoped that the sheriff would make it here quickly.

Bubba came back out of the caretaker's house with a sheet, throwing the door open with a loud thud. He reverently covered up the dead woman with the white cloth and went back inside. A few minutes later, he came back out with a large cup of coffee, Precious following at his heels. He set himself down in an Adirondack chair on the porch of the house with a large thumping noise that threatened the entire house. Precious scooted under the chair, peering suspiciously out at Neal, who was standing in the middle of the garden with a dumb look plastered across his face.

Neal, who could smell fresh coffee from five hundred feet, approached the porch as if there were a lit bomb sitting on it. His nose twitched and he moved toward the caretaker's house. He took one step onto the porch steps when Bubba said in a low but clear voice, "I wouldn't."

26

The realtor froze in place, one foot halfway to the second step. "Like to have a cup of coffee, Bubba, if I might." His own voice was almost a petrified squeak, breaking on 'might.'.

Bubba said, "Bufford's Gas and Grocery has fine coffee. Especially the pot I made this very morning." He gestured with his cup, not even looking at the other man. "It's thataway."

Neal retreated to the far side of the yard, to the position farthest away from the woman's body and Bubba, without actually being out of sight of both. Fortunately for his peace of mind, the sheriff drove up in a county car, even while he was retreating to his perceived position of safety.

Sheriff John Headrick was another big man. He stood a whopping six foot five inches and liked to add another inch by wearing cowboy boots with a little heel. He filled out his tan uniform as if he had been poured into it. His steel gray hair matched his steel gray eyes, which went along with his sun-grizzled face and skin. When he was mad, his flesh turned the exact shade of Pepto-Bismol. When he was coldly aloof, he had skin the color of weathered leather.

Known as Sheriff John to his loyal constituents and disloyal adversaries alike, he squeezed himself out of the county vehicle, studying the situation with a hardened look. He didn't miss the realtor standing in the shade of the big Snoddy place nor Bubba sipping coffee on the caretaker's porch. Finally, his eyes caught the stark white of the sheet covering the woman's body with its two pathetic boots sticking out of the long grass in the garden.

A few minutes later, he had her purse in his big hands flipping through her wallet. The rental car had been unlocked, with a woman's black purse sitting on the passenger seat for God and everyone to see. Here was her name, Sheriff John ascertained, and then just behind him, Bubba said, "Melissa Dearman."

Sheriff John looked up, his eyebrows growing together into one long piece. Neal was still skulking in the shadows, obviously cowed by Bubba's presence. But Bubba himself had silently risen from the porch, approaching the sheriff without him even hearing his footfalls.

It startled the older man and one of his hands twitched toward the pistol in his gun belt. Bubba watched the movement and stepped back with a calm and calculating look on his face. His large hands wrapped around the coffee for the other man to clearly see. Sheriff John returned his hand to the wallet and flipped it shut, replacing it into the purse with a smooth movement. "You know her, Bubba?" he asked.

"Yes," Bubba answered. He took another long drink of his steaming coffee. He didn't think he was going to be sleeping anytime soon and would need the caffeine.

Sheriff John's gray eyebrows rose up eloquently. He and Bubba stared at each other from similar heights. Bubba was one of the few men around Pegram County who could do so. Furthermore, he wasn't a man to be intimidated by the police, or the great man himself, Sheriff John Headrick.

"He was standing over her when I arrived," called Neal from the other side of the yard.

Sheriff John didn't look away from Bubba. "That so, Bubba?"

"I believe Mr. Ledbetter followed my truck almost all of the way from Bufford's, after I got off from work today," Bubba commented mildly.

"That true, Neal?"

"...Yeah." Neal didn't want to admit anything but did so grudgingly.

"Do you know what happened, Bubba?" asked Sheriff John, with a gesture toward the body.

"Did he read you his rights, Bubba Nathaniel Snoddy?" Miz Demetrice Snoddy shrieked from around the side of the sheriff's car. She had heard the news from Alice Mercer, who was active in the weekly poker games. Alice, in turn, had been called by her sister, Ruby, who had been walking her dog, Bill Clinton, when Foot Johnson had stopped in his car to tell her. Foot Johnson had been over at the county building cleaning the offices there when Mary Lou told him. Mary Lou, the operator of the emergency line, was widely known to have a large problem keeping her mouth shut about the goings on of Pegram County no matter how many times Sheriff John had warned her.

Consequently, Miz Demetrice had hauled her five-foot-nothing frame out of the ongoing poker game with a loud, "What on God's green earth is a-happening around this forsaken little pit?" and a "Wilma, don't you dare look at my cards, you chicanery artist!" Then she had driven like the dickens to reach the Snoddy place before Bubba was ruthlessly murdered in a senseless shootout involving twelve deputy sheriffs, one SWAT team, and three Pegramville police officers, as Alice had informed her were all front and present on her property.

Miz Demetrice looked around with a slight air of disappointment. To her immense disheartenment, there was only one police officer, one browbeaten real estate agent who was giving her the stinky eye, and a sheet covered lump with boots. "What is going on around here, Bubba?" she demanded of her son, shaking her purse at the man who towered over her.

"Dead woman," Sheriff John said succinctly. He towered over the petite Miz Demetrice as well, but he knew better than to get too close.

"Dead woman," repeated Miz Demetrice. She stood up straight in her best flower-print dress with her hat askew, as though she had simply come from church. Her white hair was crammed up under the hat, and the worry in her blue eyes belied the calm in her voice. She turned her slim figure toward the sheet-covered body in the garden. "There's a dead woman in my garden," she stated unequivocally.

"Yes'm," Sheriff John agreed solemnly. "Do you know who it is, Ma'am?"

"Sheriff John," Miz Demetrice gazed upon the much taller man with scorn, "that woman's got a sheet over her. How am I supposed to know who it is?"

Sheriff John sighed and turned to her son. "Bubba, what happened here?"

Miz Demetrice turned her blue eyes on her son. "Don't say nothing, boy. We'll get a lawyer. The best lawyer in East Texas. I'll bet he hasn't even read you your rights yet. Do you know how often the police abuse the rights of the underprivileged in this state alone? Who is that woman? What's a matter with you, son? Can't you speak to your own mother?"

Bubba took another drink of coffee and studied the world around him. It was a pleasant morning with only mild humidity. It was the kind of late spring morning that would have normally had him out on the

30

lake with a fishing rod in one hand, a beer in the other, and Precious snoring up 'Z's at his feet. But instead, here he was.

His mother stared at him waiting for a reply as she had finally shut her mouth. Sheriff John regarded him as if Bubba had just crawled out from underneath a rock. Neal was malingering in the shadows of the big house because he was wondering if Sheriff John could protect him from Miz Demetrice once she realized that the realtor was once again on her property. And lastly, there was the dead woman lying only feet from them.

Bubba gestured at the dead woman under the snow white sheet that flapped gently in a spring breeze. His coffee had grown cold in his cup and he dumped it out. "That there is Mrs. Melissa Dearman, Mama. She was the woman I was going to marry when I was in the Army. You know the one I found in bed with an officer. The same officer whose arm I broke right before the Army decided that I shouldn't be a sergeant anymore." He vigorously nodded his head up and down at his mother as her face filled with comprehension. "That's who the woman is."

31

Chapter Three

Bubba Goes to Jail

Friday through Monday

Miz Demetrice was herself in the mood to end all moods. First of all, that cheating harridan of a woman, Wilma Rabsitt, had managed to fill an inside straight a mere three hands into the previous night's game. Since Miz Demetrice and two other women went out and specially bought three separate new decks of cards of varying brands without telling the others what they were each buying, it was certain that Wilma couldn't have had spare cards slipped up her brassiere or under her garter belt. But then Miz Demetrice wouldn't put much past Wilma. Then old Mary Jean Holmgreen had intimated that Miz Demetrice's own son, Bubba, had made a pass at the woman at Bufford's, telling the story with much enthusiastic gusto. Around three in the morning Mary Jean and Wilma had begun winning hands like crazy, and there had been a half-hour break to discuss general perfidy in the ranks, as well a search of the premises for elicit mirrors or cameras. Alice Mercer had thought she had found one in an air vent, but it had turned out to be a petrified olive, stuck there by God knew what or who or even when. Finally, Ruby Mercer had called her sister, Alice, with the news that Bubba was about to be shot to death by a gang of roughshod, unpitying law enforcement officials, who had discovered no less than five dead bodies on the Snoddy properties and had consequently determined the Bubba was the perpetrator of such heinous acts of evilness.

Only one law enforcement official and only one dead body, lamented Miz Demetrice sourly. In all of her years on this earth she had never seen such unrelenting gossip rampaging around a town whose population was barely three thousand people. As a matter of fact, Miz Demetrice would be reporting as such to Sheriff John, except that the poker game was highly illegal, and she was the number one evil genius. So logically, how could a slightly dishonest, Southern woman divulge such information without sacrificing her own right to have some entertainment in her old retirement age?

"You cain't arrest Bubba," Miz Demetrice submitted uncategorically, hands akimbo.

Sheriff John paused in reading Bubba his rights. "Why in the name of all that's holy can I not?" His voice was gruff as he asked the question. Plain and simple, he didn't care to explain his actions to the nosiest, pestering, malcontent, and interfering woman in the state of Texas. He couldn't count the number of times that Miz Demetrice had gotten her back up over some alleged misdeed or misbehavior on the part of whomever. Now that it was her only son involved, only the almighty Lord above could protect them. *Amen*, he prayed earnestly.

"He spent all night at Bufford's Gas and Grocery, simpleton," she proclaimed, waving a finger under Sheriff John's nose. The unsaid part was, 'Hah!' "They have surveillance cameras!"

"They're dummies. George Bufford's too cheap to buy real ones." Sheriff John adjusted his Stetson carefully and turned back to Bubba, who was doing his best to ignore the ongoing proceedings. "You have the right to..."

"And I did follow him most of the way home," Neal offered from the other side of the police car. Perhaps a little bit of judicious sucking up would be beneficial to the cause of future Walmarts in the area of Pegramville and the area of monies going directly into the realtor's pockets. *Amen,* he silently prayed as well.

Miz Demetrice vigorously motioned with her hand, flashing every piece of good jewelry that she owned, which was not insignificant. "See?" *Please don't let them take Bubba to jail, Dear Lord. Amen.*

Sheriff John sighed. "Miz Demetrice. Who else would have killed the woman? You?"

"Of course not," she returned indignantly. "I never even met her. Of course, she did hurt Bubba terribly. Not that he was overly fond of the military service, but what an awful way to end one's career."

"Mother," Bubba uttered solemnly, "you're not helping me here."

"Well, my Lord," Miz Demetrice swore, "she was a-fornicating with that man in your own bed. You told me."

Sheriff John had a blank look on his face.

"And I wish I hadn't," replied Bubba.

"Furthermore, that other man was you all's commanding officer. That's called fraternizing with your chain of command. You did tell me."

"When I was drunker than ten sailors on a port call in Tokyo," Bubba grumbled unhappily. But his mother still went on.

"...I know that you didn't mean to break that man's arm, but she was your affianced one, and the good Lord above knows that a man has got to get angry

34

when he a-finds another man poaching on his property. I suppose you were simply trying to pull him off the bed, but still you must have been mad enough to spit nails. If I had caught your father with another woman, I might not have poisoned him but bludgeoned him to death on the spot..."

"Dad had a heart attack, Ma." *And we all know why he had a heart attack, don't we?*

"...That's what I wanted everyone to think..."

"Take me to jail, Sheriff." *The faster the better, Lord*, prayed Bubba. *Amen.*

"Quick, get in the car, Bubba," Sheriff John said vigorously.

But before Bubba went to the Pegram County Jail, they had to wait for the coroner to arrive, as well as several other deputies to secure the crime scene. As well, Miz Demetrice had to be convinced to leave said authorities alone in the pursuit of their duties. Then, she realized that Neal Ledbetter was on her property...again, and had to be convinced not to fill the hind end of his Sears suit full of salt rock. Finally, Bubba's dog, Precious, had to be convinced not to bite as many deputies as she could get her paws on, by being locked up in the big house by Miz Demetrice.

Pegram County Jail had been built in 1993 with the expectations that the population was booming, and they would need more jail cells. However, the town didn't exactly boom, and most of the time various prisoners were farmed out quickly or stayed at the Pegramville Police Department's jail only a block away. Technically speaking, Bubba went here because the Snoddy place was just outside Pegramville's city limits, about ten feet as the crow flies. It was a small affair with only eight cells. Two had occupants.

35

Bubba was processed in by a jail official named Tee Gearheart, the largest law enforcement official for hundreds of miles around Pegramville. He was six foot even but weighed about three hundred and fifty pounds, if he had cared to weigh himself, which he did not. His genial manner and not insignificant muscles behind the weight, allowed him to run the jail in an amiable fashion. Across most of the eastern part of the state it was known widely that if one had to go to a jail, Pegram County Jail was the place to be. Tee was a friendly and fair fella. The food was good, and the cells were clean. Enough said.

"Say, Tee," greeted Bubba cheerfully.

"Hey, Bubba," replied Tee. He pointed to the top of the counter between them. "You want to empty your pockets there."

"Sure, Tee, how's your wife?" A wallet went on the plain, white counter along with a Buck pocket knife, two packs of gum, and three lead fishing weights.

"Poppiann's just peachy. She's almost six months along." Tee's voice lowered as he mentioned, "The sonogram says that it's a boy." He chuckled in admiration. He made a motion with his large hands indicating a space about a foot long. "You should see the size of his wee-wee."

Sheriff John was standing behind the two men, watching over Bubba's shoulder which wasn't the easiest thing in the world to do considering Bubba's height. His face was contorting in ways that Tee thought might have to do with a lack of fiber in the man's diet. Meanwhile, Bubba said, "That's just great, Tee. Say, can I have the cell with the window on the north side?"

"Sorry, Bubba, but Newt Durley came in yesterday on a DWI, and well, I cain't go 'round changing cells. But Newt's going out tomorrow if his mother can come up with bail, and then I'll be as pleased as punch to move you over there. Can you sign this here form saying you came in with these items?"

Bubba signed the form. "I don't know if I care to be in the cell after Newt Durley, Tee. I remember what he did to the toilet last time."

Tee shrugged. Newt Durley probably had the same lack of fiber as the Sheriff. All those men needed was a good dose of prunes or the like. "I know. I know. Can you take off your belt, Bubba? We cain't have you hanging yourself before we get a chance to. Also, your boot laces."

Bubba slipped his belt out of the loops with a sigh and then knelt to remove his boot laces. "I never had to do this before, Tee."

"Well, Bubba, it's because you're being held on suspicion of a higher crime. Statistically speaking, men who are held for capital crimes tend to attempt suicide more. Miz Demetrice would come down here and shoot each and every one of us ifin you were to end up dead, hanging by your boot laces or such." Tee took the items with a sorry look on his large face. "Anyway, you're just in time for lunch." He smiled hugely. "Miss Lurlene Grady should be bringing down food for all the fellas in just about a half hour." That was always a good part to the day, although there was a certain something about Lurlene that bothered Tee, and what was more bothersome was that he couldn't say quite what it was.

Bubba brightened. He had dated Lurlene upon occasion. She was a waitress from the Pegram Café in cosmopolitan, downtown Pegramville, not a half block away. She was a truly blue-ribbon kind of woman. Oh, not too short, not too tall, gently rounded in the hip, hair bobbed, and brownish-blonde, with large, luminous brown eyes. Perhaps she was a few years younger than he, maybe twenty-five, but Bubba didn't think that was a problem. They were on their sixth date with a definite option on a seventh. Bubba also thought that taking it slow and easy, based on his own prior history, wasn't a problem. Her only flaw as far as Bubba could tell, and he wasn't sure it was much of one, was that she wasn't from the South, although she tried to sound like she was. With a name like Lurlene Grady, she had to come from Southern stock, but her accent sometimes betrayed her as someone who came from norther climes. But Bubba wouldn't hold that against such a good-looking woman.

Tee locked Bubba in cell number five, two down from Newt Durley, and one across the way from Mike Holmgreen. As Tee locked the bars on Bubba, he muttered, "That little Mike, you know what he did?"

Bubba knew. The eighteen-year-old had tried to burn down the high school. Actually, he had only accomplished scorching one wall because under all of the paint was cement block. But one of the sheriff's deputies had caught him red-handed with gasoline and matches. Why? All because he was flunking algebra. Bubba had heard that Mike's lawyer had worked out a plea in exchange for leniency, and the boy would be staying as a prisoner of the jail for the next month. The local police were supposed to have him over at their jail, but on account of his youth and small size, they thought he'd be less traumatized over at this place with Tee. Mike's algebra teacher even came in to give him his homework and a little tutoring every night. "He got a 'B' on a test last week," Tee reported proudly.

"Thanks, Tee." Bubba smiled at the other man.

By the time lunch came around, Bubba was in a three way discussion about the advantages of calculus versus trigonometry with Mike Holmgreen and Newt Durley. The door rattled and in walked Lurlene with three sack lunches.

"Hey, fellas," she said cheerfully. Bubba thought she was a sight for sore eyes. Her brown-blonde hair, not dishwater blonde, was caught up in a little knot. Her doe eyes sparkled as she made contact with Bubba's own blue ones. She was a comely woman even if she wasn't originally from Texas. She handed a bag to Newt Durley with a sympathetic, "At least you didn't hit nothing but a telephone pole, Mr. Durley."

Newt said, "It was Stella Lackey's telephone pole, and she came out raising such a fuss that three neighbors called the po-lice. They shore didn't believe it when I told them that telephone pole just jumped right out in front of my car."

Lurlene gave him a large and sparkling smile and moved on to Mike. "Tee says you got a 'B' on your algebra test, Mike. Good for you. You know he put it on the bulletin board with all of the wanted posters?"

Mike took his lunch with a dreamy grin. Lurlene was a sweet thing, even if she was older than he was. And just think, his algebra test was side by side with the FBI's ten most wanted felons. That was cool.

"Now, Bubba, " she came to stand in front of his cell and tilted her head in a charming fashion, "tell me all these rumors aren't true."

Bubba took the lunch from her and tossed it on the single bed. She offered a smooth, creamy cheek to him,

39

and he kissed it through the bars. "Tell me what you heard, and I'll tell you if it's true."

So Lurlene told him some things, and Bubba made various noises of disbelief, awe, and amazement as he rediscovered Pegramville's unrelenting thirst for high confabulation. Even Mike and Newt were amazed at the potpourri of rumors circulating.

By the time Lurlene had departed, Bubba was feeling better already. After all, he wasn't really under arrest; he was just waiting for the sheriff's department to get all their tape recorders going and such. After a fine lunch of a meatloaf sandwich, spicy home fries, an apple, and a large brownie, a man was just about ready for everything.

In fact, not a half hour after Bubba had finished brushing brownie crumbs off his white t-shirt, Sheriff John returned with Tee and let him out. The next three hours were spent in a small room off of Sheriff John's main office with a large mirror on one side. Bubba asked about the mirror in a congenial way, but the sheriff and his deputies weren't up to answering questions of that nature from a 'suspect.' Bubba knew it was a one way mirror, and silently vowed not to pick his nose or scratch his balls, that is, if he could remember not to do so.

Sheriff John did not participate in the questioning but remained curiously absent. Bubba thought it was patently obvious that the man was watching from behind the one-way mirror. In any case, it was a deputy named Steve Simms who did all of the talking. Deputy Simms wasn't originally from Pegram County, and Bubba didn't know much about him except that he liked to give speeding tickets to tourists a little too often using a diabolical speed trap on the far side of

Pegram County. But, Bubba realized, the man must have been promoted because here he was asking Bubba all kinds of questions about dead women lying in tall grass.

Bubba thought privately that Sheriff John should have done the questioning. First, Deputy Simms, a man of about the same age as Bubba and seventy pounds lighter, used a condescending manner that only succeeded in making Bubba clamp up like a fixture on a radiator hose. Second and most importantly, Simms gave away more information than he got. It was this information that made Bubba realize that he was in a serious world of hurt. It wasn't just a 'Hey, explain yourself, Bubba' kind of situation but one that was far, far worse.

Among the tidbits that Simms managed to let go was that Melissa Dearman had been shot between ten PM and one AM the night before. Bubba knew perfectly well that Bufford's Gas and Grocery didn't have an operational video camera surveillance system in order to alibi his whereabouts, and there were gaps that would have more than allowed Bubba to run off and shoot his ex-fiancée dead. Two, a forty-five caliber gun had been used in the killing of Melissa Dearman. Three, an M1911 Colt .45 handgun was registered to Miz Demetrice Snoddy, and it could not be produced by the same. It had belonged to Elgin, a gun he had brought back from his exploits in Southeast Asia whilst serving his country in a military fashion. Three, Simms knew that Lloyd Goshorn had wandered into Bufford's at half-past ten the previous evening. Furthermore, Lloyd had told them about the blonde-haired woman to whom he had given directions. She had asked for the corner of Wilkins and Farmer's Roads, not the

Snoddy place but the corner closest to the Snoddy estate's front gates. As well, it seemed likely that Simms had a good idea that Martha Lyles had been in just about twenty past twelve to buy lottery tickets. Perhaps Simms even knew that two drunks had been picked up by Smith's Taxi service at fifteen after two in the AM.

Simms was too surprised to put a blank look on his face when Bubba volunteered for a lie detector test. He had to stop questioning Bubba for a while to go outside the interrogation room to confer with Sheriff John. Apparently they all concurred, and Bubba was escorted back to the jail by a deputy he hadn't met before.

Her name was Gray, and Bubba was instantly transfixed. She was about as short as a woman could be without someone calling her a midget. About the size of his own mother, a woman who came up about knee high to a grasshopper. But that was where the resemblance ended. Her lustrous black hair was done up in a tight bun that coiled on the base of her neck. Bottle green eyes regarded Bubba with the calm objectiveness of any law enforcement officer escorting a prisoner. She was slim, almost boyishly so, with her uniform fitting like a glove intelligibly showing that she was, in fact, no boy. Bubba couldn't get enough of staring at her heart-shaped face with rich, pouting ruby lips. Any thought of blonde, curvy Lurlene Grady went straight out of his mind like it was cement dropped in a pond. He shook his head vigorously.

"What is it?" she asked, holding the door open for them. Bubba was in handcuffs, and couldn't do the courtesy. He was in heaven; her voice was that of an angel; soft, throaty, attractive. Furthermore, and most painfully to him, he only had the time it would take them to walk from the sheriff's main office back to the jail, which was cattycorner to the main office, perhaps two minutes at the most.

"I'm Bubba Snoddy," he introduced himself, going through the door.

"I know," she replied, obviously not impressed, following him with a guiding hand on his shoulder.

He regained his good humor momentarily. "It's just that I thought I knew just about everyone from 'round here."

"I'm new," she responded, still obviously not impressed.

Bubba had heard about the luscious Deputy Gray but having not seen her before hadn't paid much attention to the talk. The day mechanic over at Bufford's had raved about wanting to be arrested by her. His own mother, Miz Demetrice, had made a comment about the sheriff's department being sued by someone over sex discrimination in their hiring practices and promptly hiring a woman in order to counter their lawsuit. "I've heard. What's your name?"

"Deputy Gray," she said dryly and handed him over into the custody of Tee, who giggled like a little girl when Deputy Gray signed the form. That was okay with Bubba. He kind of felt like giggling like a little girl himself when she flashed those same green eyes at him.

Bubba spent a quiet Friday night in the pokey, with Tee coming in about six PM to tell him that Miz Demetrice was picketing in front of the jail, screaming something about Attica. He let Bubba out so he could go convince his mother that he hadn't been molested

43

once or even tortured with rubber hoses by the law enforcement officials.

"Not even a fingernail removed with pliers?" Miz Demetrice asked, disappointed.

"Nope. I'll take a lie detector test in the morning and they'll probably let me out," he told his mother. He kissed her on her forehead, encouraged her to drive home carefully, and scooted her off with a wave of his hands. He watched his mother slowly walk down the sidewalk, her picket sign dragging on the ground beside her and returned to the jail, where Tee was watching from the door. "Thanks, Tee."

Then Bubba slept one of the best nights he had for a long time. When morning came and he passed the lie detector test with flying colors, Sheriff John and Deputy Simms were so angry they refused to let him out of the jail until Monday.

Chapter Four

Bubba Makes a List

Monday

There's nothing in the world like the sweet, wondrous smell of freedom, Bubba Snoddy thought as he walked out of the Pegram County Jail.

Bubba had been in excellent company while he was temporarily incarcerated. Certainly, he hadn't been bored. What seemed like half the town had stopped in to chat or just to take a gander at Bubba Snoddy, the infamous Bluebeard of Pegramville, suspected murderer of no less than a dozen young virgins, until Tee Gearheart had explained to them that Bubba was only being held for questioning. Not only that, but there had only been one dead woman involved, and she surely had not been decapitated on the night of the full moon in the Sturgis Woods.

Newt Durley stayed until Saturday night when his sister bailed him out. He had been a hell of a chess player. Furthermore, Bubba had relearned some of his algebra with Mike Holmgreen which had been interesting even if Mike's grandmother, Mary Jean Holmgreen, had winked lasciviously at Bubba on her way out of the jail after visiting with her grandson.

Bubba had just plain ignored Sheriff John Headrick's irritating, accusatory glances, as the man wandered into the jail half a dozen times, knowing full and damned well that his prisoner was being held illegally. Each time Bubba had just given the older man a grin and a wave like he was having the time of his life. He wasn't yet ready to tell his mother to go find an ambulance-chaser. No one had come in to beat him or threaten him if he didn't confess. And three hours of questioning plus two hours spent at the lie detector test wasn't much to speak of in the way of a painful stay at the jail.

Tee had showed Bubba *The Pegram Herald* on Saturday with its headline story about the murdered woman, except in the paper she was still officially unidentified. The headline proclaimed in inch-high type, 'Murder in Pegramville!' There weren't many details, but the paper had tried to make it the second coming of Jesus Christ. On Sunday, the paper still hadn't identified Melissa Dearman, and Bubba wondered if *The Herald's* crack news reporting team, Maude and Roy Chance, were sleeping on the job. After all, they hadn't even tried to sneak into the jail to interview the main suspect. And they certainly hadn't cross-examined Miz Demetrice. Bubba knew full well that his mother likened news reporters to denizens from the lowest level of a murky pond and wouldn't hesitate to pull out her twelve gauge shotgun for mobile target practice if she was so inclined.

Meals were a delight thanks to the Pegram Café with Lurlene Grady providing the service. Although Bubba briefly thought of the beautiful Deputy Gray, first name unknown, and Tee wouldn't tell him, he was still enamored enough of Lurlene such that her presence was a welcome change to all the gawkers, Sheriff John's glaring, and Mike's algebra lessons.

However, when Bubba retrieved his wallet, belt, shoe laces, and the like from Tee and walked outside the jail on Monday morning, he was happy to see the daylight from the other side of the bars. He was more than happy; he was relieved.

Deputy (first name as yet still unknown) Gray even passed him on the way out and Bubba found himself tipping his hat even though he most obviously was not wearing one. He was positive that the black-haired, green-eyed vixen's lips had twitched in an involuntary smile, if only for the briefest of seconds. He was also positive that she wasn't wearing a wedding band on her left hand.

Ah, life was good, even if it was only for the moment. Bubba had other fish to fry, other smelly fish that were rotting on a comparative level with the local manure factory on a hot Texas day. Sheriff John had his sharp-sighted eye on Bubba as the prime suspect in the murder of Melissa Dearman, and it didn't seem as though Perry Mason, in the guise of Raymond Burr, was going to appear and get the real murderer to confess while on the witness stand.

Abruptly, Bubba's good mood left him. While he was inside and basically helpless, he could forget the dead woman who had once meant so much to him. Now he would be forced to remember he, or face consequences that he was not responsible for.

It was true that Melissa and Bubba had lived together in an apartment for about two months, just about three years before. It was also true that Melissa had ambitions for Bubba that Bubba hadn't even realized. Put simply, Melissa wanted more. More status. More money. More of some unnamable quantity that spoke of position and power. Specifically, she wanted Bubba to become an officer. He had more than adequate qualifications to apply for

Officer Candidate School. He had refused, not once but half a dozen times.

Bubba could understand where Melissa was coming from. She'd grown up poor, so poor that her parents had lived from hand to mouth. The Army had been her only way out of poverty, and once she'd had a taste of being someone who controlled other soldiers at the advanced rank of staff-sergeant, she wanted more. The Army was a great equalizer. Anyone could aspire to rank, if only they'd play the prestigious game of politicking.

On the other hand, Bubba hadn't grown up dirt poor, but he did understand poverty. In rural Texas, it had been all around him as a child and still was as an adult. Miz Demetrice had wanted Bubba to understand and comprehend what it meant to be poor so that he would better appreciate what he had. The Snoddy's themselves weren't much above poverty. The Snoddy Mansion was on the verge of being a rambling wreck and falling in on itself. From a distance it was only a blurred image of what it must have looked like before the War Between the States. Any of their supposed wealth was tied up in one hundred acres of overgrown land, to include ten acres of mosquito-infested swamp land, not to mention dozens of acres with holes dug haphazardly over the landscape like the crater strewn face of the moon. It wasn't much of a legacy, but Bubba had never minded.

He had told Melissa all of that years ago. The Army had been his own kind of escape away from people talking about other people so often, that it was an avowed fact that half of the ears of the population of Pegram County were burning at any given time. The Army had its own gossip system but one that left alone

48

those who cared to work and do a good job, which was something Bubba enjoyed doing. Hell, he had taken pride in doing so. But he knew once he became an officer all of that would go away, and politics would come into play. Melissa had wanted the politics of being an 'officer's wife.' She had longed for it, and finally she had gotten it but not with Bubba Snoddy.

Instead, she had seduced their commanding officer, Michael Dearman. Right in Bubba's own bed in their shared apartment. Sergeant Snoddy had returned home from work early. His first sergeant had let everyone go early, and lo and behold, what had Bubba found?

One fiancée in bed. One captain in the self-same bed with the fiancée. Two naked people in bed together. One naked fiancée doing stuff with one naked captain that Bubba thought reserved for himself and his fiancée.

Upon this traumatic scene, Bubba had temporarily lost his mind. A wave of red had roared over his vision, causing him to lose all reason, logic, and everything he held dear to his heart. The next thing he knew, he was holding Captain Dearman's arm, grasped in one of his huge fists, with the other man shrieking beside him, and Melissa wrapped around his neck, screaming into his ear, "Bubba! Don't hurt him! Don't hurt him! Please, Bubba!"

Bubba had been standing there holding the broken arm of his commanding officer with his fiancée on his back, pounding on him with her fists, and had a vision of his own father beating his mother. Elgin Snoddy had been a handsome dickens with the devil's own temper when he drank, and he drank often. Too often. Bubba had been very young when his father had had his heart attack but he could distinctly remember those times when Miz Demetrice had to cover up her pretty arms and delicate throat, even in the heat of summer. She had to hide what her husband had done to her in his drunken fits of rage, that he always felt so sorry for afterwards. Even at that tender age, Bubba had been ashamed of his own father. It had been at that very moment that Bubba pictured himself in his father's place, losing his temper so violently that his loved ones would suffer terribly. And he had been ashamed of himself.

"Oh, my God," Bubba had muttered. "What have I done?" He had let the captain's arm go, and Michael Dearman dropped to the floor like a buffalo shot with an elephant gun. Melissa had slid off Bubba's back and wrapped herself protectively around the officer crumpled on the floor. They consoled each other, naked as jay birds but uncaring of that fact.

"Oh, Bubba," she had said, looking up at him with sad eyes, "we were going to tell you. I swear. This weekend. We're going to get married. Me and Michael." She had stroked his head, as the man on the floor struggled to overcome pain and regain a little composure.

"You got your officer then, 'Lissa?" he had asked numbly. It was the one thing that had popped into his head. It had been the meanest, most cruel thing he thought that he had ever said to another human being. Although it was true, he still regretted the words.

Melissa had stared up at him with her large, blue eyes, eyes so blue they had reminded him of the afternoon skies in spring. Her chest had been heaving with exertion; her honey-colored hair was askew. She hadn't said anything to him. As a matter of fact, it had been the last time she had said anything to Bubba at all.

Bubba had called an ambulance and the police, in that order. The captain's arm looked to be broken, and indeed it had been. Bubba had spent a night in the local jail before the military police came to collect him. They called it a general discharge under other conditions than honorable. Before a month had passed, Melissa had received her own general discharge and married Captain Michael Dearman. A spiteful part of Bubba had wondered if it were in order to avoid charges pressed against the officer and Melissa herself. After all, Michael Dearman had been Melissa's commanding officer, as well as Bubba's. And Bubba had found the two of them in bed together, obviously fraternizing with each other. On another level, the captain and Melissa had been in as much trouble as he had been.

So Melissa Dearman nee Connor had gotten her officer. There had been a few people, Army buddies, who had written to Bubba once or twice. One had stopped over last year on his way to another post. They had told Bubba that Melissa and the captain seemed to be happy. She had gotten pregnant last year and given birth to a boy. The captain had been promoted to major and went to some battalion on another post taking his family with him, the temporary scandal seemingly not affecting his career ladder. To be certain, Captain Dearman hadn't been the first to marry an enlisted woman nor would he be the last. Bubba hadn't heard anything else about them, and he hadn't cared to hear anymore.

That was, until Melissa had shown up dead almost on his doorstep. She had been using a rental car. Had she flown in from wherever they were stationed now?

What had Melissa wanted with Bubba? Bubba couldn't imagine that Melissa wanted to declare her rediscovered love for him. She had been too pragmatic for that. She had had her life mapped out for her. Her husband would make major, then lieutenant colonel, and most certainly the rank of colonel. If it were possible he would wear the star of a general. Then he would retire and start as a consultant to a lucrative defense contractor, with the family at home, and her doing officer's wifely things. Perhaps he might dabble in politics, with his serene, beautiful wife at his side; his two point five children would be on his other side. That had been the world that she had been on her way to. Perhaps she had genuine feelings for Michael Dearman, Bubba didn't know and didn't care to know for the last three years. But what in the name of God had 'Lissa been doing in Pegramville looking for him?

Because as sure as the day was long, Melissa hadn't known anyone else in this small town, hundreds of miles away from the big cities and perhaps a thousand miles from where she presently lived with her husband and family. Because, as sure as night falls she was here to see him, and him alone. Because as sure as the leaves will fall in autumn, Bubba was the only one who knew Melissa and had the only reason to kill her.

Bubba was the one Sheriff John was looking at with a rapt, disconcerting eye, because Bubba almost certainly could be the only one who had any reason to kill Melissa Dearman.

And Bubba was going to jail on a permanent basis unless he could figure out who had killed Melissa and damned quickly.

Bubba snapped back to the present with a precipitous feeling that left him discombobulated. His path became clear to him. He had to solve the murder, before the Sheriff solved him, solved him right onto death row, waiting for the deadly drip to take him into the next world. It would be a place where he couldn't do a damned thing about who had really murdered Melissa Dearman.

His first stop was the Pegram Café where Lurlene was working. Bubba needed to use the phone as well as flirt shamelessly with the blonde-haired thing. After a man had spent a time or two in the jail, a pretty, young, encouraging woman was just the trick to make things seem a little more pleasant.

Lurlene dropped a plate of eggs, hash browns, grits, and bacon unceremoniously on the counter when she saw Bubba coming through the door. She threw up her arms and shrieked, "Bubba!" Then she leaped into his arms and kissed him. He was, after all, a big man, and caught her very nicely. "They let you out!" she yelled.

Bubba winced. She had yelled directly in his ear. "Yes, Miss Lurlene, I noticed that."

"Well, Bubba, what are they going to do?" she asked, still in his arms. She studied him carefully with her warm brown eyes.

Bubba looked around at a crowd of interested faces. He thanked the Lord above that the Pegram Café was a small café with only enough room for twenty people. However, every chair was full at nine in the morning on this particular morning and their attention

53

was focused fully on Bubba. He waded through the crowd, accepting the odd, "Good to see you, Bubba." "Did they torture you, Bubba? That's what Miz Demetrice said." "We knew you dint do it, Bubba." Finally, he deposited Lurlene back at the counter, where she blushed furiously, picked up the dropped plate of eggs and fixings, and went back to work.

Noey Wheatfall, the cook and owner of the Pegram Café, came out with a white chef's hat on his head and a white apron wrapped around his torso. He grinned at Bubba, and said, "Hey, Bubba, did you see the paper yesterday?"

Noey was a good-looking man, about ten years older than Bubba. He had dark brown hair cut short, and the eyes to match. He wasn't as big as Bubba, but he wasn't a short man either. He was also married with four children, all of whom could be found in the café helping out in the summertime. His wife, Nancy, also was a hard worker. She spent most of her days at the manure factory as a secretary and her evenings helping at the café. Bubba liked Nancy but had never quite taken a liking to her husband. If he had had to put a reason to it, it would have been that Noey always seemed a little too slick, a little too smiley, and a little too eager with the ladies on nights when his wife was off doing something else. But Bubba hadn't really thought about it before, and the thought only sat with him now because Noey was looking directly at him and asking, "That was some kind of headline, huh?"

"I didn't see it," Bubba lied and immediately asked himself why he had lied.

But Noey slapped him on his back blithely and said, "Meal on the house, Bubba. Being innocent is hard work, ain't it?"

"I already ate, Noey," Bubba said. "I just came in to see Miss Lurlene and use the payphone."

"Hell, use the phone in my office," Noey replied cheerfully. Then his face twisted. "Don't those folks over at the jail let you make a phone call?" He hesitated. "You should get a cell phone, boy. Just like everyone else."

Bubba smiled weakly at the other man and followed him into his office. Noey left promptly without saying anything else. He dialed his phone number and waited for Miz Demetrice to answer.

Adelia Cedarbloom answered the phone about twenty rings later. Adelia was his mother's housekeeper, as well as confidant, as well as general dog's body. She gave him a cold hello and told him that his mother was talking to their state representative at the town twenty miles down the road. "About you, course," she answered when Bubba asked why. Bubba told her that he had been released from jail and would be home presently if Miz Demetrice deigned to telephone.

"Thank the Lord Almighty!" said Adelia wholeheartedly. "I have heard about what happens to men in places like that. It is a good thing that you are much bigger than most. You know that if you went to prison, as big as you are, you could have yourself a bitch."

Bubba asked her to repeat herself. He thought that maybe he had something in his ears, because she couldn't have said what he thought she had said.

"You know, you could run the place because no one would dare mess with you," Adelia explained patiently. "When a man controls another man, that other man is called a bitch. I heard it on television."

"Have you been watching those daytime shows again, Miz Adelia?" asked Bubba.

"Of course not. There's too much trash on that show. I don't believe they could find so many people who are sleeping with their girlfriend and their girlfriend's other boyfriend at the same time. They just make that trumpery up." Adelia's voice was indignant, but obviously she still watched the show like a dirty little secret in her closet, kind of like the dirty little secrets on the show.

Bubba wasn't positive but had an idea that the dark-haired, dark-eyed forty-ish woman, who had been with Demetrice for the last twenty years, was a co-conspirator in the infamous, weekly Pegram County Pokerama. The game was getting to be so well known that they moved it to a new and previously unused location each week. The phone at the big Snoddy house rang off the hook the day before the game, so Bubba didn't dare answer it if he happened to be in the house. But mostly Bubba wouldn't answer it because Adelia would beat him to it and give him a don't-you-dare look besides.

It had been true that he had been expecting the police to show up at the Snoddy place but for an altogether different reason than the one which actually had occurred.

Adelia continued to speak on the other end of the telephone, "I'm sure glad you're coming home. All kinds of trouble makers out here lately."

Bubba sat down heavily in Noey's chair. "What do you mean, Miz Adelia?"

"Saturday night Miz Demetrice had to shoot at someone trying to steal something off the front porch. Your mama ain't so young anymore that she should be getting knocked down from shooting that blasted elephant gun. Her posterior was so bruised she couldn't sit down most of Sunday. She said that someone was messing around the property last night around midnight, too. Like that be something new around here. Precious was howling up a storm, mind you. Miz Demetrice decided to keep her in the big house last night, and weren't it a good thing, too."

Bubba digested this information. "Thank you, Miz Adelia. I'll be home tonight. I'll take care of it."

"You best do so before Miz Demetrice up and kills someone."

The phone line was buzzing in his ear before Bubba realized that Adelia had hung up. But Bubba was thinking about his mother. Miz Demetrice had a mighty fine temper when she was so thwarted. She could be vexed about certain matters for months. Last year alone she would cross the street rather than walk on the same sidewalk as Susan Teasdale. Susan's offense was that she wore the exact same hat as Miz Demetrice to the big church social on Easter Sunday. Of course, Susan had known full well that she was wearing the same hat as Miz Demetrice. She had done so specifically to infuriate Miz Demetrice for reasons that dated back three decades. It had been something about Susan dating Elgin Snoddy before Miz Demetrice, and just look who ended up marrying him and becoming the infamous Snoddy matriarch.

Bubba snorted to himself. Susan had gotten the better end of the bargain, but Miz Demetrice sure wouldn't admit that. Susan had married a Baptist preacher, who had a church on the far side of Pegramville and was doing very well, thank you. But the gist of all of it was that Miz Demetrice held a

57

grudge. Hell, she probably couldn't even remember why she disliked Susan to begin with.

But back to the point that Bubba had been so laboriously making in his head. If Miz Demetrice's one and only child had been hurt, and there had been no doubt that Bubba had been hurt badly, she would have held a grudge against Melissa Dearman, no matter why Melissa had come calling past ten PM on a Thursday night.

Bubba could picture it in his mind. Melissa pulls up to the Snoddy house and sees Miz Demetrice there, hurrying to go to her poker game. Melissa introduces herself. Miz Demetrice rushes into the house, finds Elgin Snoddy's old Army .45, and returns to shoot Melissa in the back. All in the name of revenge upon her only, beloved son.

Bubba snorted again. Then he laughed. Then he laughed harder. Noey even peeped into his office to see just what in the name of God Bubba was laughing at, and had he lost his mind? When Bubba was done laughing, he wiped a tear away from his eye. He had laughed so hard, his eyes had watered and his gut ached.

The truth was that if Miz Demetrice wanted to kill someone then she would have shot them in their face. It was even more likely she would have clubbed them right between the eyes with a baseball bat. Then she would have called the police herself and confessed immediately. The fact of the matter was that when Melissa had driven up to the Snoddy place Miz Demetrice had been long gone and at her floating poker party already taking someone's social security money from them with an evil smile.

It wouldn't be hard to verify. Probably ten women could attest to when Miz Demetrice arrived and ten more to when she left. As soon as he verified that fact, Bubba would make a list of suspects. Who had access to the grounds? Who had motive to kill Melissa? Who had a gun? Who would want Bubba framed for a murder?

Chapter Five

Bubba Still Makes a List

Still Monday

Bubba Snoddy made his list. The problem was that it was a small list. Miz Demetrice Snoddy was at the top of the list. For all of the reasons he had listed mentally before, she was at the very top of the list. She was the pinnacle of Mount Everest on the list. She had motive. She had the weapon. She had opportunity. However, all he had to do was to verify her alibi, and she would be crossed off.

Then there was Adelia Cedarbloom, listed for the same reason as his mother. She would have felt the same indignant anger over Bubba's abrupt disengagement and exit from the military service as Demetrice had. Adelia also had the motive. She had access to Elgin Snoddy's military .45 caliber handgun, the same as his mother. She might have been present when Melissa Dearman had driven up, and introduced herself. Perhaps Adelia had just been trying to scare Melissa off.   But Bubba realized that whoever was chasing Melissa hadn't wanted her near her rental car. She had been going in the opposite direction. No, it was no accident. It was murder, no doubt about it.

Then there was Lurlene Grady, listed for the same reason, but then Bubba crossed her off because he didn't think she was capable of producing a violent, shoot-someone-in-the-back anger that had been necessary to accomplish the task. Then Bubba put her

60

back on his list because he thought maybe it had been jealousy. Lurlene might have the motive. They had dated several times. Six official dates to be precise, and Bubba didn't want to forget that. She very well could know about Bubba's history. Working at the Pegram Café was like working in a gossip factory. Anyone that Bubba cared to point at on the street probably knew the story, although Bubba had only told his mother, and she had sworn up and down on a stack of bibles that she had only told Adelia. Three-quarters of the population of Pegramville probably went into the Café during the odd day, in order to catch up on their daily ration of gossip and maybe pass it on it on to the Café's waitresses or whoever else was there to listen. But what had Lurlene been doing from ten PM to one AM on Thursday night and early Friday morning? And had she felt sufficiently angered by Bubba's ex-fiancée to do such a thing? And how would she have known that Melissa would be anywhere about? Bubba would have to find out.

Bubba added another name to his list. Major Michael Dearman. In every crime drama he'd ever seen on television or at the movies, the husband was the first logical suspect. Yeppers. The spouse was the number one killer of murdered significant others. So here was the mental scenario that Bubba came up with concerning Major Dearman as the killer. Melissa had decided that Bubba had been after all, the love of her life. She was going to visit him and tell him so, begging him to forgive her and run away to live in Bubba-like happiness. The insanely jealous Major follows and in a rage, kills his wife practically on Bubba's door step, leaving the self-same Bubba to take the rap while he slips out of town unseen and unnoticed.

61

Bubba considered. Or maybe Melissa had grown tiresome. Perhaps the Major hadn't made lieutenant colonel in a record amount of time. He hadn't been nominated for such and such award. He got a bad evaluation. He was making the officers' wife look bad to all the other officer's wives, so she was on his back. So the Major wanted Melissa out of the way. And looky here, here was Bubba to take the rap. All he had to do was to get Melissa out here and then shoot her dead on the Snoddy property. Then he would wait for the bad news and let the insurance money flow into his bank account.

Sighing, Bubba scratched that theory out with a savage pen stroke. But how would Major Michael Dearman know about the missing .45 caliber handgun? He wouldn't. If he were a smart murderer and Bubba thought that he had to have some brains in order to be a major, then he wouldn't take the chance of the slug being found and identified to the correct murder weapon. But then it could have all been a spur of the moment murder.

Bubba's head was starting to ache as if he had drunk a jug of moonshine the night before.

From the Pegram Café he hoofed it home, relieved Adelia of the burden that was his dog, Precious, and retreated to his domain, the caretaker's house. He and the dog walked carefully around the crime scene area still taped off with canary yellow tape that was labeled 'Police line – DO NOT CROSS.' Bubba scowled when he saw that Melissa's rental car was still parked at the side of the house. Precious was cheerfully oblivious, content that her master was home and pranced in the only way that a Basset hound can, long ears flopping in the air and jowls going every which way.

When Bubba entered the caretaker's house, his own home, he immediately noticed that it had been searched. It was a Spartan home with only the necessities. So cleaning the house didn't take much out of Bubba, which was just the way he liked it, thank you very much. The oak plank floors only needed a sweeping here and there. Some of the oil paintings, cast-offs from the big house, needed to be wiped off upon occasion to keep dust from growing so large that an extra placemat was necessary at the dining room table. Once a year, Adelia showed up to do all of the floors and all of the windows whether they needed it or not.

It was a house with two floors and a simple veranda. It didn't look much like the small stable it had once been. The first floor was a living room with a walk-through hallway that led right to the back door. This was commonly referred to as a shotgun hallway because one could fire a shotgun from outside the front door and hit someone outside the back door, provided both doors were conveniently open and one wished to shoot the other person. The kitchen was in a cubby hole out back, with not nearly enough room for a man as big as Bubba to turn around in. On the second floor were two bedrooms. One was empty, and the other held Bubba's bed, upon which he tended to sleep diagonally or his feet would stick out on the ends, and a simple armoire.

But with all of the sparse furniture and fixings, he could tell that all of the things had been moved around. The downstairs was more obvious. The ratty couch had been moved a few feet away from its original position. The rug it sat on was cockeyed from someone yanking it up to look underneath. Pictures hung crooked. The book that Bubba had been reading had been dropped carelessly to the floor, bending some pages in the process, and left that way. He picked it up and straightened the folded pages, then replaced the book on the coffee table.

They were looking for the gun, thought Bubba. *The gun that killed Melissa.*

There was a little desk in the corner. It was called a lady's desk because it was about the quarter of the size of a regular desk. It was a delicate thing made out of mahogany and shined to a dark brilliance. It used to belong to Miz Demetrice when she had been a child. His mother had given it to Bubba when he was in elementary school. Bubba once thought he might like to give it to a daughter of his own, but he didn't think that was much likely these days. Bubba went to it and rolled up the cover. Then he got out writing paper and a pen.

He sat himself down on the couch and made himself the list of suspects. Precious sidled up to her master and lay down under him, placing her head delicately on his boot, big brown eyes staring upward. She didn't know what the issue was, but she was going to offer her dogly protection and compassion to her master no matter what the situation.

For the life of him Bubba couldn't think of why anyone else in this town would want to murder Melissa. No one knew her. She hadn't been robbed. Her purse had been sitting in the passenger seat of the rental car, all the money and credit cards intact. Tee Gearheart had told him so on Sunday when the man hadn't had anything better to do. He had also told him that the keys to the rental car had been found halfway from the big house to where Melissa had ended up in the long grass.

Bubba swore tiredly at himself. As soon as that crime scene tape came down he was going to mow that grass so low it wouldn't come back for the entire summer. He might even burn it so that it wouldn't grow back for years. That is, if he got the chance to do so.

All of the things he considered told him logically that there was only one conclusion, since it wasn't a robbery, and Melissa hadn't been molested. She had been completely dressed when he'd found her. So it was a murder. She was there. Someone else was there. Someone else had a forty-five gun, perhaps even Elgin Snoddy's own weapon from the military. Someone else had capped Melissa in the back as she was running away, and she had died instantly.

Bubba ruminated. Melissa had known she was in danger which was why she was running away. What would make her think so? An aggravated woman coming at her, yelling, with a big old, forty-five pointed at her? Sure would make Bubba run like hell if it had happened to him. Come to think of it, it probably had happened at least once when he was really, really snookered.

There was also the moral issue that was tearing Bubba apart. He desperately wanted it to be the husband who had done this terrible thing to Melissa. Then there wouldn't be a moral issue to deal with. Because if Bubba found out that his mother or Adelia had slipped out during the poker game to get something from the house, for example, then what could he do? And if Bubba found the gun hidden

65

someplace, with his mother's fingerprints on it, or perhaps Adelia's on the grip, then what?

There was only one thing to do. He would have to confess to the crime. He would go to Sheriff John himself and tell him this story: It had been a fit of anger. He had seen Melissa at Bufford's Gas and Grocery. He had followed her to his own home, where no one was home. She had parked her car. He had parked his truck. He had gotten out. She had spoken to him, standing outside for a minute. Perhaps he had invited her in, asking her to wait for a moment. He had known exactly where Pa's old M1911 .45 caliber pistol was, in the top of Miz Demetrice's closet. He had pulled it out, loaded it, and returned downstairs. Maybe Melissa had seen the look in his eyes; she had known what it meant. She had seen that look before, once before. She had run out the door, and Bubba had chased after her. She couldn't get to her car in time. Bubba was right in back of her. She could hear his breath coming faster and faster. The noise of her heart and adrenaline was almost deafening. There was another house! Perhaps someone was there to help her. She had headed in that direction. But there was a single gunshot that broke the night. She wouldn't know that the nearest neighbors were almost a mile away and wouldn't hear the blast. She wouldn't know because she was dead before she hit the ground.

Bubba would know because he had been an expert marksman in the military. He had grown up with guns. His grandfathers on both sides had taught him well. Sheriff John probably already knew that. Even though he didn't own a single one, he had access to them. Miz Demetrice had a boocoodle of guns stashed all over the mansion, most of them belonging to Snoddy ancestors.

It was the only thing that made sense. Then Bubba would tell Sheriff John that he had driven back to work, throwing the gun out the truck window somewhere along Sturgis Creek. He wouldn't remember exactly where he had tossed it.

Bubba sighed. But before he confessed to a crime he hadn't committed, a crime that he couldn't have committed, he had to find out if his mother or Adelia had done it. He simply didn't have the time to waste. The Sheriff was, even now, doing background checks on Bubba. He knew about the incident with Melissa Dearman's husband. He was probably talking to Major Dearman this very day if he hadn't previously done so. He probably had already spoken to Melissa's parents about the same incident. Sheriff John might even have a copy of the report from the night that Bubba had broken Major Dearman's arm. All Sheriff John had to do was wait for the results of the gunshot residue test that Deputy Simms had performed on Bubba's hands to come back. Then once he had pretty much summed up a time line that indicated that Bubba had every opportunity to kill Melissa and not an alibi in sight, Bubba would be indicted and arrested, posthaste. He could have been wearing gloves. Bubba probably had been planning this for years. Sure, yes, indeedy. Bubba was guilty. No doubt about it.

Bubba put the pen down onto of the sheet of paper and reached one of his big hands down to scratch Precious's ear. She tilted her head into the gesture, milking it for all it was worth, leaning her body into it. Then she looked up at her master with a baleful eye, silently rebuking him for having left her with Miz Demetrice and Adelia over the weekend. *You should have seen what they made me do,* her eyes seemed to say. *They cooed at me. A lot. Then Miz Adelia gave me a bath, and she put perfume in the water. I'm nice now, but wait until I leave you a little present in one of your boots. A big, smelly present. So there.*

"You want to play ball, Precious," Bubba cooed at her too. "Little-wubby-precious-dog."

Bite me. Precious moved her head away from Bubba's hand. It was time for a dog to play hard to get.

"I know you want to play," Bubba continued. "Get that ball."

The hell with playing hard to get! Precious exploded for the kitchen where her ball was located, baying all the way down the hall, her claws clattering on the oak floor.

"Now wouldn't it be nice if a woman were like that," muttered Bubba. Only a little thing to keep her happy, not one to hold a grudge for more than a few minutes. He shook his head and went out back where he didn't have to look at the crime scene tape or the rental car, and played with his dog.

Adelia looked out from one of the third story windows in the big house and saw him throwing the ball for Precious to retrieve again and again. She paused a moment, paper towels in one hand and a bottle of Windex in the other. Then she sighed, continuing on with her work. It was nice to see Bubba acting halfway normal again. Adelia thought, *Oh, the pain and misery that woman has brought into our lives. Now she's back, even if she's dead, to do it all again. That one will haunt Bubba from beyond the grave.*

An hour later, Bubba got a call from George Bufford in the Bahamas. Precious was lying in front of the fire place on a Mexican rug, snoring, with all four paws twitching in the air, the picture of doglike contentment. She was dreaming of large, red balls and leaping endlessly over tufts of grass.

"Say, Bubba," said George, unceremoniously. "This is George Bufford."

Bubba wasn't exactly ecstatic to hear from his boss, but neither was he surprised. He didn't know how exactly George had heard the goings on from the Bahamas where he was having a rip-roaring time with Rosa Granado, his nubile and voluptuous secretary. However, it was true that the CIA didn't have a thing on how the tiny city of Pegramville did business. "Say, George," he replied neutrally. "How's Minnesota?"

George hesitated for a moment. Bubba could clearly hear a woman's giggle in the background, and he was sure that if he listened closely he could probably hear palm fronds gently wafting in a Caribbean breeze. "Fine. Fine." He paused again. "Well, boy, I heard about your difficulties."

Bubba wasn't sure what the script was for this particular phone call. Was he supposed to plead his innocence and pledge undying loyalty to all Buffords for the remainder of his life? Instead he kept quiet. It wasn't hard. He'd been practicing that respective trait for the last three years. It seemed to keep him out of trouble more than anything else. But he considered. Keeping quiet hadn't helped him much in this most recent dilemma.

"Well, I cain't have you besmirching the name of the Buffords, now can I?" George asked finally.

Besmirching? thought Bubba. *Isn't that what you do to a virgin?*

George continued on. "After all, Bufford's Gas and Grocery has been a Pegramville tradition for forty years, brought to town by my own father, George,

69

Senior. He worked his fingers to the bone to ensure that his family had meat and potatoes on the table. Ifin when this matter is cleared up, then you can have your job back, and we'll let bygones be bygones."

Bubba's silence spoke volumes. At least it did to himself. George was beginning to think that Bubba was passively accepting of the firing when Bubba finally said, "The hell we will." Then he added congenially, "Oh, and George, the health department found a cockroach the size of a mouse inside the hot dog machine on Saturday. Maude Chance down at *The Pegram Herald* is going to print up a fine editorial next week about it. They even got a picture of it next to a ruler. That health guy said he never saw a bigger roach in all his natural-born days. Say hey to Miss Rosa will you." He hung up the phone happily. Then he smiled to himself. Sometimes it was just the small things in life that made a man happy.

Bubba woke his dog up when he tromped over to the front door. Precious snorted once loudly and scrambled to go with her master. She certainly wasn't letting that man out of her sight again to do God knew what while she wasn't around to serve and protect. She scooted out the front door as it slammed shut, just pulling her tail out in time.

Skirting the crime scene tape and the rental car, Bubba went around to the big house. He went in through the side door, calling for Adelia. A minute later, he heard her hello distantly drifting down from the third floor. Bubba walked through the kitchen, once the center of activity for this grand Southern home. There were three ovens which could be fired with coals. There were two pantries, each bigger than Bubba's living room. There was a chopping block older than Miz Demetrice, Adelia, and Bubba put together. There were three sinks on one side. One was big enough to bathe a ten-year-old child in. Bubba knew because he had that done to him when he was so muddy that Adelia hadn't recognized him right off and wouldn't let him past the kitchen. Two dozen servants could have worked in here at once and not gotten in each other's way.

Through the kitchen was the long hallway of the house. There were a great many doorways along this hallway. Down to the right was the grand dining room, where the walls were lined with fabric that once glistened with ruby and gilt shimmers. Down to the left was the main foyer where a majestic stairway curved its way upstairs, showing off the large cupola, lined with intricate woodworking of cupids and birds flying across the skies. A chandelier the size of a 1969 Volkswagen Bug hung down halfway to the stairs, its lead crystal drops refracting the light as brilliantly as it did a hundred years before. There was a formal living room, a receiving room, a wardroom, a servant's room, all to be found on the first floor.

Bubba reached the stairs in the foyer and looked up. If only for an instant one could be fooled into thinking that a soul had stepped into the past. The stairs stayed polished, thanks to Adelia, as did the gleaming chandelier above, imposing grandly upon this entry. The garnet carpets looked as well tended as they had when Bubba had been ten years old. The marble tile in the base of the foyer was as polished as ever, showing creamy strains of the imperfections in its own imposing persona. He expected to see Scarlett O'Hara lifting up her colossal skirts and rushing to the bottom of the stairs to greet him.

Instead, a woman no less striking despite her lack of hoops and ribbons, leaned over the third floor railing and called, "Say, child, you know I'm not coming down until I've finished with these windows." Adelia looked down at Bubba with a mock severe expression on her face.

So Bubba went up, taking three steps at a time. Precious woofed disdainfully and followed at her own pace. This wasn't what she called fun. Her long torso wasn't made for stairs.

Adelia waited for Bubba. Presently, he was standing beside her in what had been known as the red room, cleaning one of the windows while she did the other. It had been one of the many guest bedrooms of the Snoddy Mansion, decorated entirely in crimson, from the walls to the curtains to the dressings on the bed. In lighter moments, Miz Demetrice called it the Whore Room, not only because of the color, but because some Snoddy ancestor used to keep his mistress here while his wife was dying in her bed on the second floor. In its time it must have been a thing of dreams, this room with its scarlet colors, but now it was faded, and the gilt needed refinishing.

"How did the poker game go, Miz Adelia?" he finally asked, unable to think of some witty and unobtrusive way of getting the information he desired.

The older woman continued polishing the glass almost as if she hadn't heard him. Shortly, she said, "It went well enough. Though Miz Demetrice swore that Wilma Rabsitt was cheating." She leaned toward Bubba as he sprayed Windex on the window he was working on and whispered conspiratorially, "I think Wilma was just having a good game. For once."

"You win much?"

"I won twenty dollars," she announced proudly. "It took all night to do it, too. Once I was up over sixty. But your ma, she lost almost a hundred. Then Ruby Mercer called about you, and off she went. Everyone else got so frightened by the thought of the po-lice busting in on all of us that the game broke up then and there. There were a few who were late to work, anyway." She pointed at the window Bubba was working on. "You missed a spot."

"Thanks," Bubba said, scrubbing the spot with a paper towel. "So you were there all night long."

"I don't think your ma nor did I get up more than twice to go the bathroom. And neither of us have the bladders of young women anymore." Finally, Adelia figured out what Bubba was getting at. "Oh, Bubba Snoddy. If you want to know something you should just ask me."

Bubba blushed, ashamed to be asking a woman he had known most of his life and adored almost as long, if she was a murderer. Worse yet, he was ashamed to be asking her if another woman they both loved and adored was a murderer. Even a simple, 'What was her alibi and yours, too, by the way?' was just as bad as the other.

Adelia took pity on him. "There were seven women at our table alone, sugar. Your mama, nor I, was not out of sight of most of these women for no longer than five minutes at a time. But there's no point in giving you their names."

"Why not?" Bubba asked and looked at her.

"You can ask the deputy. The sheriff's deputy who was at our game. She lost more than your mama and laughed about it so hard, she near wet her pants."

"What deputy?"

73

"Willodean Gray," Adelia answered slyly. "You know who she is."

Bubba knew.

Chapter Six

Bubba and a Ghost

Monday furthermore then onto Tuesday – Oh, Glory!

Later that day, Bubba was forced to endure the unsolicited attentions of his mother as she returned from her trip to plead for assistance from her state representative on the scurrilous and baseless case of the formerly incarcerated Bubba Snoddy.

Miz Demetrice had been adamant. "I wouldn't leave his office until he agreed to see me." She made a noise not unlike an hmph. "Next election, I believe my five hundred dollars will go to the opposition, even if he is some liberal Yankee who moved down here a mere twenty years ago." But then she was sentimental. "Oh, Bubba honey, did they do anything to you? Those jails have perverts in there. You know what they say on the news about those jails. Men get the AIDS virus there. They beat folks with rubber hoses filled with rocks. And worse." She had rushed over from the big house to the caretaker's house and burst in without even knocking, which was patently unlike her. Then she had launched herself at her son, throwing her arms around him as if he was a life vest, and she was drowning.

Bubba gently disentangled his mother from around his waist, giving her an affectionate pat on her head. "Mama, I was alone in a jail cell for the whole time. We got our meals from the Pegram Café. I don't believe I slept better than I have for a month of

Sundays. And you know, that Newt Durley plays a mean game of chess, when he's of a sober state."

His mother looked at him skeptically. "Oh, Bubba, you're not just saying that..."

Bubba rolled his eyes heavenward, asking for guidance and perhaps some patience. "You know Sheriff John and Tee Gearheart wouldn't put up with any of that nonsense in their jail."

Precious kept in the corner, half behind the couch and eyed Miz Demetrice warily. She knew what that particular human was capable of doing, and she was staying where it was safe until the bomb had safely been defused.

Miz Demetrice considered this information. She could probably even agree with it. She knew Sheriff John. She knew Tee. Both were God-fearing, church-going men who didn't cheat on their wives or lie overly. She nodded, finally satisfied that her only beloved nestling had escaped unscathed from the villainous Sheriff of Pegram County.

By the time Miz Demetrice was done fussing over her solitary child's wretched experience, it was too late for Bubba to go to the jail to visit with Deputy Willodean Gray. His eyes almost misted with regret and then with pride. Now there was a fine, Southern name for a woman such as her. Long, inky black hair. Green eyes that could have been carved from a precious stone. A slender figure with all of the right curves delicately placed...

Bubba shook his head violently, startling his mother. Now it was time to address his mother bluntly, "Mama, did you shoot Melissa Dearman?"

His mother had been expecting the question. She knew her son pretty well. She knew what he was

76

capable of and what he was not capable of was shooting a woman he'd once loved so much he had asked her to marry him. She also knew that Bubba was the one that Sheriff John was looking at harder and harder. But also, since Elgin Snoddy's forty-five was missing, and it had been her forty-five by way of inheritance for some multitude of years, that Sheriff John, and like as not, her son, would be looking at her, too. "Of course not, dear. If I were of a mind to kill a body, young Melissa Dearman being a good example of a body who needed to be killed, I'd of taken a chain saw to her and then put her poor hapless corpse into a wood chipper." She smiled brightly. "Just like I did to your father."

"Pa died of a heart attack, Ma." Miz Demetrice smiled knowingly.

"You were at the poker game all night?"

"Of course, dear. I lost over a hundred dollars and that dad-blasted Wilma Rabsitt was cheating like a son of a bitch." Miz Demetrice adjusted her polka-dotted silk dress and finally sat carefully down on Bubba's ratty couch like the queen she was, back straight, legs crossed delicately at the ankles. Precious decided it was safe and came out to sniff her shoes. Miz Demetrice offered the hound a hand to inspect, which the dog did, and then was scratched lightly behind the long ears for her efforts. The animal made a noise of contentment and settled herself down beside Miz Demetrice just in case the human decided that more loving was in order. "Besides," his mother went on, "you already asked Miz Adelia the same thing."

"You know why."

Miz Demetrice sighed. "I know why. I didn't know what to say when the Sheriff asked where I had been all night. He's going to arrest me and Miz Adelia when he finds out."

"What about the intruders while I was gone?"

"Well, who told you...oh, Adelia has got the biggest mouth, besides my own, of course," Miz Demetrice chuckled. "Adelia left around five on Saturday, and around midnight someone was banging around downstairs as if they were dying. So naturally, I got the shotgun and went downstairs to look, but by the time I got downstairs they were gone. They must have seen all the lights coming on and scrambled the hell on out of there. I went outside and let off a shotgun blast just to let them know they weren't welcome to come a-skulking in the Snoddy Mansion no more. It's certainly not the first time we've had people come wandering over the property looking for things best forgotten a century ago. Damned, ridge-crawling, rough-necked thieves, that's what they are. And stupid to boot, listening to gossip about Colonel Snoddy and his disease ridden stories. These idjits heard you were in jail and decided the pickings were rich that night." She gave Bubba a satisfied look that told him how gleeful she was to have scared the ever living crap out of the morons who came looking for rumors on Saturday night. She would have rubbed her still-sore rump, but her son was staring directly at her with an unfathomable expression on his handsome face. "I keep that shotgun right by my bed."

"They came back on Sunday night?"

"Then I was up waiting for them. Right at midnight, I heard one of the windows in the dining room being messed with, and I let a blast go right through the wall of the living room." She snickered loudly. "I bet they wet their pants for sure."

"I missed the hole in the living room," Bubba commented. "I'll come over and sleep there tonight."

Miz Demetrice shrugged. She wouldn't admit that that would make her feel a lot better. Whoever it was, who had dared to come back after two nights, was either the world's biggest fool or the world's greediest, and certainly up to no good. "Perhaps that would be a good idea."

"I'll be over later. Try not to shoot me, too." Bubba glanced out the window. The sun was setting and vivid clouds of purple slashed over the west. "What about Daddy's forty-five?"

"Oh, you know about that?"

Bubba smiled, but it wasn't a nice smile. "What about the forty-five?"

"Sugar, I don't know when it went missing. I don't believe I've looked at that gun for five years, maybe more. I kept it in a box in the top of my closet so you wouldn't get your hands on it when you were growing up. I meant to give it to you one of these days. You and your grandpappies always liked guns and hunting, that is, when you were young. I thought it would nice for you to have something that your daddy valued. But I had forgotten about it until the Sheriff started asking about guns in the house. Even then I didn't make a connection until later."

"A forty-five was used to kill Melissa," Bubba said. "I had access to one that happens to be missing."

"Bubba, that gun has been sitting in a box in my closet for over twenty years. I don't even know if it would fire without blowing up. It was probably rusted to kingdom come."

"Could it be somewhere else in your house?" he asked patiently. "Could Miz Adelia have moved it?"

79

"No, and no. Miz Adelia never cleaned my closet. I can see that box in my closet every day I walk into it. It's right in plain sight. The box is still there. The holster is still in the box. But the gun is missing." Miz Demetrice considered, rubbing her hands delicately together. Her eyebrows rose eloquently. "Although, the Sheriff didn't seem to be too surprised that I couldn't find it."

Bubba gave up and chalked it up to someone else knowing it was there and taking it. In the spring and in the autumn, the Snoddy Mansion was open to groups of visitors as it had been for the past fifty years. Some sixty people had gone through the house, not a month past, oohing and ahhing over the architecture and the carvings. A thousand people had tromped through the house in the last decade alone. Only the Lord above and the thief knew who could have taken that gun.

Bubba escorted his mother back to the big house and instructed her to lock the doors and windows. Precious was beside him the entire time he did a circuit around the house. He found two windows which were partially obscured that he thought had been tampered with. One was probably the same window that the intruder had messed with when his mother had blown a hole in the living room wall. He studied them carefully and left them alone.

It was after ten PM when he arranged a chair at one of the windows, sitting in the dark shadows with a cup of coffee in his hands and Miz Demetrice's long-barreled shotgun at his side, with Precious at his other side. The stroke of midnight went by without as much as a peep. The only noise was crickets and June bugs outside in the grass and in the trees. Then Bubba heard the grandfather clock in the long hallway ring once for one AM. Bubba didn't hear the bells strike two, but Precious did hear someone fiddling with the window. She had been trained to hunt as a pup but never could sit patiently until her master completed the transaction by killing the prey, which was why she came to be in Bubba's possession. She waited until someone had their leg halfway into the open window and pounced. All the more unexpected it was because she didn't make a noise until after she had something in her jaws.

Bubba woke up abruptly to the sounds of claws on the floor, a man cursing violently, and Precious trying to bark and bite at the same time. Then the intruder started yelling in earnest as the dog achieved her aim by joyfully sinking her teeth into his leg.

Bubba reached for the shotgun and leaped up, shouting, "Who the hell is that?!" Upon reflection, he knew he had been half asleep, dreaming about Deputy Willodean Gray and should not have been anywhere near a shotgun.

Apparently, the abrupt noise he'd made scared the intruder more than anything because he hastily jerked his leg back out the window, causing Precious to fall backwards onto the floor with a thud and a loud yelp. Bubba, who was still groggy, ran smack dab into the window, which wasn't fully open and knocked himself down. The shotgun flew out of his hand and clattered across the room. Precious leaped up from the floor and launched herself at the window, but she was too short and the window was too high for her to get out. By the time Bubba got up, found the shotgun, and returned to the window, he knew that the trespasser was long gone.

Precious was gnawing and ripping at something near the base of the window. Bubba turned on the light in the dining room, blinked a little at the brightness and saw that Precious had herself part of a white sheet. She had ripped it from the intruder's body. Well, part of it, anyway. Bubba held it up and examined it closely. Either the Ku Klux Klan had called, and he didn't see any burning cross on the lawn, or the man had been dressed up like a ghost. The snow-white sheet had two little, neat eye holes cut out next to one another.

Somehow Bubba was sure it hadn't been the Ku Klux Klan.

Miz Demetrice came halfway down the stairs with a flashlight and a hunting rifle held capably in her slender hands. Next to her, the rifle seemed huge. She was dressed in an oversized red robe that seemed to dwarf her as much as the rifle did. Bubba scowled when he saw it. "Just how many guns you got in this house?" he demanded irately.

"Let's say that the NRA and I see eye to eye on a great many issues," Miz Demetrice issued royally. "You mind telling me what in the hell happened just now?"

Bubba held up the sheet like a banner, poking his fingers through the eye holes. Then he grinned. "We got ourselves a ghost."

"What? Another one? We got three already." She ticked them off on the hand that wasn't holding the rifle. "The civil war lady in the upstairs powder room. The little black slave out in the back ten acres, and the midnight coachman who only comes before someone in the Snoddy family dies. No one's seen that one since the week before I stabbed your father." She grumbled all the way back up the stairs, the tails of her long robe trailing behind her. "Just what we need, another goldarned specter."

Six hours later Bubba was up and on his way. Not only had he shaved, showered, and put on his cleanest, newest blue jeans, but he dragged out a pearl white western shirt, and topped it all off with his best Stetson, a dark brown one. Precious gave him an approving woof and climbed into the '54 Chevy truck that was parked off to the side of the yellow crime scene tape. He gave his own approving nod when he saw that Melissa's rental car had mysteriously vanished, presumably taken by the police to the impound lot.

With a roar and a clunk the Chevy started up, emitting about a storm cloud's worth of blue smoke. Some mechanic I am, thought Bubba. But he dismissed it. He was on the trail of Melissa's murderer. He supposed that if it had been two years earlier, he might have thanked that particular individual himself. However, he didn't know exactly when it had happened, but he had stopped hating Melissa. He could even understand why she had felt insecure about her position and wanted to feel safe. On one of his big hands was the issue of clearing his own name. On the other one of his big hands was the matter of finding out just who had murdered Melissa and why they had done it.

Understanding might ease the feeling of disquiet within him. Bubba knew it was going to get a lot worse if the grand jury saw fit to indict him. Furthermore, he knew full and well, it wouldn't take much to do just that. The county prosecutor would take the word of Sheriff John and Sheriff John wouldn't look past the most obvious suspect in the whole state of Texas. Why should they? If it wasn't Bubba himself who was the suspect, he'd be saying the same thing that half the population of Pegramville was saying, too.

It was half past eight in the morning before Bubba parked his truck in front of the Pegram County Sheriff's Department. He noted with some relief that Sheriff John was not present, known by the absence of his county car. However, he didn't know what Deputy Steve Simms' car looked like nor did he know what Deputy Gray drove. So he was taking his chances either way. He rolled down the truck windows, instructed Precious not to attack anyone dressed in sheets no matter how much they looked like the ghost of the previous night, and presented himself to the receptionist. He carried a large brown bag with him, and he put it on one of the various seats in the front office of the Sheriff's Department's offices.

The receptionist was none other than Mary Lou Treadwell, who also manned the emergency phone line. She was a-goggle when Bubba exhibited himself to her, asking for the fair deputy, *Willodean* Gray, and Bubba did indeed emphasize the lady's first name in such a manner.

He even went so far to tip his hat to Mary Lou, who knew all of Pegramville's dirtiest secrets and was not one to keep a confidence to herself. As a matter of fact, Mary Lou didn't even keep her own secrets to herself. Her hair was dyed scarlet red. She wore blue contacts, and she had had not one, but two face lifts. Lastly, she had had a boob job, going from an 'A' cup to a 'D' cup, and her husband was extremely happy about that. She would even share that singular information with anyone who was so inclined to listen on 911 calls. "It shore gets their attention away from them having stabbed their girlfriend or mother," Mary Lou would justify herself.

Mary Lou muttered, "Just a second, Bubba. I'll buzz her desk." As she dialed the telephone, she inspected Bubba with an intrigued eye. *The big man cleans up awfully nice*, she thought. *Too bad he's an ex-fiancée killer. But who could blame him, after finding her in bed with another man? In their very own bed, too.*

In the time that Bubba waited, Foot Johnson, janitor at the Sheriff's Department, came wandering through, as did a secretary, and another sheriff's deputy. All gave Bubba Snoddy a wide berth, although he was trying his best to appear as nonthreatening as possible. If he had been able to, he would have melted into the woodwork, but he was, after all, a large man. A few minutes later, the attractive deputy, Willodean Gray, appeared, coming through the magnetized doors behind Mary Lou.

Bubba respectfully removed his Stetson. Willodean placed herself in front of Bubba squarely and looked intently into his face. After a few seconds she said, "Well?"

Bubba took a list from his jeans pocket. He held it in one hand as Willodean looked first at his face and then at the piece of paper. "My mother's house was broken into over the weekend, and I thought maybe that you could look into it."

Willodean kept her face neutral. She was new to the area of Pegram County it was true, but she had been in law enforcement for five years. She had worked in Dallas for most of that time and decided recently that big city life was not to her liking. When a job opportunity had arisen, even though knew full well that she was a token woman, she had taken it eagerly.

85

For the past month, she had worked with the other deputies and Sheriff John, trying to show them that she was as tough, as capable, as good as any of them. Some of them had grudgingly begun to behave as though she was a 'real' cop, and not a ditzy female who had been hired for the gender alone, and not her ability. But here was Bubba Snoddy, lately a murder suspect, asking her to bend the rules because he was clearly infatuated with her. Finally, she asked, "Did you call it in over the weekend?"

"Nope."

Willodean waited for details and when none were forthcoming, finally asked, "Why not?"

Bubba shifted his feet around a bit. "I didn't think the sheriff's department would be too inclined to look into anything that happens out at the Snoddy place right now. For obvious reasons."

Willodean cast a look over her shoulder at Mary Lou, who was patently ignoring phone calls into her station and listening to their conversation as obviously as she could. "Say, Miz Mary Lou, you got a call there," she told the emergency line operator slash receptionist. To Bubba, she said, "Let's walk outside a bit."

Bubba said, "A moment, please." He placed himself before Mary Lou again and put the brown grocery bag before her. Mary Lou put some unfortunate soul on hold and looked inquiringly up at Bubba. "It's books for Mike Holmgreen. You know, some mysteries, trashy fiction, and other stuff my mother was going to give to the Goodwill. Will you see he gets it? That boy needs something to do all day besides play chess with other prisoners and do algebra."

He turned back to Willodean and even held the door open for her.

They were outside walking slowly down the street before Willodean said, "That was a nice thing to do for Mike Holmgreen."

Bubba shrugged. "He's not a bad kid. Just made a mistake."

"And did you make a...mistake?"

"Not the one you're thinking of." Bubba considered. "I think the worst thing I've ever done was to lose my temper when I found my fiancée in bed with another man."

Willodean almost groaned. Why didn't Bubba just notarize a motive and pass it over to Sheriff John and the district attorney? "You broke his arm."

Bubba nodded. "It wasn't a good thing to do. When I came out of being angry, you know I was so mad I couldn't see straight, I found out that I had broken his arm. And worse."

Willodean paused in her step. They had crossed over Main Street and were standing next to the courthouse. It was a huge, red-bricked affair with five floors, a clock tower, and Italianate carved faces that peered out at every level and corner of the building. It dated from 1895, and in the summer the tourists would flock to it because it was such a grand, stately place, surrounded by an acre of well-manicured greenery. But she wasn't examining the courthouse's intricate architecture; instead she looked into Bubba's face. It was bleak with memory. He was staring forward, but he wasn't seeing anything, except into the past. "What's worse than breaking his arm?" she asked gently.

"Have you ever spanked a little child, maybe a pet, a cat, a dog or the like?" he asked instead of answering.

"Yes," she replied. Her sisters had children. And she'd had pets.

"Maybe you spanked a little hard once and had a child look up at you, or a pet look up at you, and they were scared of you." He finally put his Stetson back on his head, adjusting it carefully. She didn't say anything. She thought she knew what he was getting at. "When the red haze cleared out, that man was frightened of me. That's what's worse. I had scared a man so badly he was shaking with fear. He thought...he thought I was going to kill him."

There was a cool spring breeze wafting around the courthouse. Not too many people were around at the time. Across the way, the Pegram Café seemed to be almost empty. "I was angry at Melissa Dearman once. But if I had seen her again, I wouldn't have lost my temper," he finished. "I didn't kill her. I want to find out who did."

"And the Sheriff isn't inclined to help you out," she completed the meaning he was trying to convey.

"Just so."

"What do you want from me?"

"Someone who is objective enough to see that I'm not the only suspect, or to at least, believe that maybe I might not have done it." Bubba crackled the list in his hands. "This here is my list of suspects. My mother was tops."

Willodean laughed, thinking of hours spent playing poker with various, eccentric ladies of Pegram County. "Well, that's one down."

"And Miz Adelia Cedarbloom, my mother's housekeeper," he went on, "was number two."

88

"I guess you know that I was involved in the...ah...Pegramville Women's Club activities that night," Willodean commented mildly.

"Is that what my mother is calling it lately?" Bubba chuckled. "Well, Mama claims that she murdered my father, but I don't think she would have shot my ex-fiancée in the back. Same with Miz Adelia. Maybe they would have dropped a cement block, but not shot her in the back."

"Who else you got on that list?"

"Melissa's husband." Bubba's voice was serious. "You know, the man's whose arm I broke."

Chapter Seven

Bubba Gets in a Fight

Tuesday

"What about your intruder?" Willodean Gray asked of Bubba Snoddy. They still stood in front of the courthouse, a cool breeze wafting the smell of honeysuckle over them. The shrubbery around the edifice was abundant with honeysuckle, and it was in full aromatic bloom.

Willodean was speaking to him in a different tone of voice, perhaps one that had a bit more seriousness in it. Bubba had suddenly ceased being a 'suspect' and was now a 'human being.' He liked that.

"I wonder if that person might have seen something that night. Maybe that person can tell me what happened," Bubba said, trying not to stare at Willodean's pouting ruby lips.

"Did you consider that your burglar might have done the killing himself?" Willodean chewed on her lower lip. Bubba watched, fascinated. *Just look at that lower lip. Golly gee whiz. What did she say?* "But why are they breaking in your place?"

"I suspect to scare my mother. I don't believe the fella is interested in killing anyone." Bubba took the piece of bed sheet out of his pocket. He had put in carefully into a plastic, Ziploc baggie. He sighed, considering whether to tell Willodean the rest of the story behind the frequent intruders out at the Snoddy Mansion. But damned if Bubba was going to advertise to such an attractive woman that not only was there a famous, addlebrained kook in the family tree but that his legacy was still impacting the property in terms of excessive heaps of dirt scattered here, there, and everywhere, as well as in the form of frequent and irritating intruders intent on hitting the mother lode. "Here's what he was wearing early this morning." He amended that. "Well, he was wearing other stuff, too. But this was on top."

Willodean carefully took the baggie. She held it up and turned it this way and that. Finally, she looked at Bubba again. Her lips were twitching. "I don't suppose the Klan is mad at you. People burning crosses in your yard and such?"

Bubba smiled. "There hasn't been an active Klan around here since the 1930s, and no, my grandfathers were not involved. They were too busy making a living."

She shrugged, and Bubba couldn't help but admire the slender twist of her shoulders. "What else?"

"I read that DNA evidence can be taken from saliva," Bubba said pointedly. Then he pointed at the baggie she still held in her hand. "Those are eye holes. So he must have breathed on it, maybe even left saliva on it. I figure we can identify that person. Not to mention that the windows he's been trying to get into must be covered with fingerprints. I don't believe he was wearing gloves. You could come and see if there's any there. Then run them on your database." Bubba didn't know what was wrong with him. That had been more than he had said in the last month, including at the police interrogation. He was beginning to sound like a charismatic preacher on a Sunday after the welfare checks had been delivered.

Willodean nodded. "And if you can identify this person, then you might have a witness. However, we don't really have the resources for all that. It takes a lot of money that the Pegram County Sheriff's Department is not budgeted for. Folks don't realize the stuff on CSI is a tad bit exaggerated. But Bubba, the real question would be why would anyone be trying to scare your mother?"

"I believe it's that damned Neal Ledbetter." Bubba chomped down hard on his lower teeth not realizing that a vein in his forehead popped out as he did so. He could picture Neal in the yard with him, staring down at Melissa's body. Just as innocent as you please. That man was a carpetbagger born of other shady carpetbaggers.

"Of Ledbetter Realtors?" Her voice was incredulous. Bubba could see it plainly on her face. Why would a bland, well-to-do realtor feel like donning bed linens and come a-calling after midnight? If it had been said in the bright light of day, it would sound a little silly, even to Bubba.

Bubba nodded anyway. He would explain the reasons that had led him to that conclusion. "For some reason, Neal has decided that the Snoddy property is the only and bestest place to put a new Walmart. My mother, Miz Demetrice, isn't of a mind to sell the family estates."

"A Walmart?"

"A Walmart Supercenter. Just like the one fifteen miles up the road. I don't think they would approve of Mr. Ledbetter's strategies. There's a lot of farm land around the area, but most of the farmers wouldn't let their lands go for what Neal wants to pay. But here's a big chunk of land, just aching to be sold, and alls that's on it, is a big, old, falling down, ramshackle of a place that needs demolishing before it comes crashing to the ground all by itself." Bubba sighed. "Not to mention it's convenient to the folks of Pegramville and simple to get to. A big Walmart sign could easily be seen from the freeway. It's a good piece of property for that, except that there's a woman standing in the way. Neal has always been a slimy, underhanded sort just skirting the line of the law. You can ask the Sheriff. He's been trying to get Neal for fraud for the last decade." He paused. "The money would be nice, but my mother is determined to keep the place up and running."

"What about you?"

"I think it needs a historical foundation to restore the mansion. It's a fine place, but it needs some tender loving care." Bubba thought of something else that needed a little tender, loving care and then mentally chastised himself. *Bubba,* he told himself silently, *you already got one woman dangling, and you would be a dandified fool to think you can play with two.* He scratched the side of his head just under the edge of his hat. "I'd like to see it in all of its past glory, myself. D'you know that Robert E. Lee once spent the night there on his way to Austin, Texas. And there's been two presidents there as well. Taft and Roosevelt. Teddy Roosevelt, that is. That was when the Snoddy name still had a little panache. And a little more money, too."

Willodean looked mighty interested. "But Neal Ledbetter doesn't see that?" she asked. "Nor does he care."

"No. So, he thinks he can scare my mother. Or at least that's who I think is doing that. Neal should know

93

my mother doesn't scare very easily. As a matter of fact, she thinks that someone parading around in a sheet on the Snoddy properties is next to hilarious. And it will be, until she lets go a round of salt rock right in his sheet-covered ass." Bubba tipped his hat to Willodean. "Pardon my French."

"I've heard the word before," noted Willodean. Not only that, but she had gotten to know Miz Demetrice very well over the last couple poker games, and she didn't think the older woman would be too scared by a linen-garbed idiot moaning and rattling chains in the middle of the night either. "I think I can get the forensics guy to go by your place and take fingerprints of the windows. We'll say your mother filed a complaint, hmm?"

"Perhaps that would be best," Bubba said.

Suddenly, Willodean smiled. "Sometimes you sound like a redneck fresh out of the woods, and sometimes that parlance and phrasing sounds just like a cultured fella who forgot to talk down...Imagine that."

Bubba sure liked a high-spirited woman. Willodean was such a woman. She was full of sass, and vinegar, and a little spice that makes life a lot more interesting. He mentally compared her to Lurlene Grady. Although Lurlene was a comely creature, she was more obliging, more ready to agree with Bubba and go with the flow. But this woman, she wouldn't take any kind of guff from him or from any other man. No wilting flower, she. He shrugged to the comment she had made.

They walked back toward the Sheriff's Department offices, and when they got there, out walked Major Michael Dearman.

Bubba supposed it had been inevitable that the man whose arm he had once broken would turn up to claim the body of his wife. But Bubba was still surprised. The Major was dressed in Army class 'A' attire, commonly called 'greens.' Every ribbon was in place. Every bit of gold was polished, rank and medal alike. He was putting on his green saucer cap which had a band of gold leaves ringing it, when his eyes made contact with Bubba's.

Dearman still looked like the same fella he'd been three years earlier. Although, Bubba thought that maybe having a little child would make a difference on a man's appearance. But then here was a man who had just lost his wife. How he had lost his wife was the important part, or at least it was to Bubba.

Dearman was a tall man but not as tall as Bubba. He was also leaner with long ropy muscles that indicated a man who enjoyed running in a marathon or two. Not a spare ounce of fat on this man. The skin still fit as taut over his well-formed face, but the heavy black rings of exhaustion belied the rest of his appearance. His blonde hair was cut military short with not a dissenting lock out of place. Blue-gray eyes observed everything in purified military fashion. Here was a man who had been born and raised specifically for the intent of performing well in the United States Army.

Dearman continued to stare at Bubba with a puzzled look on his face. It was self-evident that while he hadn't immediately recognized the other man, he knew his face from somewhere. It was a face Dearman should have recognized, and that was what was troubling him.

That surprised Bubba even further. Could it be possible that the Major hadn't known where his errant wife was going? That was part of Bubba's theory. Irate major knows that beautiful, young trophy wife is returning to old lover, follows her to old lover's place, and murders her in a fit of rage. That theory plainly relied on the information that Major Michael Dearman knew where his wife was going and who his wife was going to see. Because if he didn't know where and who, then he didn't have a motive for murder.

Dammitall, thought Bubba, vexed. *So much for suspect number three.* But he brightened. It could be that the Major was merely a good actor. After all, there was a sheriff's deputy standing beside him, watching the Major herself, with her own growing recognition of the general situation, even if she was a little, slender thing that looked as if a strong wind could blow her right over.

But then a couple came out from the door just behind the Major. These were two people in their early sixties. Bubba knew them, but he had never met them. He had seen a framed portrait of them sitting on Melissa's dresser for about two months every time he had gone into the bedroom. The man was balding and had a paunch. He was dressed in what had to be his best suit, a brown, polyester accommodation that looked about twenty years old, with a wide, striped tie that looked even older. He was tugging at his collar as if its tightness pained him, and he had Melissa's blue eyes. The woman looked to be his age, dressed in a flowered print with a neat little box hat over her gray hair. She still held a little snow white handkerchief in her hand with which she continued to dab at her eyes.

Her features were a picture of what Melissa would have looked like had she lived so long.

Melissa had been one of five children but the only girl. Although her family had been poor, they had loved their daughter. They had also been proud of her accomplishments while she had been in the Army. Certainly, they would have come to see about the murder of their only daughter. Maybe they would have accompanied their son-in-law to claim her body.

Bubba didn't have a long time to cogitate about these matters because Willodean hissed at him out of the corner of her perfect crimson mouth, "You need to go now."

Bubba agreed heartily. He took one step toward his truck where Precious was intently observing his every action.

Precious was quite perturbed that she hadn't been allowed to go on a walk with the other human, and she would certainly hold it against her master for as long as a minute perhaps. But then another game was afoot as the dog observed the human in the green suit and the green hat give a sudden hoarse shout that she didn't understand. Her master twisted his head about, just in time to see the man in green launch himself at him. Precious scrambled to get her body through the open window but couldn't manage it, so she began to bark and bay as if a safe were going to be dropped on her master's head, which in a way it was.

Dearman lost his hat in his launch at Bubba who he had finally recognized. Willodean stepped in between them, and Bubba reached out one large hand and shoved her out of the way. The Connors watched the spectacle as if they suspected that their son-in-law had just lost his mind.

One of Dearman's arms pulled back, his hand clenched in a fist, and let go at Bubba's head. It connected solidly, and the Stetson went off his head, flying away to parts unknown. But Bubba merely rocked back a little on his heels. Inside his mouth he could feel with his tongue that one of his teeth was loose. Dearman had quite expected Bubba to go down like the giant from the story about the beanstalk and a nondescript fella named Jack. When Bubba didn't, Dearman hesitated, unsure of what to do next.

Willodean gave Bubba a look of intense dislike, which dismayed Bubba more than being hit in the face with a fist. She reached out and spun Dearman around, expertly throwing him against Bubba's truck with a solid clanking noise. Dearman had forgotten about her and went to strike her without thinking about who he would be hitting, but Bubba caught his arm. Coincidently, it was the same arm he had broken three years earlier.

Dearman glanced back at the large man holding his right arm. He trembled just a bit before regaining his righteous anger. "Go ahead, you lowlife hick. Go ahead, do it again," he snarled, baring his teeth in a rictus grin that held no humor. "Just what I'd expect from a murderer."

Bubba's lips flattened in a grim line. "I understand why you want to hit me. And I have only one thing to say to you. I didn't kill Melissa. But you won't hit Deputy Gray. She ain't done nothing to you."

Willodean rolled her eyes. *Just what I need, a big macho protector*, she thought, incensed. "I can handle this, Bubba," she gritted through her teeth.

Bubba let go of Dearman's arm. The other man yanked it back to his side and began to rub his fist where bone had met bone. Then he stared at Bubba as if hate itself could kill the other man.

Bubba wondered how much Dearman and the Connors had been told about who was a suspect in the case, who was the only suspect in the case. He wondered if he had already been arrested, tried, and convicted in their minds. He turned on his heel and went to the door of his truck. Precious bayed once more at the Major, and retreated to the passenger side of the truck. "Deputy, I think the Major is a little...overwrought, and maybe he deserves a break on this." He paused, wincing at his own words.

Then Bubba got into his old truck, started it up, and drove away, his dog peering venomously out the back window at the lot of them.

Bubba didn't see Willodean pick up his brown Stetson and look at it thoughtfully. But then Willodean didn't see Bubba crumple up his list of suspects and throw it out the window in a fit of pique.

He drove to Bufford's Gas and Grocery where he picked up some of his belongings from the garage. The day mechanic was named Melvin Wetmore, and he was already back from being employed at Walmart. Bubba supposed that George Bufford had made Melvin a better offer.

Melvin had lately been speaking of the newest deputy in the sheriff's department. He was stuck under Mr. Smith's Mercury, yanking on something that Bubba suspected was the transmission. Melvin was a man in his fifties, as bald as a cue ball, and cross-eyed to boot. He wore glasses with lenses so thick they could cause a fire if one were to leave them in the wrong place with the sun shining. But Melvin did have an eye for females of any size, shape, texture, and persuasion, and never tired of them. Much to the surprise of most of Pegram County, the females never seemed to tire of him either.

"Hey, Melvin," said Bubba preemptively.

Melvin stuck his head out the side of the Mercury. "Hey, Bubba. I don't think George Bufford's going to be real happy about you being here."

Bubba picked up an empty box that once contained 10W - 40W oil. He put his calendar of the *Women of Texas* in it. After all, it still had seven naturally Southern women from Texas on it, of whom Bubba had not cast his male gaze upon, and God knew that Bubba could use something to divert his attention. Melvin protested, "Hey, I ain't looked at the rest of that."

"I'll say the same thing I'd say to George Bufford ifin he was here instead of boinking Miss Rosa Granado in the Bahamas: Ain't that a fucking shame?" Bubba's jaw was starting to ache, and he suspected he was going to have a black eye as well, since the Major's fist had kind of slid up Bubba's face, bouncing off his eye socket, leaving a half swollen eye. In other words, Bubba wasn't in the kind of mood to put up with any crap. He wasn't in a mood to be polite, and he didn't really care if he didn't use proper English and did use very improper swear words.

Bubba put in his set of metric wrenches. Then he put in a mallet, a set of Craftsman screwdrivers, and two shirts he had left here to change into if he had spilled various automotive components on himself and needed to be presentable to Lurlene.

Melvin commented, "You know someone played a right fine joke on me." He waited a moment and went on. "Someone called me up and pretended to be a human resources manager. Said they heard about my reputation and all. Wanted me to show up Thursday night for work." He paused for effect and swiftly changed the subject. "So they say you had a fit of rage and done shot yer old fee-on-say."

Bubba paused in his search for old items to glare briefly at the mechanic sticking his head half out from under Mr. Smith's Mercury. He put a few other things in the box, filling it to capacity, and then added a handful of Bufford stamped pencils and pens for good measure. Melvin added hastily, "I wouldn't believe that."

"Melvin," Bubba said at last, "tell George that he owes me for two weeks' pay, and if he don't pay me P.D.Q. I'm gonna sue him whether I'm in jail or not."

Melvin adjusted his thick-lensed glasses and said, "You know George ain't gonna pay no criminal back pay."

"Melvin." Bubba glowered down at the mechanic, watching as Melvin winced and scooted halfway back under the Mercury. Bubba set his jaw in place even though it hurt like a sonuvabitch. "You putting that transmission back in?"

"Yeah, damned sucker is heavy, too."

"You forgot the seal." It was a part that Melvin would need to undo all of the work he had probably done for the last hour in order to repair. Bubba couldn't help but notice that particular part sitting all by its lonesome on one of the benches.

"Oh, Christ in a sidecar!" Melvin cried, clearly dejected.

Bubba smiled to himself. The only thing he was sorry about was that he couldn't have told Melvin about the missing part until after Melvin had completely finished the transmission. He went out to his truck, put the box in the back, and went inside Bufford's to get himself some ice.

Leelah Wagonner was at the counter, and Bubba supposed that the place looked a bit more presentable than the last time he had been in here. The floor was clean and not one hot dog was blocking the mechanism of the hot dog machine. Nothing was exploding, beeping, or buzzing. It was peaceful. He sat a bag of ice down before her along with a dollar bill, having decided that staying close-mouthed was infinitely preferable than talking to most of the townsfolk about these days.

Leelah gave him some change, and smiled tentatively, "You know, Bubba, there are some folks who think you didn't do it."

Bubba wasn't in the best frame of mind, but he looked at Leelah to see if she were in earnest. She was. "I appreciate that, Miz Wagonner," he replied at last.

"But the way some talk about it, you were rightful in killing off that woman, considering what she done to you. If you had killed her, that is." Leelah looked befuddled, having confused herself. She considered what she had said, and added, "Not that I think you did. Oh, heck, I'm sorry. I don't think you did it but that Sheriff John, well, when he's of a mind, he's like a bulldog, and he ain't apt to let go."

Bubba put the bag of ice across his head. It was big enough to cover not only his eye but his jaw as well. *What it really sounded like*, he thought, *is that people are going to wait until I'm convicted before saying, 'I told you he was a murderer, even if she did deserve it.'*

Leelah waved to him as he drove off, leaving him in a slightly better mood. At the rate he was going, half the people in Pegramville weren't going to talk to him based on the fact that he might be a murderer. But if he were acquitted, then that was okey-dokey. On the other hand, if he were found guilty, then they could still feel a little righteous. Luckily for Bubba, he knew that there were people who would speak to him, people who would wait for all of the facts to come in before convicting him mentally in their minds.

A person like that was one Doctor George Goodjoint. Doc Goodjoint was a local practitioner around Pegramville, who would still do a house call, when it was necessary. What he also did was to act as a Pegram County Coroner, when it was also necessary, as well. And that was what Bubba was really interested in at the moment.

Chapter Eight

Bubba Finds a Clue

Tuesday through Wednesday

"I need to see Dr. Goodjoint," Bubba Snoddy announced at the Pegramville Family Medical Clinic and Chiropractic Care Center. Licensed Practical Nurse Dee Dee Lacour looked at Bubba as though he had sprouted horns and a tail. Bubba craned his neck around to check if indeed he had germinated a red appendage on his gluteus maximus. He had not. What a relief. Then he realized that must mean that he had a booger hanging from his nose. That wasn't a relief. He wiped his nose quickly with the hand which was not holding the sack of ice in place.

Although he needed the ice to reduce the swelling on his face, Bubba thought it also made a nice cover story for going in to see the doctor. Then the doctor wouldn't have to listen to any of Sheriff John Headrick's blather about talking too much to suspects in an ongoing murder case. As if diabolical murders happened around Pegramville on a regular basis.

There were three other people in the waiting room of the family clinic. One was Doris Cambliss, and if there was a soul in town who didn't know who she was, then Bubba thought that person surely must be deaf, dumb, and blind. Simply put, and it could not be simpler, Doris ran the brothel. The Red Door Inn, to be precise, was a thinly veiled disguise for the brothel. The brothel had been in existence since the 1850s,

104

originally opened by some of Doris's forebears. It was widely accepted that the brothel had kept the Yankees from burning Pegramville down to the foundations by Union soldiers in 1864. A troop of brothel girls had hastily scuttled out to entertain some of the Union officers. Then the colonel in charge of the company of Union troops had become infatuated with Miss Annalee Hyatt, one of the Red Door's most popular prostitutes. Miss Annalee had been raised in Pegramville, had family still there, and kind of liked the place. She pleaded with the colonel not to destroy it and did her utmost to convince the officer of her sincerity. The colonel, whose name had been lost in the annals of history, apparently thought highly of Miss Annalee's charms, and thus was persuaded. Consequently, when brothels of the west became immoral and then illegal, in that order, it was with a blind eye that the law enforcement of the area overlooked the Red Door's activities. A full length portrait of Miss Annalee, displayed with all of her charms apparent, was hanging in the living room, a testament to her influence, her ingenuity, and her breasts, not necessarily in that order.

"Miz Cambliss," said Bubba, reaching up to tip his hat and realizing that he no longer wore one.

Doris was in her fifties but looked thirty-five. She wore make-up with stunning success, knowing how to compliment her features with mastery. She wore her hair dyed jet black, no one had an inkling as to her true hair color except her hair dresser, and that person wasn't talking. She wore clothing made of silk, bearing designer labels that the local women looked on in disdain but were secretly jealous of her style and flair. Her brown eyes often twinkled with humor when she

105

saw someone eyeing her up and down with apprising stares. She didn't care what folks thought of her. Enough of the residents of Pegramville supported her behind closed doors and that was enough to make her giggle all the way to the bank.

Bubba knew from talk that she didn't run as many girls as her forebears did; the business wasn't a cash cow anymore. So she had gradually turned the Red Door into a bed and breakfast, full of antiques, and history. Half the time, people who stayed there didn't even know the real nature of the business, despite the portrait of Miss Annalee in all of her naked and pink glory.

The other customers in the clinic were a mother with her small child. The pair stayed well to one side, avoiding both Doris and Bubba as if they both had the plague.

Doris patted the seat next to her. "Say, Bubba Snoddy, welcome to my world. My blood pressure is up again." She added cheerfully, sotto voce, "I cain't imagine why."

Bubba laughed. Nurse Dee Dee scowled. The mother on the other side of the waiting room scowled. The small child stared with big eyes. Bubba sat next to the madam in one of the waiting room's nondescript plastic chairs.

"That's a fine-looking piece of work, you got done to you there," Doris commented, referring to the growing bruise and black eye.

"Thank you, Ma'am," he smiled. "How's the bed and breakfast business?"

She leaned over to whisper in his ear. "Well, I ain't seen you there since you was eighteen years old, but I have to say that the B&B is doing much better than the brothel."

Bubba spent about twenty minutes speaking to Doris about antiques, and bed and breakfasts. Doris was of the opinion that the Snoddy Mansion would make a fine bed and breakfast. Then the older woman was called in to see the doctor. "Small towns with colorful histories are big business these days," she said on her way in. "And we both know just how colorful Pegramville can be."

Bubba spent another fifteen minutes being stared at by the five-year-old child with an obvious case of chicken pox and his indignant mother before they were called in. Looking at the child mildly scratching at his face with mittens duct-taped on his little hands made Bubba want to rub like an old hound dog. He lazily scratched the side of his nose.

Doris came back out about ten minutes after that and called to Bubba as she left, "You come see me, hear?"

Nurse Dee Dee made a noise that sounded suspiciously like she had smelled something bad and was trying not to breathe. Then she motioned him to follow her into an examining room, where she took his temperature, his blood pressure, and his pulse. "What's a-matter with you?" she demanded in a sour tone that denoted clearly that she thought 99% of the patients in to see the doctor were full of tomfoolery and monkey business.

"Now that's a long list by some people's standards," he remarked idly. He started to name, "Too lazy. Too dumb. Too..."

Nurse Dee Dee, who was a short, plump woman with a lack of humor that was notorious throughout the entire county, snapped, "Today. What brings you here today?"

Bubba pointed at his eye, which was just about swollen shut. "Something came in contact with my eye." He almost smiled at her. Almost. His lips twitched.

Nurse Dee Dee muttered something under her breath that sounded like, "I'll just bet." Then she disappeared out the door. A few minutes later the doctor swept in.

Doctor George Goodjoint was an elderly man who had attended Harvard and Johns Hopkins for his various degrees, including a couple in medicine and one in philosophy. Then he had returned to practice general medicine in the small farming community he loved. He was a shade less than six foot tall, tended to stoop because of a curvature in his spine, and possessed a shock of white hair that he liked to periodically sweep back over his forehead.

Miz Demetrice had always gotten along fine with the doctor and he with her, which was why he came to supper at the Snoddy place about once a month. Bubba suspected it was because both of their spouses were dead; they had to have someone else to argue with. Consequently, Bubba tended to avoid his mother's monthly dinner affairs as if his life depended on it. No one could be sure who would attend or what would happen in the evening. But her one and only son knew nine times out of ten it was some sort of mayhem. One memorable evening ended with a duel fought with two hundred-year-old muskets and with the entire household incarcerated in the county jail another time for repeatedly disturbing the peace. All of which would occur with his mother and the good doctor egging everyone else on, and bets on exactly how many squad cars would be deployed from the Sheriff's Department.

Doc grinned at Bubba, using one gangly hand to turn the younger man's head toward him, examining the swelling on his face. "Got any teeth loose, boy?"

"Lower molar," mentioned Bubba. He pointed with one hand.

Doc reached inside Bubba's mouth with two long fingers, and liberally wiggled the tooth back and forth. Bubba grunted. "Yep," Doc said. "That's a loose tooth all right. It's my professional opinion, based on years of advanced training in the area of human medicines, and years of practice that you should have a shot of twelve-year-old scotch, and then go see a dentist. Now lemme have a look at that eye."

He peered into Bubba's swelling eye. He pulled out an orthoscope and shined a light in the impaired eye. He made several noises sounding like, "Uh-huh. How about that. Mmph." Then Doc leaned back and said, "You didn't come here about your eye. That eye is fine. Keep putting ice on it today, and it'll be okay in about a week. It ain't the first black eye you had, nor do I suspect will it be the last."

Bubba crossed his arms over his chest. "I been having problems with impotence," he deadpanned. "I believe my pecker is dead."

Doc choked until his face turned the shade of purple that was just about the color of eggplants at the grocery store. "Jesus, Bubba, why don't you just say you want to know about that Dearman girl. I know that's why you're here. Boy, you're as slow as molasses in the wintertime. Your mama was here on

Monday asking about her, and I'll tell you the same thing."

Bubba waited patiently. Finally, he asked, "Which is?"

"Not a goddamn thing." Doc barked with laughter. "Impotence. At my age, little surprises like that are enough to give a man a coronary." He patted the breast of his white jacket as if he were knocking on wood for good luck.

"Or the brandy and cigars you and Miz Demetrice share."

"Or that, too," Doc agreed, a little smile curling his lips. He flipped his alabaster white hair back over his forehead and out of his eyes. "Missed you out on Thursday."

Bubba knew what Doc meant. Doc had been out to the Snoddy Mansion to take a look at Melissa's dead body, pronounce her dead, and all that consisted of his coroner duties. Bubba had been a little too preoccupied to walk up and give a friendly howdy. For some reason.

"Sheriff John is about to put my head on a platter and serve it up to the grand jury," Bubba pointed out calmly. He gazed directly into Doc's eyes. No lie about that. It was exactly what the Sheriff of Pegram County was about to do to Bubba. Furthermore, Sheriff John was going to do it with wondrous glee in his heart and immense self-satisfaction that a murderer had been apprehended.

Doc placed himself carefully in a chair. Bubba remained perched on the examining table. The two stared at each other for a long time. Finally, Doc said, "That Dee Dee Lacour is going to come in here and ask what in the hell is taking my old bones so long to look at a little, insignificant black eye. She's a mean woman. Don't ever marry a mean woman. They make your life a living hell. Glad I'm not married to her. Bad enough that she's my nurse."

Bubba thought about what Nurse Dee Dee could do with her question and decided not to offer the thought up to Doc, just in case the older man was of a mood to follow up on the suggestion.

Doc sighed. "Melissa Anne Dearman was killed approximately at half past ten of the PM on that night. Her body temperature relates that information, however, it was a warm night, and taken statistical probabilities into account, I would give Sheriff John and Deputy Simms about an hour leeway. Here comes another however, Bubba. There was a witness who places her at Bufford's Gas and Grocery at around ten-fifteen PM to ten-thirty PM."

Lloyd Goshorn, thought Bubba. *Nothing I haven't thought about before.*

Doc went on, "So we can say with reasonable certainty that Missus Dearman died between ten-thirty PM and eleven-thirty PM. Personally, I would say closer to 10:30 PM. She died almost immediately upon being shot. There was very little bleeding from the wound so that would indicate this was so. Furthermore, the murderer shot her as she was running away and from a distance of about ten feet. It was either a lucky shot, or the shooter was a damned fine shot."

Bubba was a good shot. He placed third last year at the Turkey Shoot, scoring just below a local police officer and the mayor's sister. Sheriff John had been there shooting as well. So had Simms. So had half the town folk. But then the thirty-eight revolver Bubba

111

had used belonged to Bubba's cousin, Harv, over in Louisiana, who had come to visit with Miz Demetrice. Bubba didn't even own a handgun. Or even a rifle.

"Otherwise, she wasn't harmed. No defensive wounds. No bruising. Nothing to suggest that any other damage occurred to her before or after her death." Doc sighed again. "They won't ask me this, Bubba, but it sounds like a crime of passion. A spur of the moment kind of thing. A man in a fit of anger might shoot a lady in the back."

Bubba was getting tired of people giving him a look that suggested that while he might be justified in killing an ex-fiancée who had slept with another man in their own bed, that he was also a murderer. "I...didn't...kill...her." He clamped down so hard that his jaw audibly popped.

Doc sat up straight in his chair. "Christ Almighty, Bubba Snoddy. I didn't say you did. I'm telling you what the sheriff is going to say to the grand jury and what ninety-nine point nine percent of the population of Pegramville is thinking. Boy, if you didn't shoot her, then who in the hell would have?"

Bubba thanked the doctor, not knowing how to answer a question that had been plaguing him endlessly since he had found Melissa dead in the long grass of the overgrown Snoddy gardens. He paid the bill to a disinterested cashier, ignored Nurse Dee Dee's sullen face, and left by the same way he'd come.

Precious was just as eager to see him as she always was. She drooled on him as much as she could, before getting her fill and retreating to the passenger side to observe the local flora and fauna they passed in the truck. She stuck her head out the open window and panted lustfully.

112

Ten minutes later, Bubba was walking into his home. For most of the afternoon he slept on the couch downstairs, his big feet sticking way off the end, but there was no one but Precious there to notice. He woke up to the phone ringing and heard Adelia Cedarbloom telling him that some 'po-lice' officers had been in taking fingerprints off the dining room windows and making plaster molds out of footprints from the mud underneath the same windows.

Bubba nodded thoughtfully. Deputy Willodean Gray had come through for him. When he wandered out onto his front porch, he found that she had returned his brown Stetson and left it in one of the Adirondack chairs there. He fingered the brim where she must have touched it with her shapely hands and sighed before taking it back inside.

There was a call from Lurlene Grady, and Bubba spent almost a half hour speaking to her, though most of the conversation went in one direction, from her to him. She wanted to know all about jail, and all about being suspected of murdering someone, and had she really been his ex-fiancée, and why hadn't Bubba told her about that woman before? Bubba's answers were along the lines of, 'Yep,' 'Nope,' and 'Dunno.'

He couldn't help a brief mental comparison between two women. One dark. One light. One sassy. One talky. Bubba shook his head like a wet old hound dog. *Man, you don't want to go there,* he told himself. So he did not.

Since he had skipped lunch, Bubba went over to the big house to eat dinner with his mother. Adelia had made Yankee pot roast, which made her laugh uproariously when she did so for some unknown reason. Something about irony and the Civil War.

113

However, only Miz Demetrice and Bubba sat down to dinner in the cavernous dining room.

Bubba got a big piece of roast beef, a mountain of new potatoes, and a teetering pile of carrots and proceeded to drown the entire dish in gravy. Miz Demetrice nibbled on the roast beef and several carrots, staring at the bruises on her son's face.

"Miz Adelia is as fine a cook as ever," Bubba said.

His mother nodded. "You know, Bubba, my lawyer came by today. You know, Mr. Petrie."

Bubba knew Mr. Petrie. He didn't think much of Mr. Petrie. The lawyer reminded him of a mortician. He was always dressed in a three-piece black suit, even when the humidity and the temperature were three digits, and everyone else was positively dying from heat stroke. He wore a black derby, a black tie, and wingtips. He fawned over Miz Demetrice as if gold pieces would pour out of her mouth his hands. And damned if Bubba knew the man's first name. It was always Lawyer Petrie or Mr. Petrie, esquire. So basically, Bubba kept his mouth shut. Something about discretion being the better part of valor.

Miz Demetrice rolled her eyes at her son. "I know you know Mr. Petrie. Well, don't worry. I haven't given him control of the Snoddy fortune yet." She laughed. "You know that man still thinks we have a fortune. Anyway, he mentioned that he was aware of your plight and offered to be your lawyer."

"Lawyer Petrie does family law. Not criminal law," he added unnecessarily.

"You're my son."

Bubba accidentally bit his tongue and cursed appropriately.

"Well, I didn't get you out of a cabbage patch."

Bubba said, "No one is saying you did, Mama. Lawyer Petrie isn't an expert in criminal law."

"He's a lawyer."

"He's an idiot."

"Mr. Petrie says the grand jury is convening soon to see if you will be indicted."

"Doc Goodjoint said you were over at his office on Monday," Bubba said, spearing a carrot with his fork.

Miz Demetrice gave her son a piercing look that only a mother could give to a son. She took a delicate sip of red wine. It was a New Mexican vintage she had recently 'discovered.' "You should have some of this."

"He told me what he told you."

"Well, Bubba honey, I didn't want you to worry," Miz Demetrice explained.

Bubba sat up in the chair. "Listen, Mama. I'm in a world of hurt here. I can't explain to you how much in trouble I am in right now. I'm so screwed that..."

"I get the picture, Bubba. One doesn't need to be so graphic," his mother protested.

"I'm the only one who had any reason to kill Melissa," Bubba started, and his mother cut right in.

"You're the only one who had a reason, who doesn't have an alibi," Miz Demetrice corrected primly.

"Who better than me?"

Miz Demetrice considered her son carefully. "I'd like to think that Sheriff John has a little more intelligence than you give him credit for. Else you'd be in jail, yet."

Not much was said after that. Bubba wasn't sure why his mother didn't mention the swollen face and black eye, but he was thankful. He cleaned up the dinnerware while Miz Demetrice put leftovers away for Adelia. Then he kissed his mother on her cheek, checked all of the locks on the windows and doors of the big house, and made his way over to the caretaker's place.

It was about midnight when his phone rang. He answered it sleepily on the third ring.

His mother's voice came across the line in a high-pitched whisper. "Bubba," she whispered in a squeak. "The ghost is back. Come on over, quick!"

Bubba threw himself out of bed and tripped over his dog, who responded with a pitiful yelp. He pounded down the stairs, clad only in boxer shorts, and out the front door before Precious knew what was up. He ran across a fog-filled yard toward the big house, looking around for intruders running away. The kitchen door was ajar. Just as he was about to open it, the blast of a shotgun knocked him on his butt.

"Goddammit!" he roared. "Mama, it's me!"

Miz Demetrice stuck her head out the kitchen door. Her face was contrite. "Did I hit you?"

Bubba brushed splinters off his chest. "You called me. Where did you think I would come in at?" He looked down. No blood. "Mama, you're a lousy shot."

Miz Demetrice shrugged. "It's rock salt. I'm only interested in scaring. I came down to let you in and saw a big shadow."

Bubba glared at his mother. "In case you haven't noticed I'm a big man who casts a big shadow."

"Big baby, too," his mother said proudly. "Eleven pounds two ounces. Nearly split me in half."

He stood up, brushing off bits of wood and glass with his hands. Then he carefully walked through the debris into the house. "You leave that door open, Mama?"

"The kitchen door?"

"Yeah?"

"You locked it on your way out," she stated. "I didn't touch it."

"Someone's been in here then. It was a few inches open."

"Then my ghost is gone," she declared. "Dammit. I wanted to shoot him on his sheet-covered ass. Teach him to try and scare a helpless little old woman."

"Helpless little old woman?" Bubba repeated skeptically. "What woke you up?"

"You're not going to believe this but the sounds of moaning and chains rattling."

Bubba stared blankly at his mother.

"I told you, you wouldn't believe me."

It took Bubba almost an hour before he found what he was looking for. It was a neat, tiny sound system that was activated by a lack of motion. Twenty minutes after its sensors which were placed in the long hallway, the staircase, and the bedroom door, detected motion, the tape was activated. The speakers were hidden behind some plants, a bookcase, and a spittoon. It was a costly little affair too, not something a man could purchase from a local hardware store.

Bubba showed it to his mother. Then he played the tape. It was about ten minutes of moaning, wailing, and some chains rattling.

Miz Demetrice wasn't impressed. "We've never had a chain-rattling ghost at the Snoddy Mansion," she said indignantly. "Someone needs to do their homework a little better."

Bubba put the whole thing into a bag, put his mother back to bed, and prepared to spend the night on the living room couch, where like his own couch, his feet stuck off by too damn much.   But he didn't really care about that.

Chapter Nine

Bubba and the Subpoena

Wednesday

Trouble was Bubba Snoddy's middle name. His name might very well be Bubba T. Snoddy. He could legally change it and no one would even make a comment. As a matter of fact, they would all agree whole-heartedly and toast his decision with a keg of Coors. Consequently, because of Bubba's should-have-been middle name, he was not particularly surprised at the reaction he received when he reported the break-in at the Snoddy place to the police department on Wednesday morning. The emergency line operator, who was not Mary Lou Treadwell, laughed at him merrily and disconnected the telephone.

"Say, Mama," said Bubba mildly. He put the phone carefully back into its receiver. He didn't even slam it into its cradle, although he that was precisely was he was tempted to do.

His mother was sitting in the kitchen with him. She didn't have a crick in her neck from sleeping on a couch that was precisely two and a half feet shorter than her actual height. Dressed in a cornflower blue robe with matching slippers, she delicately sipped from a cup of coffee. The color of the robe and the slippers was almost exactly the color of her eyes, the same eyes that her son had. Her white hair was in curlers, the only time Bubba would ever see her without immaculate make-up, hair flawlessly styled, and wearing smart clothing that would put the local Sunday churchgoers to shame. Her son thought it was amusing, even if Miz Demetrice did not.

"Yes, dear," she responded. She needed her coffee in the morning, in much the same way that a junkie needed a fix of heroin. It was much the same as her son did. Foul moods from either Snoddy were common before the deliverance of the most holy of caffeine products into the blood stream. "Coffee?"

"Yes, please, the big cup. No, the big cup." She passed him the really big cup. He drank gratefully from it, sighing with relief at the influx of the much-needed addictive substance into his body. "I believe you should call the police about the break-in. They're not disposed to listen to me." He had roamed all the way around the house and had not found where the intruders had gained entrance. Obviously, they had gone out the kitchen door which Bubba had found ajar. He wondered if they had made a copy of someone's keys. He knew that his mother was prone to leaving her keys on any old table in sight for days on end because she was always losing them. Accordingly, she had at least three different sets of house keys.

"That doesn't sound good," Miz Demetrice pointed out thoughtfully. She pondered, "What do I pay taxes for?"

"Not for much," Bubba remarked dryly. His head felt like a blown-up balloon, about to burst at any second from having too much air put into it. His eye was swollen completely shut, and Miz Demetrice had made a comment about the sheer variety of colors showing on his face. ("My, I didn't know a human being could turn all of those colors, at the same time. My goodness gracious.") Coffee alone wouldn't do much for it. He knew exactly where a prescription bottle of 800 mg ibuprofen was located in his house, and as soon as the holiest of coffee was drunk, he intended to generously avail himself of the painkillers.

But Bubba knew that his state of trouble was not limited to the inclination of the emergency line operator to listen to him. His grand list of suspects had petered out. Not only had it petered out, but it was almost nonexistent, lying in a crumpled ball somewhere outside the Sheriff's Department. His mother hadn't done it. His mother's housekeeper and cook hadn't done it. And Major Michael Dearman had been surprised to see Bubba here, where his wife had died. So the chances were significant that he hadn't done it either.

The final suspect on his list was Lurlene Grady, and Bubba was almost ninety-nine point nine percent certain that she hadn't done it either. Lurlene wouldn't know which way a gun was supposed to go, much less be able to hit a moving target at ten feet. She liked her fingernails long and painted and complained when she had to open the truck door by herself.

So here was the thing. Bubba was counting on an unknown someone who was trying to scare his mother off the property as a witness. He reasoned that if their midnight ghost had, in fact, been the murderer, he wouldn't be crazy enough to come back night after night. After all, and if that were the case, he had murdered someone. If one followed that logic further, then why not murder Miz Demetrice and her know-it-all son, as well. Since the haunting attempts were just that, attempts to scare them, and half-assed at best, Bubba knew that the perpetrator had to be something just short of a bumbling idiot.

121

Just like Neal Ledbetter, the real estate agent with an eye on providing Pegramville with a Walmart Supercenter, instead of one fifteen miles away. A man with an eye for the immediate advancement of his own personal wealth, no matter who got in the way. A man who was dumb enough to wear a sheet and leave a sound system around as proof of his crackbrained plans.

Bubba looked at that very system, now lying encased in plastic wrap on top of the chef's block in the middle of the kitchen. He couldn't find a baggie large enough to put all of the pieces into it. But there it was. He had very carefully dismantled it, touching only the edges where his own fingerprints would not remain. He would deliver it to the Deputy Willodean Gray, as time permitted, and as his impending incarceration permitted. With any luck at all, a man as stupid as Neal would have left fingerprints on it, and his fingerprints would be on record for accomplishing some other stupidness elsewhere in this world. That all in account, then the beauteous deputy could interrogate the man to her little heart's desire and help Bubba out in the process.

"Mama," he started. Miz Demetrice looked up. "You could help me."

"What?"

"You could talk to Michael Dearman or the Connors about their alibis," he said.

His mother stared at him thoughtfully. "What makes you think that they'll tell me any more than they'll tell you?"

Bubba made a face. A disbelieving face. This was his mother to whom he was speaking. Miz Demetrice had an illegal poker circle going, in which thousands of

122

dollars passed every week, and every participant, including a sheriff's deputy, kept unswervingly mum about. She regularly petitioned the state's politicians for whatever bit of nonsense she was involved in, to include cloth diapers versus disposables, the promotion of a monument to Miss Annalee Hyatt (one that portrayed her ample charms in all of their naked glory), and kicking the present-day mayor, John Leroy, Jr., out of office, on any given day of the week. That one included a proposed public butt-booting ceremony, in which John Leroy, Jr. would have his hind end kicked by the man with the biggest foot in the county. But then Bubba was digressing. "You could find out if he has an alibi. You could find out if the Connors are gay, swinging, neo-nazi's who have tattoos of Charles Manson on their hinies, if you really wanted to. The Conners are the only other people who might have some motive or perhaps a clue as to who might have done it. I'll be damned if I know why though."

Miz Demetrice arched one eyebrow in recognition of the backhanded compliment. "Well, I can be influential."

Bubba nearly choked on his coffee.

A half hour later he was feeling the assuaging effects of not one but two 800 mg pills of ibuprofen. He had showered, shaved, and dressed in a spiffy manner. His best blue jeans, a pearl gray western shirt, belt with his biggest belt buckle, his least-battered boots, and his trusty Stetson. Now all Bubba needed was a dog, which was ready and waiting, a pick-up truck, which was also ready and waiting, and a cute cowgirl, which was not ready and waiting.

But a sheriff's deputy would do, thought he of the bedecked rural outfit. Then he considered. He was

123

almost, almost, ashamed of himself.   There was a perfectly good woman in that waitress, Lurlene, awaiting his manly presence, and all he could think of was a short, sassy, dark-haired woman. *And big green eyes*, he added mentally. *Nice green eyes.*

Thus, he took Lurlene out to lunch at the Dove's Nest, which was a little hole-in-the-wall restaurant inside an antique mall, in a town about fifty miles away from Pegramville, and thirty miles outside of Pegram County. She had some sort of Nuevo American salad involving grapes, ginger, and watermelon. He had a meatloaf sandwich that made his mouth water from a mile away. They talked about a great many things, which included exactly how Bubba's face had gotten beaten up, and to which Lurlene responded with sympathetic pseudo-language noises with which one would address any child under the age of two ("Poor little-widdle-Bubbie. Didums get a widdle smack on the face-ums?") But Bubba was attempting to lead up to the one thing he wanted to know. In a roundabout way that wouldn't alert an ant to the presence of an elephant about to step upon him. All subtle-like.

Bubba, however, had just about used up any amount of subtleness that he possessed.   "Miss Lurlene," he said. Here was the only start of which he could think. Certainly, it sounded pathetic, even to him.

"Yes, Bubba," she murmured, fluttering her eyelashes. Bubba had to admit that she had nice eyelashes.   They were long and only lightly accentuated with mascara. They very much supported her pretty brown eyes. *Even if they didn't compare with...stop it, you dang, old fool.*

"You work pretty hard at the Pegram Café, don't you?" Well, hey, that was just as clever as a fox in the hen house.

"It can be hard. Did you know that Shirlee Bufford is thinking about filing for divorce?"

"Shirlee Bufford is thinking about divorcing George?"

Lurlene nodded her head up and down. She took a bite of something that included bean sprouts, raisins, and an unidentifiable fruit. "She found out about the Bahamas and Hot Rosa Granado."

Bubba took a drink of his iced tea. The people at the Dove's Nest made a delicious blend of oranges and tea. It was unusual, full of spices, and tasty. Boy, are we getting off the subject or what?

"You work until ten, don't you?" he asked, about as delicate as a sledge hammer hitting thin ice.

"Sure, most nights, but not Mondays and Thursdays," she returned happily. "This salad is delicious. You wanna bite?" She shoved a loaded fork in his direction.

Bubba smiled weakly, shaking his head. Anything with bean sprouts in it was something that he considered horses, goats, and other farm animals should be eating. Not a full-grown man. If Miss Lurlene was inclined to eat it, more power to her, but not this cracker-barrel Bubba. Uh-uh. He thought about what she said. "So you didn't work on Thursday?"

"No, why?" She smiled at him and batted her eyelashes again. "Were you going to ask me out?" With her left hand she reached over and stroked his hand. Bubba noticed that her normally long manicured nails were short and brittle for a change but immediately forgot that he noticed it, as she was

125

slowly caressing his hand. "But you were working, silly."

"I was just wondering if you saw anyone suspicious at the Café," he mumbled. *How did Jack Lord do it all those years ago? Where's Danno? The hell with Danno, where's Sherlock Holmes? The CIA?*

"Mrs. Wheatfall works late that night by herself," Lurlene responded without hesitation. "I don't know where Noey gets hisself off to. I hear he's got a thing going with one of the girls over at the Red Door Inn."

Not likely, thought Bubba sourly. Miz Doris Cambliss, the madam, didn't care for riff-raff like Noey in her boudoirs. If those girls just looked at Noey, they might catch something. But then something occurred to him. "You mean Noey Wheatfall doesn't work Thursdays either?"

"It's not a real busy night," Lurlene said. She ticked things on her hand. "There's the Pokerama, which you ought to know about. There's the auto race over in Merill County. Then, there was that bar down on Oakley Street. What's it called? Grubbo's. Now that's an odd name. Well, the manager down there started a dime night. You pay your entrance fee, and then all drinks are a dime each. Every man in the county under the age of fifty was there. Excepting you, I suppose. And well, Noey, too. Of course, it was awful crowded with the live band and all. He might have been there, for all I know. I had at least a dozen rum and cokes."

"You went?" Well, duh, cowboy.

"Sure, darling." She paused, almost purring. "You're not jealous, are you?"

So there was Lurlene's alibi. She was dancing and drinking the night away at Grubbo's with most of the male population of Pegramville, whose wives were off practically giving their money away to Bubba's mother at her highly illegal, weekly Pokerama, even while Miz Demetrice called it a 'social event' of the Pegramville Women's Club. Meanwhile, Bubba was supposed to be jealous of Lurlene's extracurricular activities, but he was too busy feeling guilty instead, for thinking of another woman.

Bubba mentally crossed Lurlene off his list. Now all he had to do was confirm Major Michael Dearman's alibi, if indeed, he had one.

Bubba dropped Lurlene off at the Pegram Café. She gave him a kiss on the lips that would set half of the jaws in town a-flapping. And, considered Bubba, half of the jaws were a-goggling out the window of the Café as he opened the truck door for her. At least a dozen people had their faces smashed up against the window, like a row of precocious little kids.

Precious jumped out of the back of the truck while Bubba watched the rather attractive back side of Lurlene entering the restaurant. The dog trotted around to the open door and dragged herself up, casting a beleaguered look at her master. Certainly, she enjoyed a ride in the back of the truck but only at her convenience, and didn't that human woman with the blonde hair smell like too much flowers and spices? The dog sniffed her own crotch. Not a nice dogly smell like herself.

The next stop was the Pegram County Sheriff's Department. Bubba pulled up and was pleased to notice that half the employees were gone to whereabouts unknown. He went in, spoke to Mary Lou Treadwell again and waited for Deputy Willodean Gray to emerge from the depths of the interior offices.

127

She came out of the door, and he smiled hugely. *My, isn't she a perty woman?* he asked himself. He even answered himself, *Why yes, she is.*

Willodean stared at Bubba for a long moment with an odd expression on her face. He chalked it up to the bruises on the side of his face. Bubba held the package of stereo equipment out. She looked at it and then back at him. "Why aren't you at home?" she asked slowly.

Bubba wasn't sure how to answer that. "Because I'm here?"

Willodean shook her head. She looked at Mary Lou, who was sitting at the desk with her chin resting on her hands, gazing at the two of them as if nothing in the world could be more interesting. As indeed, at that moment, nothing could. "Look," Willodean said in her very best deputy voice, "you need to go on home."

"There was another break-in late last night, around midnight," Bubba said, not understanding what it was that she was trying to say to him.

"Your mother called me about an hour ago," replied Willodean.

Bubba held out the sack. "Here's the stuff. It's kind of specialized. I bet we can go to Radio Shack and figure out who bought it."

"We? Oh, no," she said hardily. "You need to get on home before...well...you just do."

Bubba shrugged. "You'll let me know about that equipment?"

Willodean rolled her eyes. But she said, "I'll let you know. I'll see you later, Bubba."

On the way home Bubba saw the Snoddy's nearest neighbor, Roscoe Stinedurf, out by his mailbox. The Stinedurfs had lived in Pegram County just about as

128

long as the Snoddys but in somewhat less fortunate circumstances. The present round of descendants had themselves a set of mobile homes that formed a little circle on their five acres of property adjacent to the Snoddy lands. For sure the mobile homes didn't look as stately as the woebegone Snoddy Mansion, but the Stinedurfs generally kept things neat and tidy. No rotting carcasses of Edsels or Chevy trucks there. Not even a pack of half-wild dogs that might chase the mailman halfway back to Pegramville. Just the mobile homes, or what the Stinedurfs called them, manufactured homes, with little white picket fences and a big garden. In the back, Roscoe and his clan kept a herd of goats, some cows, and a chicken coop, replete with cluckers.

As neat as the place was, Roscoe seemed to have a few extra wives that most of Pegramville wondered about, which was why there were all the extra trailers. At least they weren't married to anyone else, and all of the children looked like Roscoe, with his whip-thin body and hawked nose. Sheriff John and the police had ignored the situation because no one seemed to be abused or neglected. The kids always went to school and everyone had clean clothes on their backs. The women went to church together and never had a black eye or an unsightly bruise. None of the Stinedurfs complained, so what was the problem?

Miz Demetrice lifted her nose upon occasion, talking about the traditional family unit, but Bubba didn't care much one way or the other.

Bubba pulled up beside Roscoe and said through the open window, "Hey, Mr. Stinedurf."

Roscoe was a man of few words. He said, "Hey, Bubba."

129

"You see anyone running around after midnight who shouldn't be around?" asked Bubba, not one to be engaged in a long conversation.

"Nope," Roscoe said, similarly inclined. He started to walk down the quarter-mile road with his mail in his hand, but he turned back to Bubba. "You goin' to sell your property to Neal Ledbetter?"

"That's up to my mother," Bubba said promptly. "Why?"

"We decided to sell out," Roscoe said. "But Neal Ledbetter wants to buy out all the property around here."

"So ifin he don't gets the Snoddy place, he don't buy nothing," concluded Bubba.

Roscoe nodded. "Just so." And he resumed his long-striding walk down the road. Bubba thought there was little to no malice involved. Roscoe was interested in selling his land for a profit. He would buy a similar property to put his women, children, animals, and trailers on. Or maybe instead of trailers they'd have a circle of neat little houses. It was no sweat off Roscoe's brow. Or he could stay right there. A bit more money would be nice, but it wouldn't be the end of the world if he didn't get it.

Bubba watched the Ichabod Crane-like man walk away then started off home himself. Precious had her head resting on the edge of the passenger seat, as she sat sprawled across the remainder of the seat, dead asleep with a croaking snore. Some watchdog she was.

As he rounded the corner that preceded the Snoddy Mansion, he saw rows of cars backed up. Police cars. There were at least five of them. This was where nearly the sheriff's entire department had gone, except for Deputy Willodean Gray. Bubba's heart

130

dropped into his stomach until he saw both Miz Demetrice and Adelia standing on the front veranda of the big house watching police officers going back and forth, as healthy as any woman around.

Miz Demetrice waved frantically at Bubba when she saw him. He parked the truck on the side of the road and got out, allowing Precious to follow him at her own half-asleep pace.

His mother didn't wait; she met him half way down the huge green yard. She said, "They came right after you left, Bubba. They had a search warrant. They just finished the big house, and now they're working on your place."

"What are they doing?" asked Bubba curiously. He could see Sheriff John directing people from the caretaker's porch. But he couldn't make out what the man was saying.

"Searching the place for that damned gun of your father's," answered Miz Demetrice with a snarl. "Honestly, I have no idea where it could be though. I haven't a clue as to why they came back to search, again."

There was another car that came up just then. It was an old Ford Mustang that looked to be on its last lingering legs. It belched a cloud of black smoke that ascended heavenward as the driver's side door opened. A kid no older than twenty got out. With a curious expression, Bubba recognized the kid to be none other than Mark Evans, who had spent considerable time and effort quitting Bufford's Gas and Grocery over the phone on Thursday last. When he saw Bubba, his Adam's apple visibly went up and down as he swallowed convulsively. He approached Bubba and his mother as if something dreadful would happen to him.

Mark was a young man who still had a rash of acne across his face and looked to be five years younger than his actual age. Bubba couldn't even fathom why the young man would be showing up on his front door step, or at least, the front of the yard. "Bubba Snoddy?" he asked.

"You know who I am," Bubba said affably. "This here's my mother. As I recall you had a few things to say about her. Since I'm certain you all aren't acquainted, I figure you might be interested."

Miz Demetrice gazed keenly at the young man but said nothing. She knew very well that the people of Pegramville talked about anything and anyone at any time and didn't take offense.

"This here is Mr. Mark Evans, Mama. He done spent considerable effort quitting from Bufford's Gas and Grocery on Thursday night. You know, the same night my ex-fiancée got herself murdered." Bubba curled his lip into a parody of a smile. "Mr. Evans was right riled up."

"You would be too if old Bufford had threatened to fire you on account of a little under-the-counter...business," Mark spit out. Then he shut his mouth. A second later, he opened it up compulsively and added, "Good thing someone tipped me off."

Bubba stared.

Mark swallowed nervously again. Both Miz Demetrice and Bubba watched his Adam's apple bob up and down, and up and down. It was hypnotic. "You are Bubba Snoddy?" Mark asked again. His voice was almost a squeak.

"Sure," Bubba answered, puzzled.

Mark handed him an envelope. Then he galloped back to his Mustang, just a gangly teenager still growing, yelling across his shoulder, "You've been served!"

Bubba nodded to his mother before he opened the envelope. "I guess he found himself a new job, serving legal papers."

Miz Demetrice gazed upon her son as if he had suddenly turned green. "Well," she said after a long minute, "what it is?"

"I've been subpoenaed to the grand jury on the matter of Melissa Anne Dearman," Bubba said nonchalantly.

Chapter Ten

Bubba Goes Back to Jail

Wednesday through Thursday

As it turned out, the subpoena would have to wait. There was a bit of excitement over at the caretaker's house when one of the officers yelled from out back. It drifted over to Bubba and Miz Demetrice, "I foooouuunnndd something!"

Sheriff John Headrick, although normally graceful for being such a big man, stumbled over his own legs trying to get off of Bubba Snoddy's front porch and around the back of the little house. But first his little squinty eyes sought out Bubba's large frame, like a hound dog follows a very intriguing smell. He eyed Bubba like he eyed all criminals with an unspoken warning, 'Don't go anywhere, right now. Hear?'

Bubba glanced at his mother curiously. She looked back at him, equally inquisitive. He shrugged with a definitive I-have-no-idea-what-they-are-talking-about expression on his handsome face. He offered his arm to his mother, having to stoop a bit in doing so. She took it, and they strolled up to the veranda of the Snoddy Mansion, with its fifteen Grecian columns supporting the upper deck. He gave a little assistance to his mother as she mounted the steps and handed her over to Adelia Cedarbloom.

Adelia said, "Wonder what they found?"

Miz Demetrice said, haughtily, "Donuts, undoubtedly."

134

Adelia guffawed loudly. The police weren't friends of the Cedarblooms any more than the Snoddys.

Bubba shrugged again. Then Adelia said, "Well, I best be getting back to the house cleaning. Them lead crystals on the chandelier ain't gonna unfasten themselves and take a plunge in my bucket." She guffawed again at her own joke.

"I think you need to give Miz Adelia a raise," Bubba said wryly.

Miz Demetrice gazed at the back of Adelia as she entered the oversized front doors of the mansion, struggling to get one side open. Presently, she gave the door a solid kick with her foot, and it swung open. "I shall consider it," his mother noted waspishly. "I already pay her double what any other housekeeper gets around these parts."

Obviously to Bubba, Miz Demetrice was feeling a mite curmudgeonly. "That Sheriff get his paws on your little black book?" He was referring to Miz Demetrice's list of poker numbers, which included names of participants, dates of games, money earned, and places where games had been and were to be held.

Miz Demetrice sniffed at him. Then she whispered to him, "It's in my garter."

"Jesus Christ, Mama," he expelled forcefully, taking a step backwards. "Did you have to tell me that?"

"They searched through my drawer of privates," she said indignantly. "I nearly bashed Sheriff John's head in with your grandfather's mahogany cane. Their warrant didn't say anything about that man putting his grubby, no-account fingers through my underwear. I'm going have to take a flame thrower to the whole lot. Sheriff. Hah."

135

"Speak of the devil," Bubba muttered, as just that individual came striding around the edge of the big house with two deputies following closely on his heels. One of the deputies was Steve Simms, and he was smiling so widely it seemed as if a little kid could fall right in.

"Don't you try to run, Bubba Snoddy!" Simms yelled suddenly from halfway across the yard.

Bubba sighed. "Who's running?" he asked, mildly. It was quite the humid day outside, and he wasn't inclined to exercise lately anyway.

Even Sheriff John was mildly annoyed. As the three men reached Bubba and Miz Demetrice, he said, "Put a cork in it, Simms. Bubba ain't going anywhere, 'cepting with us." Sheriff John held up a clear evidence bag with a gun in it. "Do you recognize this, Bubba?"

Miz Demetrice took a step forward, peering closely at the gun in the plastic bag. "Why, that's your father's .45, Bubba," she muttered. She pointed at the handle. "You can see where he made notches for every...well, he made notches for...it wasn't men he killed, anyway," she finished abruptly, a faint stain of red colored her face. "It was for every time he went to Tokyo on leave. That rotten dead bastard. If I hadn't garroted him before, I'd certainly garrote him now."

"Actually, I don't believe I ever saw it before," Bubba mentioned. He hadn't. His mother had kept it hidden away, and for some reason the demon-like child he had been, hadn't thought to search his mother's closet for goodies such as that. Either that, or he had instinctively known what she would have done to him had she found out that he had been in her closet. Who said children were stupid?

"It was hidden in your woodpile," Simms stated, looking directly at Bubba. Simms held his five-foot, eight-inch frame up as tall as it would go. Both of his thumbs were tucked into his gun belt, and Bubba longed to comment that he could never get to his service revolver in time if he kept his thumbs there. But that was like going into Miz Demetrice's closet. The police would not care for a statement like that. Bad things would happen if such was uttered. "Anyone could have put it there!" Miz Demetrice shrieked. "It's not like it's locked up. Half the county has been wandering through the mansion on tours and such, and knows about every inch of the two houses."

"Be that as it may," started Sheriff John.

Miz Demetrice interrupted, "That's circumstantial evidence, Sheriff John." She was possessed, as if she was a woman on a holy mission. She shook one of her tiny fists at the law enforcement official as if that would take care of business all by itself. Unfortunately, it did not.

Sheriff John sighed a deep sigh indicating that he sincerely wished he was anywhere but in this place at this time. "Bubba, you're under arrest for suspicion of murder. Turn around, please."

Precious, who had since woken up from her trip, had chased Mark Evan's Mustang down the road for about one hundred feet. She had almost caught it when she decided that from the smell of it, it wouldn't be worth eating. She had sniffed her way back to the Snoddy place, taking time to mark each and every one of the police cars' wheels, when she heard Miz Demetrice yell out something and came on the double. She parked herself in front of her master and bayed at the police officers, long ears flying out.

Sheriff John said agreeably, "You want to control your dog, Bubba."

Simms took a step forward and pulled a leg back to kick Precious out of the way.

Bubba said, *"I wouldn't do that."* It was a quiet, cold voice that warned of a great many things. If there was a rule in the south, another man didn't mess with someone's truck, his dog, or his woman, in that precise order.

The exact pitch of Bubba's voice made Simms shiver just a second. He reconsidered his actions. He didn't really care to kick a dog, but this whole arrest was getting to be a farce. The Sheriff was being cowed by a damned dog and old lady Snoddy alike. It was making Simms impatient and itching to wipe that obsequious look off the suspect's face. But then there was Bubba, bigger than life, well, bigger than a whole lot of life, looking down the end of his patrician nose at Simms as though he could wrap the other man up in a bow ready for Christmas. "Uh," Simms said, his limited range of vocabulary abruptly failing him.

Miz Demetrice reached around her son and grabbed ahold of Precious's collar. The dog continued to bay and bark, but the woman dragged her back a bit. Bubba reached down and scratched his dog on her ear. She whined and suddenly sat down on the veranda, looking balefully between her master and the other humans in their uniforms.

Bubba turned around and presented his wrists to Simms. Simms extracted his thumbs from his gun belt, which wasn't a quick thing to do, and fumbled for his handcuffs. He couldn't seem to get the fastener unconnected. Sheriff John watched for a long minute, swore, and handcuffed Bubba with his own set. "You

138

give those cuffs back to me after he's processed, Simms," was his only tired remark.

Then Bubba went back to jail. He was carried away in the back of a county car as his mother yelled mild obscenities and vague threats about lawyers, and governors, and such.

Tee Gearheart was ever-present at the jail with an understanding grin on his big face.

"Say, Bubba," Tee said, not unlike the last time Bubba had been there, while Simms took the handcuffs off Bubba's wrists.

"Say, Tee," said Bubba. "How's your wife and the baby?"

"Still okay," said Tee. "It's less than a week since you last asked. He's kicking her like a mule though."

"Here's my wallet, and hey, I been looking for that pocket knife," he passed over the contents of his pockets, methodically patting each pocket for anything he'd missed. He added a lead sinker, a Susan B. Anthony dollar, and a large green button he'd found on his porch this morning. "Oh, yeah, you want my belt, too. I ain't got boot laces today."

"Yeah, Bubba," Tee said. "That's a nice belt. We need the hat, too."

"You tell those people who keep the stuff not to dent that hat. I bought that hat in El Paso."

"They wouldn't do that to you, Bubba," Tee said. "You want to sign right here."

Bubba signed the form, and said to Simms, "The sheriff wanted those cuffs back, hear?"

"Make sure you take a picture of his ugly mug so he cain't blame us for them bruises," Simms sputtered, unable to think of any kind of witty repertoire with which to respond.

139

Tee laughed at the odd expression on Simms's face. "Bye-bye, Deputy," he called, waving a hand the size of a dinner plate at the perturbed deputy. "Come on, Bubba, you can have the cell with the window. We had to rearrange the cells again because we have to get ready for a woman or two."

Bubba walked in front of Tee toward the cell indicated. "A woman?" he repeated. Tee didn't get too many women in the jail. Every now and again someone might be picked up for a DUI or bashing in their husband's skull a mite too much, but mostly it was only men.

"Yeah, somebody's wife finally complained to somebody over to the capitol about the Red Door Inn, and they're doing a raid this evening," Tee said amicably. "Not that I go by there on account that I am lawfully and honorably married and very much in love with my darling Poppiann, but it's a crying shame. That place is a monument to Miss Annalee Hyatt." Tee placed his hand reverently over his heart.

"I saw Miz Cambliss yesterday," Bubba said. "I bet somebody told her. She'll have her girls playing tic-tac-toe or something when them boys show up."

"It's the locals who're doing the raid tonight," noted Tee. "Their hearts won't be in it. But they don't have room at the city jail, so they want to reserve a few of our cells. I have a prison matron coming in tonight just to take care of them."

"Say, Mike," Bubba said, as Tee locked him in. "How's that algebra?"

"I got an 'A' plus," Mike Holmgreen said proudly. "It's my first one."

140

"Good for you, Mike," Bubba returned, leaning on the bars. "Say, your grandmother ain't coming by, is she?"

"No, she came yesterday. Say, Bubba, what happened to your face?"

About nine PM that night, Bubba watched as a female prison matron escorted Doris Cambliss to the cell farthest away from his side. It was blocked off with linen curtains so that she could have some privacy. Apparently, she had been at the Red Door Inn by herself, because none of her girls were with her. Of course, that meant that she had been tipped off, and Bubba wasn't surprised at all.

"Evening, Miz Cambliss," Bubba greeted as she walked past, with the matron holding her arm tightly. The prison matron glared at Bubba. Bubba smiled at her, too, for good measure, even though she looked to be a mean, spiteful woman.

Doris said, "Hey, Bubba. You didn't tell me you'd be in here today."

"You know those damned pesky po-lice officers, Ma'am," he said. "You never know when they're going to take it upon themselves to search an honest, God-fearing individual's property."

"Yeah," agreed Mike, simply because he felt like he was missing out.

Bubba grinned at the teenager. "You met Mr. Mike Holmgreen, Miz Cambliss?"

"Pleasure," floated back to them across several empty jail cells. The matron locked the cell and wandered back out, glowering at Bubba as she did so.

"Ma'am," said Bubba. He would have tipped his hat if he had had one. But this time, unlike others, he remembered that he did not.

141

"Bubba," Doris called in her throaty voice, "I cain't believe they'd arrest me on suspicion of running an establishment of ill repute."

"Me neither, Miz Cambliss," Bubba called back. "But these people have a mind that they've determined some responsible, aboveboard kind of folk just have to be doing something wrong."

"But I heard them deputies talking about you, dear," she said. Bubba could see her face pressed up against the bars. She sure didn't look right in the jail. She was dressed in a yellow silk dress with matching shoes, looking as pretty as any woman could, with her jet black hair in a stylish coiffure and her make-up immaculate. "They said the gun they found didn't have your fingerprints on it."

"Deputy Simms?"

"The little ferret-faced one?"

"Yeah, that's him."

"They sounded a mite worried about your case and arresting you a bit prematurely, shall we say?" She laughed softly, amused by the general ineptitude.

Bubba considered this carefully. He had, after all, never seen his father's M1911 .45, much less handled it or fired it. How much evidence could these people provide depicting innocence on his side before they decided that, just maybe, Bubba hadn't actually shot his ex-fiancée, Melissa Dearman? He had passed his polygraph test. He didn't know about the gunshot residue test but knew damned well they couldn't say he had shot a weapon when he hadn't, and now, none of his fingerprints on the murder weapon.

Someone was trying to lay the blame at Bubba's feet.

But he suddenly thought of something else he could ask Doris while he was in the position to do so. "Say, Miz Cambliss?"

"Yes, Bubba?"

"I don't suppose you recall which of your gentlemen callers happened to visit on last Thursday evening," he said as tactfully as he could. Could the police officers twist that into an illegal statement if they happened to be listening? He didn't think so.

Doris thought about it for a minute. Either she was going to say that she didn't know what Bubba was talking about, or she was going to answer him, depending on how she took it. "You thinking of someone in particular, Bubba Snoddy?" she called after a long pause.

Mike was watching Bubba with great interest.

"Noey Wheatfall," Bubba said.

Doris let out a laugh. "No, sugar. He was barred about six months ago. For a minute I thought you might be talking about our regular Thursday night customers. I got one who's a mite attached to, shall we say, infant garb."

Bubba had to think for a second about just what Doris meant by someone who was attached to 'infant garb.' Abruptly, his face twisted with understanding. "Who?"

"You know, Neal Ledbetter," she said. "And Mr. Mike Holmgreen, if you ever feel like you want to visit the Red Door Inn, it is best to keep a tight lip on anything we say here."

"Yes, Ma'am," Mike called weakly. It was true that he had plans for the Red Door Inn. He had been planning on it since he was sixteen years old and found out about the place.

"Neal Ledbetter was at your place on Thursday night?" asked Bubba.

"Sure, until after two AM. I had to kick him out myself." Doris's laugh was like her voice throaty and sexy. "Every damned Thursday night because his wife is off playing poker with your mama."

"Appreciate that, Miz Cambliss," replied Bubba. "They got anything on you?"

"No, and I'm planning on suing the socks off them, dadblamed po-lice officers. They're going to have to let me go as soon as my lawyer shows up, and they don't have a damned bit of evidence to show that I'm anything but an honest bed and breakfast owner." Doris's voice was positive and self-assured. Bubba knew that someone had warned the madam long before any law enforcement official had even stepped a single foot into her establishment. They would have to do a lot better than that in order to catch her red-handed or, in her case, red-doored.

Bubba let out his own belly laugh. Mike continued to look at him curiously. "What's the matter with you, Bubba? What's so funny?"

Bubba waved at Mike with one hand and went to sit on the tiny bunk in the corner. Here he was, inclined to put Neal Ledbetter on his list of suspects simply because he wanted to buy out Miz Demetrice so bad, and the man was off at the Red Door Inn playing in baby diapers with Doris Cambliss's girls. He laughed again. Wait until he told his mother that. He couldn't wait until he saw the reaction on her face. It would be something like her watching the Jerry Springer show for the first time. He could hear her words in his head, "Good God, what is wrong with that man? He's a grown man, wearing diapers. How could a grown man wear diapers? Is he mentally deficient or something? Good God, what is wrong with him?"

But on the other hand, Doris had just delivered something to Bubba that would get Neal off their backs. His mother was not going to sell the land, and Neal needed to get used to the idea. She didn't care if her neighbors were pissed or the town got up in arms over the whole misadventure. And if the truth were told, the townsfolk would be more upset if they lost their Thursday night Pokerama than missed out on getting a Walmart Supercenter. At least, most of the women would be, and that counted for a great deal in Pegramville.

It's too bad, thought Bubba ruefully. Neal would have made a fine murder suspect for him. He had the motive. He had the gall to carry it off. But then, he didn't have the opportunity. He had been busy. Bubba sniggered again.

Bubba spent the night at the jail before Miz Demetrice was able to round up Lawyer Petrie, who argued before the Honorable Judge Stenson Posey on the issue of playing fast and loose with evidentiary rules. Judge Posey was the only judge who lived and worked in Pegram County and knew everyone very well indeed. Sheriff John got into the argument, and Miz Demetrice was so disposed as to do a bit of her own yelling. Then the bailiff had to prevent Miz Demetrice from shaking a fist in the judge's face. Bubba watched the whole affair with a bemused expression on his face. When it was all said and done, Judge Posey was inclined to let Bubba out on bail. His Honor said to Sheriff John, "You got a lot of jack."

Sheriff John considered the esteemed man on the bench who was wearing a black robe and thoughtfully stroking his white beard. Sheriff John said carefully, "No one else had any reason to kill that woman."

Said Judge Posey, "Motive alone does not make a crime. Let me count what you have. Mr. Snoddy passed the polygraph. Oh, you didn't think I'd hear about that, huh? No one saw him driving from Bufford's to the crime scene or vice versa at the time of the crime. He had a negative on his gunshot residue test, which might indicate he didn't fire a weapon. There were no fingerprints on the weapon which was found, hidden outside of his house."

"He was lying on the polygraph and besides it ain't admissible in court," Sheriff John barked.

"Well, you still gave it to him," Judge Posey answered.

"We ain't found a witness yet," Sheriff John cried. "Yet!"

"I cain't take evidence from a ghost, now can I?" Judge Posey asked politely.

"He could have been wearing gloves," was Sheriff John's rejoinder.

"Oh my Lord, another O.J. Simpson," His Honor returned with feeling.

"Why wouldn't he wipe off the damned weapon?" Sheriff John demanded.

Judge Posey leaned over his great desk, eyeing the Sheriff with a sober, steely look. "If I were a prosecutor, which I am not, I might be so persuaded to answer a question like that. But as I am not, and you are the man who gathers the proof of wrongdoing, it is thusly up to you to gather the evidence that might prove Bubba Snoddy guilty beyond a reasonable doubt in this court of law." He smiled suddenly. "On a personal note, I believe you got plenty to indict the

146

man, but there ain't a jury of twelve around here gonna convict him. Just a little personal note there."

Sheriff John glared impotently at the judge.

Judge Posey looked away from Sheriff John and leveled his judicious gaze upon Bubba. "Say Bubba, I ain't seen you in here since, oh, let me think..." He rubbed his beard. "Was it when that feller from California mistook you for a Dallas Cowboy? Or was it when you had a haul a load of those trespassers from you all's lands?"

"Trespassers," Bubba answered shortly.

Judge Posey laughed. "I recollect ever since that article came out in People magazine, ain't been a week gone by that some idjit goes out to the Snoddy Mansion to dig a hole." He chuckled again. "You should have put up those signs. 'Trespassers will be eaten. Survivors will be prosecuted.' Watch out for that killer Basset hound of yours. That might do the trick."

Bubba muttered, "I'll give it some thought, Your Honor." He didn't even want to think about the throngs of people who had wandered out to Snoddy properties to see what they could see. All because of that old addle-pated ancestor of his, Colonel Snoddy, a man who had come back from the War of Northern Aggression with a wagon full of...

Bubba bit his lip. To hell with that train of thought. So he folded his arms over his chest and waited for the bond to be written for him. When he got all of his possessions back from Tee, he was holding that big green button in his hand, wondering where it had come from, and why it looked strangely familiar.

Chapter Eleven

Bubba Narrows Down the Suspects Some More

Thursday

As it also turned out, Doris Cambliss had spent the night in the Pegram County Sheriff's Department Jail, several cells right down from Bubba Snoddy. Since Bubba was incarcerated first, he got to go up before His Honor, the venerated Judge Stenson Posey, before she did. Bubba was waiting on paperwork to be completed and his mother to sign over what Sheriff John Headrick called a wretched and obscenely low amount bail of $25,000, and a slap in the face of law enforcement from the judicial system. While that was happening, Bubba watched as Doris appeared in front of Judge Posey.

Although it was a tiny court, it seemed as though most of the town had managed to cram themselves inside the room. The church-like pews were so jam-packed that skinnier individuals stuck between larger ones appeared as though they would pop up like cheap champagne corks. Wiser folks stood in the back and craned their necks to see the impending fireworks.

Some of the people had come to visit Bubba's evidential hearing, to include his own mother, Miz Demetrice Snoddy, and her avid clan of poker-crazy grandmothers. Mary Jean Holmgreen was there, and she waved at Bubba when he accidentally caught her eye. Much to his dismay. Other poker aficionados included the sisters, Alice and Ruby Mercer, and Wilma

Rabsitt, a woman who Miz Demetrice was convinced cheated on a regular basis. And even the gorgeous Deputy Willodean Gray was present. Willodean, noted Bubba with some disheartenment that he didn't care to put a name to, was sitting next to Lurlene Grady, who also waved happily at Bubba.

Ma's been busy with the telephones of late, decided Bubba. He smiled at his mother, trying to decide whether to be annoyed or amused.

Also there for Bubba's hearing was Major Michael Dearman, dressed in all of his military flair, and accompanied by Mr. and Mrs. Connor. The Connors seemed a little lost throughout the entire event. Dearman paused to glare at Bubba before he led his in-laws, who continued to look confused, out the court room doors.

Then there was a smattering of those who were there for the indictment against the notorious Doris Cambliss and her Red Door Inn. There was general interest, like Sheriff John Headrick and Deputy Steve Simms. There was personal interest, from Lloyd Goshorn, the around-town handyman, from Neal Ledbetter, sans any kind of infant apparel, and Roy Chance from *The Pegram Herald*, scribbling on a note pad as if to save his life.

There were quite a few other people wandering in and out of the court room. It was a regular circus. Or an insane asylum. It really depended on how one looked at it.

His Honor, Judge Posey, dismissed the case of Doris Cambliss almost immediately. Not only had the local police officers failed to find any type of evidence that would indicate that she was running a brothel, but they didn't have enough evidence to keep her in jail for even twenty minutes. In his soft, gentile, Southern voice, Judge Posey apologized to Doris, even while he knew full well that she was quite guilty of the crimes of which she had been accused. In the South, there was a gentle tradition of 'it's only a crime if you get caught doing it.' Sometimes it was known as the Eleventh Commandment. Thou shall not get caught. As the devious and cunning Doris had not only been not caught, she had gotten one over on the local law enforcement.

Then her own lawyer served the local police chief of Pegramville, Sheriff John, and the prosecuting attorney with a $2.3 million dollar lawsuit, citing wrongful arrest, police discrimination, and the predacious destruction of Doris's general character. Otherwise, the lawyer was saying that the two individuals had besmirched her good name.

Sheriff John looked at the papers with horror and exclaimed, "Just why in the name of God are you suing me?"

Bubba wondered how they had come up with a figure of $2.3 million dollars.

Doris's attorney replied in a smooth, smarmy tone of voice, ever ready to instruct law enforcement on legal machinations. "She was in your jail, was she not?"

Sheriff John said with feeling, "Goddammit."

Judge Posey said, "Now Sheriff, there are women and, well, no children, but there are women present. I don't care for that kind of talk in my court room."

Sheriff John, who had an annual budget of about $1.5 million dollars, and had a vivid and depressing visual image of said monies being flushed down a

150

toilet, said, "$#@*&%!!" Then he added for good measure, "Bleep. Bleepity, bleeping bleep."

"Sheriff, get out of my court room before I cite you for contempt," Judge Posey said, his voice no longer so soft and Southern. He smiled at Doris. "Sorry about that, Ma'am."

Doris smiled back. She knew that she would have to drop the lawsuit, or she wouldn't get any protection from the law enforcement around Pegramville. But she didn't mind seeking some well-deserved revenge in the form of ulcers and sleepless nights for the next few weeks to come. She waved at Judge Posey, who visited the Red Door Inn on Sundays after church whilst his wife was attending a weekly church board meeting.

About a half hour after that, most of the people had cleared out. Lawyer Petrie was long gone, seeing no more viable work or monies that could be squeezed out the Snoddys. Bubba walked out with his mother, his Stetson firmly on his head, and the strangely familiar green button in one of his pockets. He pulled it out to look at it, puzzling over why it was bothering him. Lurlene was hanging on his other arm, talking animatedly. "I knew they didn't have anything on you, Bubba. It's so nice to see justice do just the right thing. How do you think I look in this yellow dress? I think it washes out my skin. Did you hear that the library got broken into? Someone was messing with all of the old papers in the back room. All of the Civil War stuff. I suppose some of them papers are valuable, but they must smell awfully bad."

Miz Demetrice was talking at the same time. "Thank God for small favors. Lawyer Petrie warned you, didn't he? Bubba, did you get any sleep? Did you

151

talk with that Cambliss woman? Did you know that Elgin Snoddy used to go there when it was her mother running the place? He used to say he was going to an Elks meeting, but since when do they have Elks around here? Honestly, boy, you don't say much."

Bubba finally showed the button to his mother and asked, "You recognize this?"

Miz Demetrice shrugged. "It's just a button."

Lurlene clamped her mouth shut, annoyed that Bubba wasn't dancing attendance on her. She looked at the button and still said nothing.

Bubba looked around and then excused himself from the two women. Both women stared at his back as he walked over to Deputy Willodean Gray. She stood just outside the county courthouse steps, waiting for someone. She said to him, "I don't have anything on that equipment, Bubba."

"How about the fingerprints on the window sills?" he asked, entranced by her lovely face. Black hair the color of onyx. Green eyes formed from purest glass. Lips that begged to be kissed. He sighed inwardly, certain that he had just felt the sweetly stinging impact of Cupid's arrows to his backside.

"One was Miz Adelia's. Another's was your mother's. Did you know that she was once arrested at San Francisco for picketing Bill Clinton? Never mind. There were some unidentified ones, but we'll need a body to go with them." She bit her lip, and Bubba stared, fascinated. She clarified, "A live body, not a dead body. Listen, Bubba, I got to go."

Bubba nodded. "I need that intruder. I need him real bad."

"I know, Bubba," she said, looked around him, caught sight of something she didn't like, and took a step back from him. Bubba looked back and saw Deputy Steve Simms talking with the District Attorney. Neither one of them saw Bubba talking with Willodean. She added, "I'm glad for you though."

She turned and walked quickly away. Bubba looked back at his mother and Lurlene and found both of them watching him in turn, enthralled by the whole event. He strolled back to them, pasted a smile across his face that erased about five years of stress and asked, "Shall we go to lunch, ladies?"

During the course of lunch at the Old Gray Goose Inn, which specialized in chicken-fried anything the size of a large dinner plate, Bubba found out that the Connors would share nothing with Miz Demetrice. She was the mother of the devil as far as they were concerned, and for all they cared, he could fry in the electric chair.

"I didn't have the heart to tell them that Texas executes by lethal injection," Miz Demetrice said sadly.

Lurlene had ordered another salad. She paused with a fork full of lettuce and blue cheese dressing and pointed it at them for emphasis. "If you're gonna execute someone, at least give him a choice."

The rest of Bubba's chicken-fried steak covered with thick, creamy gravy suddenly didn't look so appetizing to him. Lurlene went on, "I hear that Gary Gilmore got to choose between being shot, hanged, or electrocuted. Now that's a progressive state."

Miz Demetrice, ever one to get involved in an open discussion, said, "Well, they do allow polygamy there."

"No they don't," Lurlene asserted. Her features flushed with red. Abruptly, her half-southern accent vanished, and she spoke as though was from some Midwestern state without any discernable accent at all.

153

"Utah doesn't allow it. They just don't prosecute it much."

"Sounds like they allow it to me," Miz Demetrice muttered. "Where did you say you were from, Lurlene?"

"I was born in Georgia," she stated proudly. "But then my Daddy brought the family to Washington. State, that is."

"Ah," Miz Demetrice murmured understandingly, with a note of pity that Bubba hoped Lurlene couldn't detect.

Lurlene waved her fork warningly. "What's that supposed to mean?"

"Nothing, my dear," Miz Demetrice said innocently. "I was merely trying to place your accent."

The younger woman suddenly sat up straight, having abruptly discerned that Miz Demetrice was trying to yank her chains. "This is very good salad," she said brightly, showing her teeth like a pit bull about to go for the femoral artery. Her accent returned to pseudo-southern. "How's your steak, Bubba?"

Bubba studied the lumpy, congealed mess that he formerly thought very palatable. "It was good." He paused and said to his mother, "What about the Major?"

"Sorry, dear," his mother said. "He took one look at me, and said I could go straight to hell." Her blue eyes studied nothing at all for a moment as she considered her own statement. "Well, it wasn't exactly what he said, but that was the gist of it."

Bubba nodded tiredly. Miz Demetrice could find out a number of things but only if she had a foot in the door. Given a little time, he didn't doubt that his mother could wiggle her way into the Connor's lives, as well as Major Dearman's, finding out every tidbit of information that he needed to know. There was a problem, however; he didn't have the time to waste. Bubba had thought what occurred at the court house ought to have made him feel better. The Honorable Judge Posey had given away a lot of useful information. One, the polygraph results had been officially confirmed. He had passed. Or in technical terms, nothing he said was determined to be deceptive in nature. Two, Bubba's gunshot residue test had been negative. Three, none of Bubba's fingerprints were on the murder weapon. However, here was the bad part. Sheriff John had every intention of continuing to pursue Bubba as his main suspect. If maybe the evidence didn't point right to Bubba, then the sheriff was gonna find some more that maybe did point right to Bubba. And that was even if Sheriff John had to point out to the jury that the evidence pointed right at Bubba. As if anyone in Pegram County didn't already know he was the main suspect and had already been arrested for the deed.

Sheriff John was looking for people who might have gone to Bufford's Gas and Grocery and found it empty during the critical time period. Bubba knew that they wouldn't find any, but people might be confused after a week or two and think maybe they had passed the store that particular night and maybe it had appeared empty.

Furthermore, Bubba was sure that Sheriff John or Deputy Simms could find someone who thought maybe that they had seen Bubba's green Chevy truck driving that way around that time, even if they weren't sure it was, in fact, on the correct night of the week. Bubba drove down that road all of the time. Sometimes when

155

he had taken a break from mechanicking, he would drive himself home for a dinner break, and to watch the news and Jay Leno. If Sheriff John pushed hard enough, someone was going to say, "Well, maybe it could have been Thursday night last. No, wait, I'm sure of it. No, I'm not. Yes, I am sure." Then in court the witness would be bull-doggedly determined that on the night in question the evil, wrongdoing Bubba Snoddy had been driving down by the creek toward the Snoddy place with an iniquitous expression on his face, as if he were unshakable in his attempt to murder the woman who had once done him so wrongly.

Bubba had a lot of zippola. Sheriff John had a lot of circumstantial evidence which could theoretically send Bubba to a place that Texas was famous for, Huntsville, where the murderers are real regularly like, fried on a stick. Or injected, if that made a body happier.

His Honor, Judge Stenson Posey, might be right about a jury of Pegramville citizens not being able to convict him, but Bubba sure as hell didn't want to get to that junction to find out whether His Honor was correct.

Bubba was abruptly brought back to the moment when Miz Demetrice said loudly, "I have got to do things in preparation for tonight, dear." In secret mother talk that meant that the Pegram County Pokerama was back on despite possible rigid persecution by John Q. Law. Perhaps the danger of being caught added to the excitement of the game. She had to make many phone calls, to decide where to hold the illegal event and to round up tonight's bringer of food and snacks. Poker was on again! The Pegramville Women's Club was back in action. Crime and evildoing abounded in abundance in the tiny town.

Lurlene hinted that she would like to spend some time with Bubba alone, but Bubba was equally determined to proceed with the elimination of suspects. If his mother couldn't talk to Major Dearman, then there was nothing stopping Bubba from doing so.

So Bubba dropped his mother off, delivered Lurlene to her apartment, and ignoring her look of spiteful resentment, and went searching for the Major. He hoped that his former commanding officer hadn't already left with Melissa's body.

He started off with Mary Lou Treadwell of the Sheriff's Department, who told him that Michael Dearman was checked into the Red Door Inn. She wasn't reluctant about giving out such information at all. *Nosiree, Bob.*

Bubba clicked his tongue and then chastised himself. The Major probably didn't have a clue as to the true nature of the bed and breakfast. When Bubba showed up there, he found Doris Cambliss dusting off the front desk, an 18th century Pennsylvanian Dutch desk with delicately carved nooks and crannies. She systematically polished it until it glowed.

"Why, Bubba Snoddy," she exclaimed, a chamois in her hand, "I didn't think I'd see you again so soon."

This afternoon, Doris was dressed conservatively in a silk flower print with ivory Jimmy Choo pumps on her feet. A lovely ivory silk scarf was wrapped around her slender throat. Doris appeared every inch the prosperous bed and breakfast owner. Not a madam, to be certain.

"It's nice to see you outside of the jail, Ma'am," Bubba said politely. It was.

"And you as well," she returned. It was, too.

157

"I'm looking for one of your bed and breakfast clients," Bubba said courteously. "Major Dearman."

Doris studied Bubba for a long moment, as if analyzing his expression could determine his intent. "You're not going to hurt him, are you?" she asked after sincere cogitation.

"No, Ma'am. I just want to find out a few things," Bubba said. He held his Stetson in front of him like a little boy. *Like a little boy who towers over a much smaller woman and doesn't take advantage of the disparity*, Doris considered.

Doris thought about it for a while longer and then silently determined that Bubba probably wouldn't hurt the man under the circumstances. Too many witnesses and such. "He went out around three. Said something about wanting to get, how did he put it, shit-faced? That was it. Shit-faced." She shook her head sadly. "Not a very nice term. But very succinct."

Bubba processed this information. There were about ten bars in town. There were two restaurants which served liquor, as well. There were three liquor stores where the Major could buy a bottle or two and proceed on his own to a location untenable to Bubba. "Do you know where he went?"

Doris continued to study Bubba. She hoped that the younger man wasn't in a mood like his daddy could get before him. Doris had known Elgin Snoddy and felt sincerely sorry for Miz Demetrice, for all her soft, gentile nature. But in the end, Elgin hadn't broken the woman's spirit, and Bubba wasn't one to go around striking down those who couldn't fight back. Bubba had gotten in a fight or two in his day, but she couldn't recall him ever being mean or malicious. However, he was on the verge of being put in jail, never to be let out

158

again if Sheriff John had his way. Who knew what he was capable of doing? She finally answered, "I believe he was going to cruise down Main Street, which means about three bars for you to search."

Bubba found a very much drunken Major Dearman in the last bar in which he looked. It was a little dive named, like a million others, the Dew Drop Inn. Bubba, who was getting tired of drunken Pegramville residents asking how it felt to get even with the woman who done him wrong and the smell of cigarette smoke permeating every bit of his clothing and hair, almost didn't go in. He thought that it was true that the Major could have gone anywhere. Even to dime night at Grubbo's, where Lurlene herself had an inclination. He was scowling as he parked his truck in a metered slot.

But he walked into the Dew Drop Inn, allowed his eyes to adjust to the dimness, and looked around. There were about ten people in the bar. Indeed, the place probably would only hold twenty at best. A few were leaning up against the bar. A few were at tables. But it was the solitary man in a green uniform at the back of the bar pounding on the juke box that caught Bubba's attention.

It was Major Dearman. He was three sheets to the wind. As drunk as a fiddler, pie-eyed, soused, jug-bitten, stinko, pissy-eyed, or in other words, staggering, blind, crapulent drunk. As Bubba watched him, he was wondering why the man hadn't already been transported to the hospital for alcohol poisoning, for it was surely only a matter of time. The folks at the emergency room would have to pump out his stomach and then things would really get messy.

The bartender, a man whose name Bubba couldn't remember, yelled at the Major, "Hey, soldier boy, it don't respond to fists! You gotta put quarters in it!"

The major said, "I did, Goddammit." Then he fell on his table with an audible thump. It was unclear as to whether or not the table would take the abuse, but it did.

There was a conspicuously large amount of space in-between him and other customers at the Dew Drop Inn. A large number of empty tables circled the area in which Dearman sat, isolated and drunk.

Bubba turned to the bartender. "You got coffee?"

"Sure," the bartender said. He didn't care if someone got stinking drunk in the place unless they started puking their guts out. In that case, he threw them out faster than he could yell, "Get the hell out, you lush!" He produced a cup, filled it with steaming coffee, and pushed it over to Bubba.

Bubba slid a bill over to the man, "Keep the coffee coming, and don't call the police."

The bartender shrugged. Bubba slid another bill over the bar. The bartender nodded.

Bubba placed the coffee before Dearman. The Major raised bleary eyes to the cup and said, "Hey, Irish coffee."

He took a sip and swore, "There isn't any Irish in this coffee."

"Say, Sir," Bubba said, reverting back to days in the military where every officer was a 'Sir' whether they deserved it or not.

Dearman's bloodshot eyes lifted to examine the man standing next to his table. The problem was that he had a hard time focusing on anything at all. All he saw was a big dark, blur. "Hey, buddy boy, sit on down.

160

Can you believe the people in this bar don't want to have anything to do with me? That one," he pointed at the bartender, then his hand pointed at the rest of the bar, "said I was a bad drunk." He breathed alcohol-laden fumes on Bubba who almost ralphed. "Can you believe that?"

Bubba sat down in the chair across from Dearman. He thought that maybe having a table in-between them might prevent a drunken rush from the officer once he finally figured out who was sitting down with him.

Dearman took another drink of the coffee. "Hey, this isn't Irish," he said again, his words slurred. He squinted at Bubba from across the table. "Do you know why I came to this shitty little town?"

Bubba signaled the bartender for another cup of coffee. It was going to be a long evening. "I got an idea."

"Tha's right," agreed Dearman. "Everyone's got an idea. Somebody puts a fucking hole the size of a fist in my wife." He thumped his chest hard with his fist, indicating the location of the hole. "Then the judge, that lowdown, briar-hopping redneck, lets the other lowdown, briar-hopping redneck go." He waved his hand through the air, bouncing it up and down, like someone skipping away from the courthouse. "Just like that, la-de-dah-dah-dah."

Bubba encouraged Dearman to take another drink of coffee.

The Major did. "This still isn't Irish, I gotta let you know."

Bubba clamped his jaw down tight. Dearman was so drunk he didn't know what he was saying. He didn't have a chance of sobering him up enough to get anything out of him. By the time he got enough coffee

161

in him, he would recognize Bubba and then, all hell would break loose.

Said Dearman, "You look familiar." Then he laughed uproariously. "But then so does that wall."

"I heard you have a kid," Bubba said.

Dearman brightened. He fumbled for his wallet. Checked all of his pockets. Some of his pockets he checked twice because he couldn't remember if he had checked them. "Can't find my wallet. Wonder if I left it at the Inn."

Bubba scowled blackly and looked over at the bar. Tom Bledsoe stood with his back to Bubba and the Major. His reputation was well-earned. He would be around for a few months until he got caught stealing something or other, or someone got tired of him shoplifting in the market. Then he would disappear to jail for a few months. He was, as Sheriff John would say, a re-peat o-ffender. "Say, Tom," Bubba called darkly.

Tom Bledsoe was a man in his late thirties. He cast an eye over his shoulder at Bubba and Dearman, and then at the door, silently calculating odds in his head.

Bubba said coldly, "I can beat you to the door, Tom."

Suddenly, Tom spun and approached the table, holding out the Major's wallet. "I was just joshing him, you know."

Dearman took the wallet and looked blearily up at Tom Bledsoe. "Hey, thanks. Don't know where I left that."

"Sure," Tom said with false cheer. Then he looked at the expression of Bubba's face and promptly left the tavern.

162

Dearman flipped the wallet open. "Here's my kid. Michael Dearman, Jr."

Bubba looked at the picture. It was a wallet-sized photo of a toddler who grinned into the camera, wearing a sailor suit and a sailor's cap. He was white-blonde, and in his features, Bubba could clearly see both Melissa and Michael Dearman. "He's a good looking boy," Bubba said sincerely. His heart did a little leap for the child that could have been his and Melissa's. But more importantly, his heart did a little leap for the poor child who would grow up without his mother. Then there was guilt there. Guilt because Bubba was looking to clear his name, not to give peace to a little boy who might want to know why someone felt it was necessary to murder his mother. *Damn whoever did this.*

"Sure he is," Dearman said. He pulled the wallet back over to him and examined the picture again. "Didn't want him to wear the sailor suit, you know. Wanted him to wear something army. Camouflage or something. But the wife thought it would be cute." His words died away as he considered what he was saying. His wife would never pick out clothing for Michael, Jr. again. He took another long drink of the coffee and didn't complain about it being non-alcoholic. "Who're you, anyway?"

"Used to work for you," answered Bubba.

Dearman squinted at Bubba again. "You used to work...for me?"

"Yep."

"The only one who worked for me around here was that damned, big old country boy, Bubba. Bubba-Wubba-Bubba." Then he giggled drunkenly. Bubba sighed.

163

"I'm Bubba Snoddy."

"Well, if you are, I ought to kill you. I already hit you once. I could do it again." Dearman thumped his chest again like King Kong. "You killed my wife," he said amicably.

"Maybe you did," Bubba said softly.

"Me? Kill Melissa?" Dearman seemed amazed at the statement. "I loved Melissa." He started to cry, copious tears and sobs tearing away at him, as if his heart were breaking.

Every single person in the tavern almost immediately took a step backward. Now Bubba understood why they were giving him leeway, and it wasn't because he was being aggressive. There was nothing, repeat nothing, like a sloppy, crying, depressed drunk to make a bar seem like the most demoralizing place on the face of the Earth.

"I could never kill Melissa," Dearman sobbed. "She was...she was wonderful."

"If she were so wonderful, why was she coming to see me that night?" Bubba asked incredulously.

"She felt guilty!" he suddenly screamed at Bubba. "She never could forgive herself for the way she treated you. She wanted to apologize so she could forgive herself, and we could get on with the rest of our lives. She was coming here to apologize!" Dearman lowered gradually until his voice was of a normal level, as if he were talking to his friend. "We talked about it. But I didn't think she would actually come here. She waited until I went to Italy for a three-month temporary tour of duty. She took the kid to my parents. She waited until I wouldn't find out about it. Then you still killed her."

164

Major Dearman covered his face again and started to sob loudly.

Chapter Twelve

Bubba and the Errant Bullet

Thursday through Friday

Bubba Snoddy carefully scrutinized Major Michael Dearman. Dearman was officially a drunken mess. The jacket of his uniform was unbuttoned. His tie was half on, wrapped once around his neck but not tied in a knot. The pins on his medals had broken, leaving the grouping hanging crookedly down his breast. His dress shirt was stained with some unknown substance. And only the god who watched over drunks knew where his saucer cap was presently located. Clearly, he had been at the Dew Drop Inn for a long time consuming drink after drink, until he could barely stand up or even focus. How much of a liar could Dearman be? How much of a liar could a man who was so drunk be?

Bubba believed Dearman when he said Melissa had been coming to apologize for what she had done to her former fiancée. Despite her shortcomings she had had her own sense of honor, her own sense of right and wrong. When Bubba had been angry with her, and that had been for a long time after the incident, he hadn't been rational enough to see that. It was true that she had wanted more from life, but he had never consciously thought that Melissa was simply a golddigger. He knew that she had to have had genuine affection, if not love, for the man she chose to marry. Even if Bubba had walked in on the two of them together, it hadn't been her plan that he find out that way. She would have told him privately, in a manner that wouldn't have been welcome but neither would it have been cruel. She had loved Bubba in her own way, as well and had never wanted to hurt him like she had. So it had eaten away at her until she had felt compelled to tell him that she was genuinely sorry for what she had been responsible, the breakup of their union, as well as Bubba's precipitous exit from the military.

Bubba had loved Melissa once. He had thought he couldn't feel compassion for her, even dead. But he was wrong. Furthermore, he felt compassion for the man who had also loved her.

Dearman was still sobbing on the other side of the table. His hands covered his face as though the simple action could take away all of the pain from his sight. It would be a long time before that would happen.

Bubba sighed. He silently noted that he was doing a lot of sighing these days. "Come on, Sir. I'll get you back to the Inn." *Please, God, don't let him throw up in my truck or on my dog.*

Dearman peeked through his hands. "What, another bar? Why not?" He wiped tears away from his eyes with the back of his hands like a little kid would do. Then he blew his nose with his sleeve. Bubba tried not to wince and failed. "It's not like I have to go home," Dearman added. His face crumpled again. "Oh, God."

Bubba put one of Dearman's arms around his shoulder and helped him up. The Major went on speaking conversationally, "You know, since you killed my wife, life sucks."

Sometimes, reckoned Bubba solemnly, *life has the strangest way of coming back and kicking one on the*

167

butt. It's the ironies that make life so interesting.
Dearman wasn't a lightweight, and most of his not inconsiderable weight rested on Bubba. Together they stumbled through the tavern toward the door.

The bartender said, "Say, Bubba, you going to take him back to the Red Door?" Privately, he was hoping that Bubba wasn't taking the man out to kill him because surely some of the blame would come back on himself. "Or maybe to another bar?" he asked hopefully.

"Back to the Red Door. Alive and kicking," Bubba said, breathing heavily from the effort of moving the Major about, "if not puking."

"Puking?" Dearman repeated thoughtfully, halfway out the front door, one hand on Bubba with the other on the door frame. "Don't mind if I do." And he did.

"Ah, Jeez," the bartender complained loudly, screwing up his face. "Throw up outside! Outside!"

"How much did he have to drink?" Bubba asked suspiciously, watching the Major heave and then heave again.

An innocent expression appeared on the bartender's face. *A veritable angel*, thought Bubba sardonically. "A bottle of Jack Daniels," the barman said cautiously.

Bubba stared at the man, silently willing him to finish the total. "And," continued the barkeep, "a bottle of vodka."

The sound of vomiting carried clearly inside the bar through the open door. Several patrons made gulping motions. One covered his mouth as if that would prevent a chain reaction. Bubba's own stomach twisted in sympathy for the man. "And three Long Island Iced Teas. But that's it, I swear."

Slamming the door behind him, Bubba reached down to support Dearman in his efforts to dispel most of the contents of his stomach. No matter how bad it was, it was the best thing for the man to do. *Much better than having one's stomach pumped out*, thought Bubba, twisting his face at the smell of alcohol and vomit inundating the air.

At least he hadn't eaten anything, Bubba thought. That would have been really nasty. His own stomach made a noise that indicated that if he wasn't careful, parts of chicken-fried steak would be joining the rest of the liquid on the sidewalk.

Dearman seemed to be done. "I think that's all," he slurred. "Thank you, Jesus."

"God, I hope so," Bubba said forcefully. He helped Dearman into the truck, which put Precious in her own nasty state of mind because some strange human was sitting on her seat. Not only that, but the human smelled terrible, and his smell overpowered every other smell in the truck. Sitting between the two of them, she whined pitifully, trying to put herself as close to her master as possible.

Dearman peered at the dog with bloodshot eyes. "What the hell is that? A gremlin?"

Precious growled a little, and Dearman promptly shut his mouth and tipped forward. Bubba said, "Why now?"

Dearman groaned. "Why now what?"

"Why would Melissa come see me now? Why not a year ago? Why not a year from now?" Bubba tried to concentrate on the questions that suddenly plagued him. How much of a coincidence could this all be? Melissa comes into town on the one night that Bubba's all alone at Bufford's and as a pile of suspicious thoughts flowed into Bubba's head, Dearman answered him.

"You called her," the Major muttered forcefully.

"The hell I did." The hell he did.

Dearman groaned again. "After court today, the Sheriff said they had a phone record of you calling her last week. Your number. The Snoddy Mansion number. You must have begged her to come." Then he pitched forward, hit his head on the dash, and passed out. Bubba made Dearman as comfortable as possible and started the truck.

Then Bubba drove him back to the Red Door Inn where Doris Cambliss helped Bubba put the man into bed. Dearman had regained a semblance of consciousness and was mumbling about a potpourri of subject matters, from his dead wife, to Monica Lewinsky, to why the color blue was the best color.

Doris huffed and puffed as she covered Dearman up with a quilt. She waved a hand in front of her face as if that would disperse the smell of alcohol. "I'm going to have to fumigate this place. How much did he have to drink?"

"Too damn much," Bubba said sincerely. "Might want to put a bottle of aspirin around for him, because when he wakes up, he's going to be one sorry son of a bitch." He added, "Maybe something for him to vomit in, too."

"He's sorry now. I'll check on him every so often to make sure he's doing okay," she assured Bubba, still waving the hand in front of her face.

They stood in the west wing of the Red Door Inn. The house was built with three distinct wings. The middle part served as the common living areas, such as the kitchen, living room, dining room, and such. The two other wings stuck out like those of a bird. Both sides were set up for occupancy. In the years since he had been in the Red Door, it had changed considerably. Bubba asked curiously, "How do you keep your client separate from your...ah...clients?"

"Separate wings, dear," Doris answered with a shrewd look. "The noise doesn't carry."

"Mind if I pay my respects to Miss Annalee Hyatt?" Bubba asked with a smile. He always liked to take a gander at her portrait when he was in the Red Door Inn, which wasn't all that often anymore. It was some portrait. Life-sized and in all her glory, Bubba could see why a Union colonel would fall for her, lock, stock, and barrel.

Doris laughed heartily. She was used to men staring at Miss Annalee. "Sure thing, sugar."

Bubba left Doris and found his way to the middle wing of the Inn. In a fancified living room with a car-sized fireplace was the portrait of Miss Annalee Hyatt. The portrait itself was hung in a prominent area, surrounded by red velvet panels and was framed with gilt-edged wood. One couldn't even walk into the living room without casting a gander at Miss Annalee's portrait. Her notoriously well-defined figure was poised as if for the centerfold of a magazine not yet published, bending over a large, red velvet-covered chair, showing off every bit of her charms. Her hair was brownish-blonde and fell to her waist, or it would have if she had been standing up straight, her eyes were like a warm brown, like a bar of Hershey's chocolate. She stared out at the observer with those gorgeously inviting eyes that one longed to drown within. It was said that the portrait was true to life and had not exaggerated Miss Annalee.

171

Miss Annalee had had many admirers. Bubba was certain of that. One was the Union colonel. And there had been another colonel as well, who longed for her favors. Truthfully, if the more distasteful rumors were true, then Colonel Snoddy had been another one of Miss Annalee's ardent swains.

Bubba stared at the life-sized portrait, and something suddenly troubled him. He couldn't put his finger on it, but it was like something was screaming at him to figure it out, and he had earmuffs on. Troubled, he looked at the portrait for a long time.

It was after eleven PM when Bubba pulled away from the Red Door Inn. Something about that portrait left him scratching his head like a chimpanzee aching for a banana. He just couldn't put his finger on it.

Bubba dismissed the thought uneasily as he happened to drive by the Sheriff's Department and saw Deputy Willodean Gray exiting the building all by her lonesome. In actuality, he drove by the station every time he thought of it, but this was the first time he had hit pay dirt. He pulled up beside her while rolling down the window. "Hey, Deputy Gray," he called.

Willodean cast her green eyes upon Bubba and rolled them in a manner that would have put off a more discerning man. Bubba reasoned that there could be many reasons she was rolling her eyes, to include working at least twelve hours this day, having a murder suspect clearly infatuated with her, taking all kinds of male-oriented crap from the other deputies, and/or a variety of reasons.

Bubba smiled winningly at Willodean. It was his best smile, the one he had practiced endlessly in a mirror when he had been sixteen years old. It was the smile which had broken the hearts of cheerleaders all across Pegram County. "I wonder if you could answer a question for me, Ma'am?" "Gentility without ability is worse than plain beggary," Miz Demetrice said regally on more than one occasion. It still sprang to Bubba's mind once in a while. One needed to be tactful and quick-witted in order to get the answer that one might need.

"No, I won't go out with you, Bubba Snoddy," Willodean answered tiredly.

"That wasn't it," Bubba said. So much for that smile. "I wanted to know if it's true that Major Dearman was really in Italy when his wife was murdered."

Willodean abruptly stopped walking and turned to Bubba. The expression on her face clearly showed the surprise of his question. He stopped the truck from motion and pushed Precious back across the seat. She was intent on smelling up the latest human to cross her path, even if that included clambering over her master to get to that human. "Good looking Basset hound," Willodean commented mildly. She allowed Precious to sniff her fingers first, and then scratched her head appropriately.

"Her name is Precious," Bubba said. "You didn't answer my question."

Willodean's eyebrows went up. "Precious? That's not exactly the name I would have pictured you giving a dog."

"Rambo didn't seem to fit a Basset hound," Bubba said wryly.

She laughed, and Bubba sighed...again. It was a nice laugh. An honest laugh. He almost giggled. *What in God's name is wrong with me?* he asked himself.

"Bubba, I can't just keep giving you information like this," Willodean stated. "If the Sheriff finds out, I'm history. There's a strict rule about nonessential communication with suspects outside of interrogation."

"Look, Deputy Gray," Bubba started, "you're the only one who's willing to talk to me. Sheriff John and Deputy Simms ain't looking for anyone else to have done this thing to Melissa. If I didn't do it then the most logical suspect is the husband, am I right?"

"You're right, but he was in Italy. Without a doubt."

"I figured as much. I don't think he hired anyone to do it either. He's as broken up as a man can get over the death of his wife. I think I don't have a single suspect anymore."

"What about Neal Ledbetter?"

"He was at the Red Door Inn during the time period." Bubba grimaced. "He might be trying to scare off my mother, but he didn't kill Melissa."

"Perhaps he has an accomplice who was there that night," she suggested.

Bubba nodded. "Yeah, but how do I find that out?"

"Well, I've got some time tomorrow to spend tracking down the origin of the stereo equipment, and if we can place him as the one who bought the stuff, I can shake him down for why it was in the house, attempting to oh, defraud someone out of their rightful property." She reached up with a delicate hand to scratch her head. "But right now, Bubba, I need to get some sleep. It's been a long day."

Bubba nodded again. "I'll wait until you're in your car."

Willodean stared at Bubba again but finally went to her car without saying anything else. She climbed in a Jeep Wrangler and drove off without acknowledging Bubba again.

Bubba patted Precious's head. "She's cute, ain't she?" The dog didn't agree or disagree but merely watched as the Wrangler's lights disappeared into the night, vexed that she didn't automatically get her way.

Miz Demetrice wasn't at home when he got there, which was hardly surprising. It was, after all, Pokerama night, despite all the police involvement of late. Who was his mother to come between the card-sharking women of Pegram County and their Thursday night fun? Not that Snoddy matriarch. On the contrary, she would be there egging them on in the face of danger. "So what if the police are all over my son," she'd say or even yell boisterously. "We deserve Pokerama! Come on, Ladies!"

Bubba took his dog on a patrol of the big house. Miz Demetrice had reported no further break-ins since the last time, and he wondered if he had managed to scare off their would-be ghost. All of the windows and doors were secure. He left the front veranda and back porch lights burning brightly but didn't think that would deter an individual if he was intent on burglarizing the place.

But that wasn't it exactly, considered Bubba. Someone wanted to frighten Miz Demetrice off. A little old lady alone in her mansion should be pretty easy to scare. It made Bubba more and more angry. It also made him laugh because those people didn't know how determined Miz Demetrice could get. If it were Neal Ledbetter, then he would have a hard lesson learning that Miz Demetrice wasn't going to leave

Snoddy Mansion unless she wanted to leave, which presented another problem.

If I were someone who wanted the old lady out, Bubba thought watching Precious patrol the bushes near the front veranda, *and the old lady wouldn't be scared off. Then what would be the next step?*

Why I'd have to kill her, answered Bubba. That would be the only answer. *If I wanted something badly enough.* He rubbed the side of his face a little. The bruising was starting to go down. He could see just a bit out of his left eye where it was all black before. In a few days the colors would begin to turn from purple to greenish-yellow and then eventually disappear.

Precious was on the trail of something mobile. In the light from the veranda, Bubba saw a rabbit explode from a bush and hightail it across the yard with Precious in close pursuit. But the dog's stumpy legs were no match for the rabbit and gave out halfway down the driveway. She snorted and sniffed around for a minute, then began trotting back to her master.

Bubba didn't care for the path his mind was taking him in, but it was logical. All it depended on was how far someone was willing to go. And since Melissa had been killed by someone, then it was also logical that that was how far someone was willing to go. So why not Miz Demetrice next? Why not, indeed?

He leaned down to scratch his dog's head and beckoned her to follow him back to the caretaker's house. He was tired, hungry, and smelled like he had taken a bath in a distillery. When Bubba was done with a meal, a bath, and feeding his dog, he went into his bedroom and slept like the dead, snoring so loudly that even his dog didn't care to be in the same room.

However, not long after Precious was baying loudly.

"Shut up, you damned dog," Bubba muttered irritably. Wasn't it a nice dream he was having with Deputy Willodean Gray wearing a white negligee, and her long black hair cascaded over her shoulders, and...

Precious bayed again and scratched at the door.

Bubba opened an eye. The door was shut. The dog had inadvertently closed it in an effort to get out. She was up on her hind legs, scratching away, and baying clamorously. She looked over at Bubba and realized he was awake. Down she went and up on the bed she clambered. She stood astride her master's chest and licked Bubba's face, trying to tell him that someone was outside.

His eyes were an awful chore to open, but Bubba did so, looking at the clock on the night stand. Its luminous digits said it was fifteen minutes after four AM. He brushed the dog off of his body. Precious thumped to the floor and returned to clawing at the door. Bubba rolled out of bed, clad only in boxer shorts, and pulled the door open. Precious disappeared out the door, down the stairs, baying all the way.

Bubba pulled the baseball bat out from behind the door and followed his dog. Precious was a little frantic now, as she nudged her body against his front door. She snuffled around and pressed her body against Bubba's legs. Bubba commanded her to shut up. The dog, who wasn't one to obey commands overly, did so immediately much to her master's surprise.

All of the lights in the house were off, and Bubba looked out into the night. The back porch light on the big house was off, unlike the way he had left it. He knew his mother wouldn't turn it off, so it was a good bit of figuring that told him that their little inquisitive buddy was back. Additionally, he couldn't see Miz Demetrice's car parked in its regular spot.

Bubba went out his own back door, taking the time to slip his size-twelve Reebocks on his feet. He whispered to Precious, "If you can keep quiet, you can come."

The dog panted at him. Bubba made a face. "Keep your big trap shut, understand?"

Precious seemed to be in some accord with her master, even if she did not nod or otherwise acknowledge this command.

Bubba slipped around the side of the caretaker's house, keeping to the deep shadows. Precious followed at his heels, for once in complete harmony with him. He was hoping that the nightly visitor would keep doing whatever it was he was doing inside the house instead of being frightened away. He wasn't worried about the man having a gun since he or someone else had planted it in Bubba's woodpile sometime before.

But hey, thought Bubba, *there's that rifle, and the shotgun, and didn't Mama own three eighteenth-century muzzle loaders, too?* He looked at the baseball bat he held. Then he looked at his boxer shorts, a cloth rendition of Old Glory emblazoned across his lower body. Oh, the hell with it, decided he, determinedly swinging the bat once into his fist.

Bubba got past the wide open yard by scuttling around his old Chevy truck. He almost dropped the baseball bat once when Precious abruptly stuck her cold, wet nose on the back of one of his calves. The closer he got to the house, the louder the sounds of

178

noises could be heard in the house. This was undoubtedly the noise that had awakened Precious.

Someone was methodically tossing the house looking for something. Bubba considered this for a long minute. He was standing next to the back kitchen door, where he could see, even in the darkness, the light bulb of the fixture had been removed and dropped to the ground, where it had broken into many pieces. He tried the door. It was open.

Among the things that I need to do, considered Bubba seriously, *is to change the locks*. He didn't know how their burglar got a set of keys, but the locks hadn't been changed or renovated for forty years. Some of the Society for Preservation of the South had sets in order to come and go from the house during the spring and fall tours. Bubba had a set. Miz Demetrice gave Doc Goodjoint a set ten years before. Miz Demetrice and Adelia both left their keys all over kingdom come, from the grocery store to hanging from the locks themselves. They had been duplicated so many times that every man, woman, and child in Pegramville could have their own sets.

Inside the house was full of darkness. The sound of banging drawers drifted down the long hallway. Bubba had spent his whole life, or most of it, clambering up and down every nook and cranny of this house. Their curious friend was in the living room searching the built-in cabinets that dated back before the Civil War. He was throwing the empty drawers on the floor. Something glass broke on the Persian rug-covered floor.

Precious emitted a low growl beside Bubba, evidently picking up on her master's anger.

Bubba had every intention of sneaking up on the unsuspecting burglar or whatever the hell he was. Then he might proceed to break some bones and generally make everyone an unhappy camper before he called the Sheriff's Department to pick up the trash.

He was halfway down the long hall when the noises abruptly stopped. Precious made a keening sort of growl that lifted the hairs up on the back of Bubba's neck. When he reached the door to the living room, he carefully looked around the edge and saw nothing.

There was no one in the living room. But the drawers to the built-ins were askew. Some were on the floor. Some of the fine crystal that Miz Demetrice collected was shattered on the floor around the marble and brick fireplace.

Bubba couldn't understand how the man had gotten past him. There wasn't another exit to the living room, and the windows were fastened shut.

Precious let out a howl as someone crashed by the bushes just outside the window. Bubba yelled at his dog to follow him and took off down the long hall, ran out the kitchen door, and around the side of the big house.

The mysterious burglar took careful aim at Bubba's half-naked figure and shot at him.

Chapter Thirteen

Bubba and Another Dead Body

Friday

The bullet missed Bubba Snoddy by a gap equal to the national deficit. Instead, it hit the side of the house with a loud zing and ricocheted off one of the tall columns supporting the top veranda. The sound of the gunshot whirred like a maddened bee and echoed loudly into the sultry night.

Bubba ducked, a little after the fact, but he still ducked.

Precious decided that the whole thing was too much for her and hightailed it back around the side of the house, peering over her shoulder as if a much larger animal with huge teeth was nipping at her heels.

In the woods to the north of the Snoddy Mansion Bubba could hear someone fumbling around as he or she scrambled down a path of their own making. Bubba cautiously lifted his head but he couldn't see any kind of light in the woods. The burglar had waited to shoot Bubba and then was taking off through the woods, apparently without a flashlight. Or perhaps they chose not to use one in order to remain undetectable in the gloom that was nighttime.

Bubba rose to his feet, yelled for his dog to heel, and took off after the unknown individual. Precious kept back from her master a good long distance. She knew that discretion was the better part of valor. Someone was in the woods with a gun, and she knew that guns would hurt any dog no matter how good they were. Her master was clearly out of his mind. If she had been human she would have stuck her tongue out at his back disappearing into the tree line. But she wasn't. So she didn't.

Bubba made almost as much noise as the burglar. He tripped over a fallen tree in the heavily overgrown thicket, full of every kind of growing ivy from honeysuckle to poison ivy and surrounded with dozens of trees from birch to cedar. Unseen animals took off for quieter locales as he clumsily blundered through three bushes and narrowly avoided a precariously leaning cedar. The woods on this side of the property hadn't been cleared for over a hundred years, and Miz Demetrice liked the look of it, so it was left untouched. In effect, it was almost a dark, green jungle of trees, and that was during the daylight hours.

Cursing and jumping around like a fool with a lit match in-between his toes, Bubba decided that having a flashlight would have been a good, if not tremendous, idea. He stopped for a moment, and the woods had become silent. Not even a cricket or a June bug was sounding off. The presence of strident humans had hushed the lush copse.

His shin hurt like the devil, the skin on his arms felt like it had been scraped with sandpaper, and he was groggy from having so little sleep of late. Bubba was not only aggravated, but he was beginning to get really angry.

The woods went on for several almost impenetrable acres in this direction as Bubba knew well from childhood excursions. On the other side of this lot was Farmer's Road and a little strip mall where Miz Demetrice was inclined to purchase vegetables from a vendor set up next to it. It would be a good place to park a getaway car where people wouldn't look at it overly instead of alongside the road beside the Snoddy Mansion, where everyone and his cousin would remember it being parked.

Bubba decided that boxer shorts with Old Glory or not, he was headed for the strip mall to lay in wait for the burglar. The man might be hiding under a shrub right now, and Precious was next to useless. Nevertheless, the intruder would have to come out of the woods sooner or later. There couldn't be that many cars parked at the strip mall at four in the morning. Bubba knew he could narrow his focus down considerably.

He slipped through the forest, avoiding long strands of poison ivy that draped off trees like curtains from a window. His running shoes crunched a little on the vegetation-laden floor, but that couldn't be helped. Carefully, he headed toward the north, following what he could see of the North Star. After a while, there was pink in the east, and the stars began to disappear. The crickets and cicadas resumed their noisy music, then the birds began to sing as well, but Bubba never heard his intruder again.

Precious followed her master with a little whine of protest, but as she calmed down, she began to be happier about her location. Despite having gotten out of a warm bed she was in the woods with her human and having a good old time. This was clearly a dog's life.

Bubba hefted the baseball bat in his right hand. He was beginning to think that he had gone in the wrong direction when he suddenly saw the street lights of Farmer's Road through the dense trees. Although the sun was coming up it was still twilight, full of long shadows and pockets of unfathomable darkness.

He wasn't the only one there. Off to his left someone else burst through the thicket and launched themself in the direction of the strip mall. Bubba bellowed appropriately and took off in heated pursuit. Precious howled and followed, ready to bite whatever was causing her master anxiety as long as they didn't have a gun.

The intruder, who apparently thought that he or she lost Bubba in the woods, screamed like a girl whose brother opened the bathroom door while she was on the toilet with her panties around her ankles. Then the person turned and shot awkwardly at Bubba again, missing by several bushes, two trees, and a provoked armadillo. Birds flushed from the trees, attempting to escape the noise of the weapon.

Just before Bubba was the person who was so intent on scaring Miz Demetrice. The individual was barely visible in the dim night, a medium-sized figure dressed in black clothing. Bubba was just about to jump right on the intruder, rifle or not, when a large hole in the ground appeared before him, and he fell in, hitting his head on the side as he fell. Actually, the hole was already there, but if one asked Bubba at later time, perhaps when he had regained consciousness, he would have said, "That hole just jumped right out in front of me," just like Newt Durley's telephone pole.

But he was unconscious. Therefore, he didn't see the black-clothed person holding a rifle, run across Farmer's Road, like the devil himself were behind him, and climb into a vehicle, which abruptly started and drove off. There were no witnesses except maybe Precious, who wasn't saying anything to nobody.

184

When Bubba came to, he heard whining which sounded like a broken fan belt. "Gotta adjust that fan belt," he muttered. "Sounds like it's 'bout to slip like it was running on snail snot." He opened his eyes. He knew he was in a hole because it was now daylight, and full daylight at that. Presently, he could plainly see that he was in a hole. There was black dirt all around him with roots and rocks interspersed in the earth. He knew that he had hit his head on something because he had a headache akin to someone pounding on his skull with an iron mallet. The whining, incidentally, came from Precious, who was lying on the side of the hole, her head resting on her paws, as she continued her vigil above her master, gazing down upon him with soulful brown eyes. Her unsaid question would have been something like, "Just what in the hell are you doing in that hole, hmm?"

"On a scale from one to ten," Bubba said conversationally to his dog, "I would have to say that this day is a one. A one being the worst day I ever had. I thought that would have been the day I broke the Major's arm, but I was wrong. That was a one and a half. *This* is a one."

Precious lifted her head and cocked it, listening to her master's voice. At least he was awake.

Bubba climbed out of the four-foot-deep hole, bringing the baseball bat with him. All he was dressed in was a pair of boxer shorts with the picture of Old Glory across them and badly tied Reeboks. There were scrapes from the brush and trees across his body. There were mosquito bites punctuating several muscle groups. And he smelled like the earthy scent of eau de locker room. "Holy Jesus, I'm ready to go to town," Bubba said with a weary chuckle and immediately wished that he had not done so. His head pounded like a demon was playing on kettledrums inside.

He surveyed the hole he had fallen into and the immense tree root that he had cracked his head against. Someone had been digging on the property. Daylight trickled down through thick trees and vegetation; they were rays of light mottled with dust motes. Around him were a few other holes, all dug within the last few days judging by the color of the freshly turned earth.

Rubbing the sore spot on his head, not a sore spot, but a lump the size of a tennis ball, Bubba puzzled over the hole. It wasn't a grave. It didn't look like much at all. But there in the dirt pile next to the hole was a six-inch-by-a-foot piece of rusting iron. It looked like an old piece of a tiller. He picked it up, looked at the hole again, and then back at the rusting metal in his hands. He walked over to the next hole. In the dirt next to that hole was another piece of rusting metal on top. It was unidentifiable except that it was rusting iron of some type. Clarity came to Bubba suddenly. Someone with a metal detector was using it in the woods to find things long buried. Once they had recovered what was clearly a piece of junk they had stopped digging and discarded the trash.

Lucidity uncluttered Bubba's mind so abruptly he almost gasped. He knew what their ghost was after. It all made perfect sense now. But he bit the side of his mouth. What didn't make sense was Melissa's death. She couldn't have seen anyone digging in the dirt, could she? But she could have seen someone searching at the house. The one night that Miz Demetrice, Bubba, and Adelia Cedarbloom were certain to be gone. The one night that someone could have had a free hand in finding something hidden. But there was the fact that the police had a phone record of someone calling Melissa from the Snoddy Mansion. Someone had to know that she had been coming.

Bubba dropped the piece of tiller on the forest floor. Precious pounced on it, sniffing it eagerly. She was one hungry dog and felt as though her sacrifice to protect her master throughout the night was not properly appreciated. She dismissed the metal as inedible, not to mention, undesirable, and woofed softly to Bubba. *Feed me, dammit.* She put a wet, sloppy nose on his leg.

He reached down with a long arm and scratched Precious's head. She leaned into it. *Now that's more like it. It's not Alpo but it ain't bad.*

The pieces of the puzzle were still rumbling around in Bubba's head. Some things began to make sense, and other things that he hadn't connected to the whole situation were promptly connectable.

But who's behind it all? he asked himself. Who, dammit, who?

Bubba walked to the edge of the forest where he could clearly see the strip mall. His intruder was all too likely to be long gone. But he looked out all the same. His mouth dropped open. Apparently, he had been lying in the hole for a long time. As he surveyed the mini-mall it appeared as though everyone but the kitchen sink was present going about their daily business.

Off to one side were Miz Demetrice and Adelia arguing with the vegetable vendor over oranges. Adelia's old Volvo was parked next to the vendor's cart. Roscoe Stinedurf was filling up his truck with gasoline at the gas station on the other end of the strip mall. One of his wives, Bubba couldn't tell them apart, was sitting in the cab of the truck nursing a baby. Neal Ledbetter was standing outside of the copy place, talking with, of all people, Lurlene Grady and none other than Noey Wheatfall, owner and operator of the Pegram Café.

Bubba could faintly recall Lurlene talking about Noey's plans to open up a new restaurant on the other side of Pegramville, and this was clearly it.

Finally, up drove Sheriff John Headrick in his county car, and beside him sat Deputy Willodean Gray. They both got out and started talking to Roscoe Stinedurf as he continued to fill the tank of his truck.

Bubba closed his mouth with an audible snap. Everyone was there but the Major, and then his mouth dropped open again. Out of the dry-cleaning store walked Major Michael Dearman, looking distinctly green in his gills, but there he was all the same. He was carrying his uniform in a plastic bag.

Almost everyone who even remotely had something to do with the mystery of who murdered Melissa Dearman was there. Bubba was intelligibly dumbfounded.

Precious whined loudly again. Bubba stepped back, broken from his reverie. He wanted to get back to the house before anyone saw him wearing only his shorts and Reeboks. He was sure he'd never hear the end of that if he didn't beat his mother and her housekeeper home. God help him.

That wasn't his only immediate problem. Bubba's subpoenaed testimony was due at one PM that day, and he couldn't miss it. He looked up and decided that it was late in the morning. Besides which, the temperature was not at its hottest. Either that or a man should go around in boxer shorts more often.

It was to his benefit that no one saw poor Bubba as he made his way back to the caretaker's house, with Precious following at a cheerful pace. When he got inside his house, he discovered that while he had been chasing someone around the woods, someone else had been searching through his own house. After all, he had left it wide open.

Bubba looked around his home in dismay. It was as if the Sheriff and his merry men, and one pretty woman of course, had come by to do their search again. Except this time, whoever it had been, had left things a little in disarray. Nothing was broken. Not that there was all that much to disarrange, but everything was either on its side, or on the floor, or put in backwards. He knew it hadn't been the Sheriff and company.

Willodean had been correct in her estimations. There was an accomplice. A devious accomplice who had waited until Bubba had been lured by the sound of the first guy banging around in the big house. Then what? Led him out into the woods where Bubba was supposed to get lost like the dumb redneck he was. Or fall into a hole?

Bubba needed ibuprofen. And a shower. But first he fed his dog. She was grateful.

An hour later he felt almost human. All that was left was to find some clothing that appeared halfway presentable. He discovered that he didn't have any clean jeans. So he finally found a pair that he had worn the day he had come from the jail. They had been kicked under the bed by none other than Bubba himself, whose idea of laundry was to wait until each piece of clothing could stand up on its own or until Miz Adelia took pity on him, which was more often than the former.

He picked up the jeans and the green button fell out of the pocket onto the floor with a little ping. Bubba picked up the button and looked at it. It still looked like something he ought to recognize. He had assumed it was one of his mother's outfit's buttons, but she had denied ownership. He shrugged. Perhaps it was Miz Adelia's. He put it in back in the pocket of the jeans.

Therefore, Bubba was mostly clean and presentable when he appeared before the Pegramville Grand Jury for his testimony. He was asked to present his side of the events of the night that Melissa Dearman was murdered. He was also asked about his involvement with her during his time in service.

Bubba admitted all. After all, it was hardly a secret now. "Yes, I was engaged to Melissa Connor...Yes, I broke her husband's arm. Only he wasn't her husband then...No, I didn't shoot Melissa Dearman...No, I don't know who shot her, but I'd like to...Because it ain't right, even if she did sleep around on me when we were affianced...Thank you, Mrs. Barnstable, I appreciate that...No, Mr. Rittenhouse, I still didn't kill Melissa."

Finally, he was allowed to leave. Sheriff John was waiting outside as if prepared to arrest Bubba again. That thought confused Bubba. He already thought he was under arrest for doing Melissa in. The indictment itself seemed to be a way of saying, "Oh, by the by, you can go ahead and officially arrest Bubba Snoddy now. Here's our golden stamp of approval."

190

Surprisingly, Sheriff John merely stared at Bubba for a long minute. Bubba's natural inclination was to stare back. Their similar size made it easy for them to do so. However, it was Bubba who looked away first. He didn't have time for manly games of show. Perhaps the Sheriff thought that some sort of police officer psychology would allow him to pierce Bubba's mind with vengeful eyes that impelled the suspect into confessing all.

Naw, thought Bubba. *That would be stupid.*

Bubba stopped at the library which was about three blocks down from the Pegram County Courthouse. It was a right smart little building built in 1986 with funds provided by the Lion's Club, the Optimists, and Miz Demetrice's group of avid gamblers, who put aside their obsessions for a time, to raise money for a worthy purpose. Federal funds provided monies for one librarian and two aides. And most of the books in the library were not too old.

"Miz Clack," Bubba greeted the librarian. Nadine Clack was sitting at the front desk shuffling through books. She was a short woman, not even five feet tall, and plump to boot. Despite the fact that she was in her early forties, her hair was completely white. Then there were the gold-rimmed Ben Franklin glasses that all librarians seemed determined to wear, that Nadine did, in fact, wear. Finally, it was a known fact to all of Pegramville that Nadine was not a woman with any kind of sense of humor, which put her in the same ilk as Nurse Dee Dee Lacour. Some would call her mean, but Bubba didn't think that. She was stern. But she was never cruel. Little children kept quiet in her library. Hell, so did everyone else.

"Bubba Snoddy," Nadine said as she surveyed him through the spectacles which had slid down to the edge of her nose, causing her to tilt her head far back to see him.

He looked around. The library seemed as empty as a crypt. He mentally chastised himself for using the comparison. It didn't do a bit of good to make that kind of judgment. That was like asking God to kick a fella in the ass and pretty please with sugar on top, too.

"Heard you had some break-in's too," he noted, all friendly like.

Nadine stared up at Bubba though lenses that made her eyes look as large as a bug-eyed critter from the red planet. She waited for him to come to the point.

"The archive section?" he asked.

Nadine nodded slowly.

Bubba came around to the side of her desk and sat down so that he wouldn't be the cause of the crick that would surely result if she continued to look up at him in that fashion. "Look, Miz Clack, I know you've heard I'm in a bit of difficulty of late."

She nodded again. The expression on her stern face didn't soften a bit.

"I wonder if you can tell if any of your old papers are missing," Bubba continued, even while she nodded.

Nadine didn't say anything else so Bubba added, "That would be Civil War era papers, maybe diaries from Colonel Nathaniel Snoddy, maybe?"

Nadine finally spoke, "That's correct, Bubba. I didn't care to share that particular information with your mother." So Nadine didn't care to have a situation with Miz Demetrice. Miz Demetrice rubbed

Nadine the wrong way and vice versa. Bubba could surely understand that.

Bubba raised his eyebrows. "Well, I can appreciate that. Anybody been asking about those papers lately?"

"No, dear, I suspect that's why they stole them instead. The Sheriff seems to think that it's kids pulling a prank, but it's obvious that he's a plain fool." Nadine rested her arms on her desk and carefully adjusted her glasses on her nose. *The better to see you with, my dear,* he thought and almost laughed. *My, what big eyes you have, Miz Clack.*

Bubba sat back in the straight-backed chair. He wasn't surprised about the missing Snoddy papers. Nathaniel Snoddy had been his great-great-something-grandfather and had been prone to writing everything down. And that meant everything. He had written the weekly grocery lists and kept them in his diaries. He had written the state of the weather every day. He had even written about his conquests of women, irrespective of his thirty-year-long marriage to the long-suffering Cornelia Adams Snoddy. Miz Demetrice had gleefully cleared out most of the rotting papers by donating them to the historical society, which in turn stored their materials at the library, hoping that Nadine would eventually sort them out. Apparently she had.

"That old legend again," he muttered darkly. It seemed to surface every so many decades or so. The last time had been when there had been an article in...

"*People Magazine,*" said Nadine, succinctly. "There was one person who displayed a certain interest in that edition. You know which one, the June edition of 19-something or other. He sat right over there not a month ago and made three copies at the Xerox machine." She pointed at the table and machine, helpfully.

"I thought Miz Demetrice told you to burn every copy," returned Bubba grimly.

"Now, that is not the attitude to display in attempting to uncover information from me," Nadine warned in a level voice.

"Because of thrice-damned gossip, I fell into a really, really deep hole early this morning, dug by some asinine fool," said Bubba. It had seemed like a bottomless pit at the time.

"Neal Ledbetter," Nadine said, clicking her tongue. "Mr. Ledbetter seemed very interested in the Snoddy properties of late."

Bubba's face was black with anger. He politely thanked Nadine, who watched him exit the library with a certain amount of concern. She was so concerned that she telephoned the fool of a Sheriff about the incident.

Consequently, it was Sheriff John who found Bubba with Neal Ledbetter's corpse in the realtor's office.

Chapter Fourteen

Bubba and the Fire

Friday through Saturday

The truth was that Bubba Snoddy found Neal
Ledbetter's corpse in the offices of Ledbetter Realty
just about 45 seconds before Sheriff John Headrick
found Bubba.

Bubba was standing in front of the only desk, in
what was a tiny office, with one of his hands held out,
ready to shake a warning finger at Neal on account of
his actions of late. But Bubba was really late. For that
matter, so was Neal. Literally.

Someone had blown a hole in Neal's head. He sat
in a high-backed, leather chair with his head leaned
back against the rest as if he were taking a break. His
eyes were shut, and if Bubba hadn't seen the blood
splatter on the wall and the tiny hole in-between Neal's
eyes, he might have thought the other man asleep.

It was about thirty seconds before Bubba could
believe what he was seeing. The office door had been
open. The radio on Neal's desk was playing an eighties
pop station out of Dallas, something about ninety-nine
red balloons. There was a Cross pen in Neal's right
hand as if he had just signed a real estate contract with
a client. He was dressed as he always dressed, white
shirt, black tie, and a gold watch around his left wrist.
Bubba presumed absently that the dead man had a set
of slacks on underneath the desk, which was not
visible to him, and he wasn't about to step around to

look. There was a cup of coffee sitting on some paperwork just to Neal's left. It was only that little dot there on his forehead, the color of a dark penny and no bigger than the tip of Bubba's pinky, that proclaimed to one and all that something was wrong.

But the bright afternoon light that streamed through the only window showed there was a huge circle of blood on the cream-colored wall directly behind Neal's head. It was as if someone had taken a paint brush heavily laden with crimson paint and flicked it against the wall. It was slightly above his head, as if someone had shot the realtor from below where he was sitting, or, realized Bubba abruptly, if Neal had been standing up when he had been shot.

Bubba was frozen. Here was his suspect, and he was as dead as dog meat. He was deader than the Dead Sea scrolls. He was as dead as Abe Lincoln's corpse. He was really, really, really dead. And the worst part for Bubba was that he finally realized in all the time he stood there that someone was going to very likely yell accusingly, "Hey, Bubba Snoddy shot this one, too!"

Then Sheriff John stepped into the office behind him. Murphy's Law, number unknown: Whenever a person is standing in front of a murdered individual and has a motive, and was very recently known to be angry with said dead individual, then the local law enforcement will, in fact, step into the room at the most inopportune moment. With the following qualifier: whether one did the deed or not but especially if he didn't. Bubba was going to have to write Murphy a note about the latest law.

Bubba didn't move. He didn't even hear Sheriff John softly open the door and step into the small office, standing behind Bubba as quiet as could be. Bubba continued to stare at the body as if he had never seen one before. The truth was that before viewing his father's at the mortuary and seeing Melissa Dearman in the yard, he hadn't. This was twice in a month, and he was not exactly fond of the experience. Only morticians and police officers were supposed to be looking at dead people, certainly not Bubbas.

The wind from the open office door shifted the air around the room, and Bubba got a whiff of what a dead man smelled like. He had smelled death before. In the rural area that Pegramville was located, there were hunters galore, and it was common to run across something having been cleaned or something recently dead. Bubba reckoned that it had in no way whatsoever prepared him for the real tamale. He was in a closed space with a man who had been dead for at least several hours, and the quick, fast food he'd grabbed just before testifying at the Grand Jury didn't want to keep itself down.

There was a sound like a gulp that issued forth from Bubba's mouth. "Ulp-urp," he said. Sheriff John accurately summed up the situation and stepped aside for Bubba, even while holding the door open, standing as far back as his large body could allow him to in the small space available.

Bubba stumbled into the parking lot, one hand over his mouth. Then he lost everything that he'd eaten that day and some of what he had had the day before. He was bent over the side of his truck, resting one hand on the chrome bumper, heaving his guts out, when someone reached down and gently soothed the hair back from his forehead. He was too sick and miserable to look up.

After a while, someone said, "All done?"

Bubba nodded wretchedly. A hand passed him a handful of wet wipes. He used them to clean off his face. He looked up and saw Deputy Willodean Gray looking down at him with a good deal of compassion in her lovely face.

"It doesn't smell very good," she murmured, correctly guessing the reason he had been so sick. She had on the other hand, seen quite a few dead bodies and knew better than to stay in a confined space with one that had been dead for more than a few hours.

Bubba shook his head. He wasn't sure if it were from being violently ill or the sight of the beautiful black-haired, green-eyed deputy that made his knees shake, but he didn't dare try to stand up. "I didn't do it," he muttered.

Sheriff John nodded at Bubba as he stood behind Willodean. "I don't think you did, Bubba."

"Well that's about the best news I heard all month long," Bubba grumbled, knees still aquiver.

Sheriff John twisted his face up. "Don't be thinking that I believe everything you got to say, Bubba Snoddy. That man's watch is broken. The time is stopped at one PM on the nose. I seen you myself, and so did twelve people on the Grand Jury. It sure would be a feat to be able to kill this man and testify at the same time."

"How can you be sure he died at one PM?" asked Bubba.

"Shut up," muttered Willodean out of the side of her mouth. "Are you trying to get a one-way ticket to Huntsville?"

Sheriff John smiled grimly. "Doc Goodjoint will tell us the time of death. After all, the body was inside for

198

four hours, give or take. It shouldn't be hard to come up with a Basel temperature for him."

"A what?"

"Bodies cool down after a person has died. Whatever Neal Ledbetter's temperature is now, will tell us how long he's been dead," Willodean explained helpfully.

"Miz Clack gave me a call from the library about you being a mite touchy about Neal Ledbetter," Sheriff John interrupted, pausing to glare at his deputy. She returned his look with a level one of her own. "She seemed to think you might do the boy some harm. Although that would kinda be hard to do seeing as he's already as dead as dead gets." He crossed his arms over his massive chest. "That's a pretty dead kind of fella."

"I didn't kill him," repeated Bubba. He finally felt well enough to rest against the front of his Chevy truck. He wiped the sweat beads from his forehead.

Sheriff John ruminated for a long minute, obviously thinking about what it would take to have Bubba be the murderer. He decided that Bubba must not be because he himself had seen him at the County Courthouse, as plain as the nose on his face. Sheriff John wasn't a dummy; he knew something funny was going on. What he couldn't figure out was whether or not Bubba was involved. Two murders in Pegram County just doubled their homicide rate for the last year. It made an elected official look kind of bad, and here was his token female deputy consorting with the prime suspect of one of the murders.

Ticking off other miscellaneous items of reprehensible transgressions, Sheriff John thought about some of the things that had been occurring of late. Murdering, consorting, illegal gambling rings he couldn't get a hand into, law suits against him for wrongful arrest of a madam, and God knew what else was going on in Pegram County, which he considered was directly headed for hell in a hand basket. And here he was, a man who was supposed to be on top of all of this. He would be lucky if he got voted for animal control officer next election.

"It's true that Neal Ledbetter always had some shady deals going on," Sheriff John grumbled. "His wife could have shot him for all I know." He clamped his mouth shut, amazed that he had said that to a suspect of the same crime.

Bubba rolled his eyes, feeling sorry for the woman of which Sheriff John was speaking. Her name was Nita Ledbetter, a teacher who taught elementary school alongside of Martha Lyles, the lady who had come into Bufford's Gas and Grocery to buy lottery tickets because of a dream. Nita seemed a shy, non-talkative type of woman, who was mousy and plain, preferring to stay in the background of everything she was involved in. She taught school, went to church, and sometimes donated goodies for bake sales. Her only peccadillo seemed to be her weekly participation in the Pegramville Women's Club's poker game. He personally didn't think that Nita would know the right end of the gun to point at her husband in order to shoot him. Sheriff John knew that as well as Bubba did.

"Look, Sheriff," said Bubba at last, his stomach rumbling tyrannically at him, threatening an imminent repeat of recent rebellion. "You going to arrest me for this?" He waved a hand at the formerly alive-and-kicking Neal's office.

"What did you want with him?" Sheriff John said gruffly.

"I think he was the one who was messing around on my mother's property," Bubba said.

Ignoring Bubba's answer, Sheriff John peered at him suspiciously, suddenly seeing him for the first time clearly. "You know, every time I see you, you look more and more beat up. I know that Melissa Dearman's husband took a swing at you, but what's that big lump on your forehead?" Sheriff John eyed Bubba as if examining the bumps and scrapes on him could provide the answers to mysteries yet unsolved. Willodean looked closer at Bubba's head.

"Tree," answered Bubba succinctly.

"Tree?" repeated Sheriff John.

"A tree?" echoed Willodean.

"A tree," confirmed Bubba. "And a big hole."

"Get the hell out of here, Bubba," Sheriff John instructed at last. He was disgusted that he couldn't pin anything on this man. It was like Bubba was coated with Teflon. Nothing stuck. "Try to stay out of trouble."

Bubba issued forth a grunt of acquiescence and briefly smiled at Willodean. "Thank you, Ma'am." *Damn it, there goes my knees again*, he thought as he glanced at her lovely face.

Willodean nodded to him.

Bubba tiredly tipped his head. He had gotten sick in front of the most beautiful and effervescent woman he had ever met. He was more battered than a prize fighter after ten rounds. He had stared at a dead man for a long time. He had smelled a smell that he never wanted to smell again. He was the suspect in not one, but two murders.

Bubba wasn't sure why he didn't tell Sheriff John about the intruder last night, or the recent holes dug on Snoddy lands, or his suspicions that this whole affair was happening because of some asinine legend about Colonel Nathaniel Snoddy, Confederate colonel and confirmed womanizer. It didn't sound real to him. So why would Sheriff John believe him? Naturally, he would not.

He climbed into his truck, and Willodean handed him his brown Stetson again. Bubba didn't even remember where it had come off of his head. She whispered out of the side of her mouth, "I've got to talk to you about that equipment."

Bubba glanced around her at Sheriff John, who was staring at them both. Willodean was worried about her job. *Rightfully so*, thought Bubba. The Sheriff wasn't a man to condone an employee's alliance to anyone but him. "Call me tonight after you get off work," Bubba said. He needed to talk to her about one particular mechanic by the name of Melvin Wetmore and a young man named Mark Evans, lately a process server. Willodean didn't say anything, but a muscle in her cheek twitched. Attractively so, if Bubba had been asked, but he hadn't.

Bubba spent Friday night with his mother, eating a succulent chicken dinner prepared by Adelia Cedarbloom. He talked about Neal Ledbetter, and Miz Demetrice talked about Thursday's Pokerama. She had won almost a hundred dollars from Wilma Rabsitt and gosh darn, was Wilma put out about that.

"Mama, don't you care if I go to jail for murder?" Bubba asked, perplexed.

"Bubba, they don't convict innocent men," Miz Demetrice said, her devotion to fairness and justice

202

dripping from her voice like gravy off chicken-fried steak. "Now I don't care for the police because they are all communist, Nazi organizers, who never caught the back side of their mother's hands as children, but they don't convict honest, God-fearing men in a court of law. You see, those people are our friends and neighbors, and they know that Bubba Snoddy isn't a murderer." Her son found her logic dotty to say the least.

"What makes you think that I'm honest or God-fearing?" asked Bubba facetiously.

"Bubba Snoddy! Don't you blaspheme in this house!" Miz Demetrice shouted, rising up in her seat. She, who wasn't above taking the Lord's name in vain upon occasion, sat back down with a mild, "Goddammit."

"Has there been anyone around asking about that old legend?" Bubba asked after a long silence that involved the eating of the main course. Adelia's chicken supreme was, of course, as tasty as ever; the chicken was apt to melt in one's mouth.

"Which old legend?"

"The Colonel."

"No one's said much about that for years. Not since that awful magazine article." Miz Demetrice cleaned her face daintily with a cloth napkin. Something occurred to her suddenly. "It was probably that badly behaved Neal Ledbetter, God rest his soul. He's been in this house a dozen times over the last five years. Coming at the spring and fall openings to gape at the place he couldn't buy, mentally figuring out how much it would cost him to tear it all down, and what could he get on eBay for the fixtures. I'd bet you he was the one in here trying to scare me off."

Bubba rested his chin on his arm which in turn was resting on the table. It was bad manners, but he didn't particularly care right now. It was true that his mother could be slow at times. "Do tell."

"This could explain Mrs. Dearman's death, as well. She saw him, and he had to shoot her to cover up."

Bubba had thought of that, too. It didn't figure. He had come to the conclusion that there were at least two, possibly three, people involved. There was one who pretended to be a ghost and who was clumsy and ran like the very dickens when confronted. Then there was one with a gun who broke into the house and disappeared after a chase in the woods. And the third one was the one who broke into Bubba's house while the second one distracted him. The second and third ones were the ones who were capable of murder.

But there was something else that Bubba had thought of since that conclusion. On that morning when Bubba had found Melissa, Neal had been as shocked as the other man to see that woman's dead body there in the grass. He had stood across the garden as far away from the body as he could get, shaking in his boot straps. What had he been scared of? That Bubba would kill him, too, or that his accomplice had done something so horrible that if they were caught then it was going to be the lethal injection for all of them.

Neal hadn't been a murderer. Maybe he had been a ghost. Maybe he had been the first accomplice or perhaps the third one.

Precious moved around under the table by Bubba's feet, nosing his leg for a bite or so. Bubba recalled that the dog had had her teeth in the intruder's leg. Perhaps that would prove that Neal had been on the property, breaking into the mansion. Maybe the police would find the missing diaries of Nathaniel Snoddy at Neal's house. Maybe they would clear this all up by themselves. But Bubba was still under indictment. He was the one who would be tried, long after Nita Ledbetter buried her husband in Longtall Cemetery on the highest hill in Pegramville. And someone else might still have something to lose.

Or something to gain.

"Maybe you ought to go visit Aunt Caressa in Dallas tomorrow," Bubba suggested.

Miz Demetrice studied her only child with an air of insolence. Truly, her boy was getting too big for his britches. "Now why would I want to go and do that for?" She thought about it. "Caressa may be my sister, but she snores like a cat throwing up a hairball."

Bubba abruptly put the fork full of chicken supreme he had in his hand back on the plate.

Miz Demetrice went on. "Not only that, but she keeps her house temperature on 105 degrees minimum. She's three years older than me and half-senile besides. It's about 100 degrees outside in Dallas, and she has to have the house even hotter. If I ever get that way, I give you permission to have the doctors pull the plug." She made an undignified noise and resumed eating.

Bubba was lost in the vivid mental picture of his aunt snoring like a cat throwing up a hairball. He didn't think he would ever be able to look at his aunt the same way ever again. There was nothing like his mother to spoil a persona for him. She had done the same thing once when explaining why the folks on Gilligan's Island couldn't exist there and continue to have unspoiled clothing, coconuts that worked like radios, and people who wandered in like it was Grand Central Station. It had broken his five-year-old heart to find out that was so.

"For one thing, someone took a couple of shots at me this morning while you were off gambling away like a drunken sailor on shore leave."

Miz Demetrice laughed. "That's not what a drunken sailor on shore leave would do, dear." She sobered. "Someone took a couple of shots at you? Here?"

Bubba nodded. "Bullet hole near the southern end of the veranda. Remind me to point it out to you."

"I'm a-loading all my guns tonight," Miz Demetrice declared faithfully. "I'm going to put some big holes in some trespassing son of a bitch."

Bubba rolled his eyes. Now there was another vivid mental image, with his mother knocked ass over tea kettle from using one of the Winchester twelve-gauge shotguns.

"No salt rock tonight, by God," Miz Demetrice swore.

"You want me to spend the night over here again?" Bubba asked cautiously. He wasn't sure if he wanted to be in the same house as his mother while she was loaded for bear. Why, he might sleepily get up in the middle of the night to go to the bathroom and lose one of his lungs in the process.

"I'll be safe enough," Miz Demetrice vowed.

"You know, when I thought I had the fella cornered in the living room, he up and vanished. The next thing I knew he was outside, and the windows were still closed and latched," Bubba said. "How do you suppose he got outside without me seeing him?"

"In the living room?" Miz Demetrice said with a concerned expression on her face.

"Yes."

"Colonel Snoddy's secret passage," Miz Demetrice said tiredly. "I wonder how he found that."

"A secret passage," Bubba said. "I never knew about a secret passage in the house."

"Well, there was the priest's hole that really wasn't a priest's hole," replied Miz Demetrice. "The Snoddy's have never been Catholic, as you know. However, Colonel Nathaniel Snoddy's wife, Cornelia Adams Snoddy, used to help runaway slaves as they headed for Missouri. It was by the stables or such. But I believe your great-grandfather found it to be infested with rats and had it filled in, in the twenties. Then, there was randy Nathaniel's living room door, behind the portrait of Cornelia on the east wall of the living room. It was his idea of a joke. He would light out to meet a fancy lady or two, by sneaking out behind his wife's portrait. I believe I read about it in one of the Colonel's diaries." For that matter, so had Elgin Snoddy, who had used the secret door himself when on one of his binges. *Not that it had been necessary*, Miz Demetrice considered. She would have helped him out the front door at that point in time because he had been such a self-centered bastard. *No wonder I threw a toaster in his bath*, she thought, with a little nod of her head. "It's a simple mechanism that swings on a pivot point. Truthfully, I'm surprised it hasn't rusted shut. You can block it off after dinner. Push a credenza in front of it. He won't come back in that way."

"That makes sense," Bubba said, thinking about missing diaries. "Our boy was breaking in the window and using the secret door at the same time? Now that doesn't make sense."

"It does if there's more than one person," his mother said virtuously. It surprised Bubba that Miz Demetrice could be so devious at times and so nonsensical at others. But this fit in with his thoughts that more than one person was involved. Had Neal Ledbetter been working with an accomplice after all? Had this other person withheld information from Colonel Nathaniel Snoddy's diaries? If he had, had the accomplice been keeping information to himself? It seemed so, or Neal wouldn't have been breaking in through the windows in the dining room but using the secret passage in the living room.

Three hours later, Bubba was in his bed snoring much like a cat throwing up a hairball. Precious, who wasn't the most observant of dogs, was snoring in the same manner on the end of his bed, where her paws fought for purchase against Bubba's long legs. When all else failed, she would simply drape herself over his legs and allow them to lie where they might.

The stately grandfather clock made of white oak in the long hall of the Snoddy Mansion had just rung the one bell, signifying the end of the witching hour. Miz Demetrice, who normally slept like the dead, was up and prowling around a darkened house with a shotgun cradled in her arms. When she carefully and quietly walked down the long darkened hallway, she saw a faint glow coming from a window in the kitchen.

Miz Demetrice frowned. She knew almost precisely what time it was and knew that it wasn't even close to being dawn. She stepped outside to see what the glow was and found that the caretaker's house where Bubba lay sleeping was on fire.

"Holy cra-diddly-ap!" she yelled, quite out of character for her.

Chapter Fifteen

Bubba Gets Rid of Miz Demetrice

Saturday

Thump. Thump. Thump. It was, Bubba Snoddy determined at a later time, the most amazing dream he had ever had. Even in the days of adolescence he had never had a dream like that one. There was Lurlene Grady flapping her eyelashes at Bubba in the most provocative manner. Her burnished,-blonde hair wafted back from her face by some sultry breeze. Her soft brown eyes stared at him as she affected a seductive pose not dissimilar to the one Miss Annalee Hyatt took in her infamous portrait at the Red Door Inn. Then Deputy Willodean Gray came striding into the dream like a Grecian goddess, her black hair streaming behind her, twice as long as it was in real life, and her luminous green eyes flashing. Then the two women proceeded to wrestle half naked in a ring full of Jell-O pudding.

Chocolate flavored, Bubba decided. It looked pretty tasty to him. The pudding, that was.

It seemed as though Lurlene had the upper hand, for she had Willodean in a half nelson, and was about to stick the law enforcement officer's head under the Jell-O pudding in a decidedly unsportsmanlike manner. But somehow, perhaps with the aid of the slippery substance in which the two women were grappling, the splendiferous Willodean oozed out of the blonde's grasping hands and turned the tables on the other woman.

It seemed astounding that in the dream, although each of the women's bodies was concealed with fudgy, chocolate sliminess, their hair was blowing free in that same sultry, sweet-smelling breeze. In mere seconds Willodean had Lurlene pinned to the Jell-O laden floor of the ring, and the referee, none other than Miz Demetrice, Bubba's own mother, was screaming, "One! Two! Three! Four!" even while she flipped her hand down once, twice, thrice, to indicate the count.

Then, oddly and very fishily to Bubba, something was hitting the back of his head. Thump. Thump. Thump. It was as if someone was walloping him with a wooden paddle in the direct center of the back of his head, a few inches beneath what had been his fontanel. He thought that dreams never really made sense, but this was ludicrous. He opened his eyes and discovered, to both simultaneous disappointment and relief, that he was no longer dreaming.

His long body was encased in a blanket, and someone was dragging his body, wrapped up in that same blanket, down the stairs, causing his head to hit each one of the risers. Thump. Thump. Thump. "Hey," he protested, but all that emitted was a strangled squeak. He could hardly breathe, and he could hardly see because of the viscous, black smoke that almost completely enveloped the stairs and the two people on it.

The person dragging him let his legs go so suddenly that they hit the steps with a loud bang. "It's about time, dad bless it," Miz Demetrice snarled. "Do you know how big you are?" She coughed in the thickness of the smoke, waving her hand in front of her

211

face as if that would dissipate the murk. "You were a big baby, I'll say, but Jesus Christ Almighty, you weigh a ton now. I know that you aren't fat, but my God in heaven above, I never realized how much of you there is to try to drag down the stairs." She paused to cough again. "And in case you haven't noticed, your house is on fire!"

Bubba fought to escape the trap that was the blanket that was wrapped around him. The air was heavy and full of noxious, suffocating fumes. *That sure would explain a lot of things,* he thought inanely. *My house is on fire. Gee golly whiz.* "Get this blanket offa me!" he croaked.

Miz Demetrice reached out one hand and yanked, tumbling her son down the remaining five stairs to the ground floor but retaining the blanket in her sure grasp. For a moment she looked dismayed but then brightened, muttering, "I should have done that to begin with." Her voice got louder as she called, "Are you all right, Bubba darling?" She went down the stairs, nearly tripping on her son as she reached the bottom.

Bubba didn't know how much more abuse his poor body could take. He had been hit, bruised, and now battered by a fall down the stairs, and who was going to believe that his mother had done that last thing? Not to mention that he was breathing in enough smoke to kill him. "Where's my dog?" he rasped.

"She was smart enough to head for the hills as soon as I tumbled her out of bed," Miz Demetrice said urgently. Then she pinched her son's ear by one slender hand. "We're leaving."

"Ow," Bubba protested, crawling to his feet, gasping in the smoke that surrounded them. "I'm going. I'm going."

Outside he simultaneously rubbed the back of his head and his ear. He could hear the fire trucks in the distance and police sirens, too. He stood beside Miz Demetrice clad in his blue Smurf-covered shorts watching as the caretaker's house burned readily. "I liked that house," Bubba muttered, still coughing occasionally.

Miz Demetrice draped the blanket around Bubba's shoulders. "Me too, dear."

"Uh-thanks, Mama," he said, hiding his sentiment with a coughing hack. The back of his head hurt, and his ear had been twisted half off, but hey, she had saved his life. Who was he to dispute that?

His mother shrugged. "You know, Bubba, I never would call you fat. But my Lord, son, how much do you weigh?"

Bubba, who hadn't weighed himself in years, shrugged back. He knew what pants size he wore. His belly was as flat as a wash board and had just about as many ripples. He could bench press two hundred pounds if he was so inclined. He still went running in the mornings when he wasn't being investigated by the Sheriff's Department for murder. He was a big man. Besides diet was a four letter word.

Besides all of that, Miz Demetrice wasn't exactly expecting an answer. After all, she knew a great many four-letter words that she would have readily used if someone had asked about her own weight. Instead, she said, "Arson?"

"Yeah, but why not the big house?" Bubba said back.

213

"You know why."

"I 'spect I do," Bubba sighed.

The fire trucks ripped onto the property as if they were late. Miz Demetrice had called them from the big house before she had rescued her only son and his only dog from a house fire. Precious showed up to bark at the fire trucks as they pulled in beside the mansion. A county car pulled in behind the fire trucks, which contained a young sheriff's deputy that Bubba did not know. Roscoe Stinedurf wandered over from his property to see what in the blazes was going on and found out it was exactly that, blazes. One of his wives and two of his teenaged children had come, as well, gaping up at the burning house and the firemen spraying hundreds of gallons of water on it from a tanker truck.

About an hour later, Bubba was still wrapped up in a blanket and watching from the big house's kitchen door as Sheriff John Headrick pulled up behind the rest of the government vehicles to add his two cents worth. Miz Demetrice had made her way to a shower to alleviate sore muscles and was going to bed, in that order, having resolved that intruders would not be returning to the Snoddy place anytime soon. Bubba was waiting until the firemen had the fire at the caretaker's place put out.

The caretaker's home, his residence, wasn't burned as badly as he had feared. Someone had splashed gasoline, or something equally ignitable, on the backdoor and around the exterior of the back of the house. Then they had lit it. The smoke had poured upward inside the house and certainly would have killed Bubba and Precious by carbon monoxide poisoning, if not by fire directly, if Miz Demetrice hadn't interfered in the most motherly way she could have.

As Bubba stood there, about six firemen were puttering around the house, going in and out of the front door. A bit of watery smoke could still be seen wafting up from the rear of the house. Things were just about wrapped up for that fire.

Sheriff John stepped up to the kitchen door, underneath the porch light, which had been replaced by Bubba himself the previous evening, before he had had chicken supreme with his mother for supper. "Say, Bubba," Sheriff John said in a neutral fashion. The shadow caused by the porch light caused the big man to appear a little meaner than usual.

"Hey, Sheriff John," Bubba said, his voice still hoarse. No words to be wasted here. He didn't have a lot to say to Sheriff John, and Bubba suspected that the sheriff didn't have a lot to say to him either.

"Chief Andrews says that fire is plumb near out," Sheriff John said casually. He most certainly was not casual.

"Someone was trying to kill me," Bubba opined genially. He, also, was not genial.

"You see anyone?"

"I was asleep," Bubba said. "Would have stayed asleep, too, for a real long time, ifin my mother hadn't dragged me out of bed." His hand returned to rubbing the sore spot on the back of his head. Any more bumps, scrapes, or bruises and he wouldn't be able to live with himself. He wouldn't be in worse shape than if he had jumped from an airplane without a parachute. And he didn't even want to think about the effects of the smoke-related lack of oxygen that Miz Demetrice had rescued him from. He'd be expelling black-tainted goop from his lungs via his membranes for the next month.

"That's what the fire chief said." Sheriff John stared at Bubba's face in the bright light of the porch. "You look like hell." Bubba did. He had black streaks of soot running down his face, all over his hands, and his hair stood up straight on half of his head, kind of like that kid from *The Little Rascals*. Not only that, but Sheriff John could smell Bubba as if his nose was glued underneath his armpit. It wasn't a pleasant smell either. Finally, there was the fact that the other man was standing in the doorway in a pair of boxer shorts with what appeared to be little blue critters on them and only a blanket draped over his shoulders to cover himself up with.

"It's been a long few weeks of late," Bubba agreed.

"Fire chief says it's arson," Sheriff John also said, casually. He still really wasn't casual.

"Said someone was trying to kill me," Bubba said stubbornly. He was really stubborn. He'd learned it from the stubbornness master of the universe, Miz Demetrice.

"You said that," Sheriff John concurred. "But I'm thinking that maybe you set the fire yourself."

"Why would I do that?"

"Insurance money?"

"Miz Demetrice only has insurance on the mansion." Bubba nearly grinned at Sheriff John, happy to prove him wrong on some account. That would be easy to verify with Miz Demetrice and with their insurance agency. The Snoddy Mansion was a historical relic with a whole lot of old, historical stuff inside it. It didn't matter that the place was falling down but that almost everything inside it had some

216

kind of significant value to it. The caretaker's house was just a little house on the same property, changed from stables less than a hundred years before. Nothing historical about it, unless an individual counted the time that Miss Annalee Hyatt's daughter visited and spent the night there back in the early 1900's, in order to be honored by the town for the 40th anniversary of her mother's heroic exploits.

"Deputy Gray says you've been having all kinds of problems out here," Sheriff John said.

Bubba considered this information. Evidently, Willodean had let the cat out of the bag for whatever reason. It wasn't a secret, but Bubba didn't think that Sheriff John would be receptive enough to receive such information or take much credence in it.

"That equipment that you found, that stuff she was checking out for you, had been purchased by none other than Neal Ledbetter," Sheriff John offered. "At Radio Shack. And some at a specialty shop up the freeway about twenty miles."

Which explains why Willodean told you, thought Bubba. Murdered fella just happens to be the one who broke and entered the same mansion as where one murder suspect named Bubba lives, or lives real close to. She couldn't keep that to herself. Not legally, not even morally. He couldn't even feel the least bit sore at her. *But maybe that's because she's so damned cute.* His mind went blank for a second. *Stop that*, he chastised himself, thinking of chocolate Jell-O.

"Told you I thought he was trying to scare off my mother," Bubba said. "Walmart Supercenter, my lily white ass!"

Sheriff John chuckled. "Now that would be a real trick. Neal Ledbetter wasn't the cleverest of fellas, was

217

he?" He was referring to the fact that someone trying to scare Miz Demetrice off would like be trying to put mascara on a wild elephant.

Bubba didn't say anything.

"He wanted the land for a Walmart," Sheriff John said, answering his own unasked question.

"A Walmart *Supercenter*," Bubba grumbled, but Sheriff John went on.

"But why not just pick another site. There's plenty of land around here that would be a good spot for a Walmart. Plenty of people willing to sell, even to a little dickhead like Neal Ledbetter." Sheriff John considered. "Good spot here, though. Prolly the best spot.

Now, Bubba knew it had been more than just the Walmart Supercenter. Now he knew. Then, he hadn't. Sheriff John didn't know. Bubba didn't think he would ever get it. "You find anything interesting at Neal's place?"

"Like what, Bubba Snoddy?"

"Chains, old papers, a written confession of why he might have killed Melissa," Bubba said very seriously. He pulled the blanket close around his shoulders.

"Sorry," Sheriff John said insincerely. He almost smiled. "Just because Neal Ledbetter might have wanted the place as a Walmart doesn't mean he up and shot Melissa Dearman in the back."

"Walmart Supercenter," Bubba said and then added, "But you think I did." It wasn't a question.

"I think you could have." Sheriff John's voice was coolly objective. "I cain't dismiss you because you some laid-back good ol' boy who putters around as a mechanic down at Bufford's Gas and Grocery most nights, dates a waitress, brings her back before ten at

218

night, and don't drink 'til you pass out every Friday and Saturday night."

"What in the hell does that have to do with the price of tea in China?" Bubba resisted the almost overwhelming urge to slam the door shut in the sheriff's face. "You think I go around acting the way I do because all the while I was planning to commit a murder, maybe years in the future. Hot damn, I didn't know I was that smart."

"A lot of people around here don't know you have a college degree," said Sheriff John. He hooked one hand in his belt loop, just like Deputy Steve Simms did. Now Bubba could plainly see where the deputy had gotten the habit.

"Who would go and tell you such foolishness as that?" Bubba knew when to play dumb. A fella went and got a degree from a university, then all of a sudden he was some kind of nerd, and didn't that look bad around a place like Pegramville? Even if his degree was in something mundane and dull as history, which was about as non-committal as a college student could get, except for maybe liberal arts.

"Your mother spilled the beans," Sheriff John said.

Bubba made a face. Miz Demetrice had the biggest mouth at the most inconvenient times. Sure, she could run an illegal gambling ring, keep that secret, keep the local police right off of her back but a little thing like a degree, she had to share to every cotton-picking body in the world. "So now I'm a citified fool, who coolly planned the death of my ex-fiancée for three years. How'd I get her here?"

"Don't know. The Dearman's nanny says that Mrs. Dearman told her that she needed to take care of some personal business in Texas and she would be back in a few days, at most. There's a record of a phone call to the Dearman residence from the mansion. You could have told her a bunch of lies to get her here. That you still loved her, that she was the center of your universe, that maybe you'd just up and kill yourself if you didn't see her one more time."

"Then why did I leave the body out in the open for everyone to see?" asked Bubba. Just when he thought he was getting ahead, Sheriff John blindsided him with another theory that calmly put him as the cruelest man set on revenge that ever lived in Pegram County. *"A meaner man never existed," they would say for years to come,"* thought Bubba. *"He was so mean that he even...gasp...kicked his poor old Basset hound."*

"Because Neal showed up unexpectantly," Sheriff John answered, victoriously. He had that answer all ready to go. "He saw you just before you were going to cart that body off to hide it somewhere. God knows that you have a hundred or so acres of land, not to mention half of it swamp. And perfect for hiding a body. Hell, your father and about a hundred others dug enough holes on it to plant a thousand bodies in."

"Jesus Christ, I am one bad son of a bitch," Bubba said bitterly.

"Then you set the fire on your own house as a diversionary tactic," Sheriff John said, "in order to occupy the investigators with the so-called individual that's been trying to scare you and your mother off the Snoddy lands."

Bubba let out a deep sigh. He wasn't about to suggest to Sheriff John that maybe Bubba himself snookered Neal into buying that fancified equipment to make sounds in the mansion, too. Even if it was sarcastic in nature, it would be like handing his head over to the Sheriff on a silver platter. And he wasn't going to bring up Melvin Wetmore, Mark Evans, and the elusive Mary Bradley because Sheriff John would probably blow holes in those theories, as well. "I guess you got it all figured out. Now what?"

"I'm waiting for some ballistics on the bullet that killed Neal. We dug it out of the Donut Shop beside Ledbetter's Realty. We'll need to confiscate all of the weapons in the house, Bubba, for comparison." Sheriff John smiled widely, kind of like what Bubba imagined the grin of a great white shark would be like, right before it ate someone.

"You got a warrant?" Bubba asked nicely.

Sheriff John patted his shirt pocket. "You want to read it?"

"You know what?" Bubba was as tired as a man could be without falling on his face flat out on the floor. "I do." And he did, much to Sheriff John's consternation, from front to back, and in slow excruciating detail, pausing to look up every third word in the family's oversized *Webster's Unabridged Dictionary*. By the time Bubba finally finished the warrant he could hear Sheriff John's top teeth grinding away at the bottom. An hour later, Sheriff John left the mansion with every single gun in his legal possession. Miz Demetrice had been woken up and followed Sheriff John around the house, saying, "You going to leave us without protection, Mr. Sheriff Man? This is just another example of po-lice harassment. Just wait until I talk to Lawyer Petrie. He eats people like you for breakfast and poops 'em out at lunch. I'm going to call every congressman from Texas about this morally deficient outrage! Did we wake up in the Soviet Union this morning? Do we live in communist China now?

This is exactly the reason that we have the Constitution of the United States of America! We have every right to bear just as damn many arms as we can buy!"

To Bubba's amazement, Sheriff John didn't even lose his temper once. He merely collected all of the weapons, which included some that Bubba didn't know about, much less even knew what to call them, placed them in a box, wrote out a receipt for them, and presented the paper to Miz Demetrice.

She leaned out the kitchen door, dressed in her scarlet robe, and screamed at the county car as it pulled away, "I bet you don't do this right next to an election year!"

Bubba went to the telephone in the kitchen and held the receiver in one hand, while he flipped through the yellow pages.

Miz Demetrice watched him with something akin to astonishment. She was so furious that she couldn't believe that her son was so calm. She had figured that everything would be just hunky-dory once Sheriff John figured out that her son, Bubba, was just the most innocent man on the face of the planet. All they had to do was wait it out, and then, Sheriff John would say, 'Okey-dokey, you can go on home. Sorry about all the accusations, and name-calling, and general defaming that went on. We'll print a retraction in the paper.'

But it didn't happen. And even worse, it didn't look like it was going to happen. Then there was her son, looking like nothing had happened to him, and although he was as black as a coal miner he was going down one page of the telephone book with his index finger. He made a call, poking on the numbers as if he had all the time in the world. He waited and then asked, "I sure would like to know when the next train to Dallas is?"

Miz Demetrice's mouth dropped open.

"It is? Well, that's just great. Can you tell me if you have any seats on it? You do. Yes, it's an early train, isn't it?" Bubba tapped on the cover of the telephone book absently. "I know the weather has been a little mild here...thank you, I think I'm a nice fella, even at five in the morning. Good-bye, now."

Bubba disconnected the line with one blackened hand. He dialed again and listened to the phone for a long time before someone answered on the other end. "Miz Adelia? Yes, I know what time it is...a dream about what...Tom Cruise...Is that right?...No, I ain't never dreamt about Tom Cruise...Maybe Sylvester Stallone once...but that was completely innocent...Listen, we had a fire out here...No, everyone is okay...Ma is her normal self...That's right, as mean as hell...I'm a gonna put her on a train to Dallas this morning, and I don't want you to come to the house for the rest of the week...I'll give you a call...Consider it a paid vacation." He looked up as Miz Demetrice started to say something loudly and then abruptly shut her mouth. "You just rest up for the week, and when Miz Demetrice comes back, we'll all be ready to take on her orneriness then. Bye, Ma'am."

Miz Demetrice stared at her only son with what he termed the glare of doom. It was a look perfected over years of sheer biliousness, practiced on hapless shopkeeper, card cheaters, and mayors who didn't toady to the Snoddy matriarch as the rightful ruler of her own universe. She had used it on her son on the odd occasion when it was warranted, until her son had figured out that it was only a look and nothing that

223

could hurt him personally. Unless one counted the grudge Miz Demetrice could hold for months, and in some cases, years.

Bubba gave her back a look, measure for measure. "You're going. If I have to carry you kicking and screaming."

"You don't think I'll kick and scream?" she asked slowly, dangerously.

"I don't care if you tell people I beat you with a big stick, you're going. So you might as well get dressed and pack your clothes. I'll call Aunt Caressa." Bubba would have smiled at the expression of utter disbelief on his mother's face, but he knew that if he did, he would suffer for the remainder of his natural life, if he even had one after that.

In the end, Bubba escorted Miz Demetrice to the Amtrak station with minimal fuss. He smelled like smoke, dressed in jeans rescued from his blackened bedroom, and Precious wanted to fight over the passenger's seat. But he passed his mother onto the train conductor like he was presenting the Queen of England to the President of the United States of America.

Miz Demetrice took turns scowling at her son and the train conductor, who was clearly flustered.

At the train station there was at least ten families seeing someone else off on the seven AM train to Dallas. Half of them couldn't wait to call someone about Bubba's mother escaping his clutches to run off to Dallas. By the time the news got back to Mary Lou Treadwell, operator of the emergency line, the story was that Bubba himself had hijacked the seven AM train with an Uzi submachine gun and taken one hundred screaming hostages.

It was all the same to Bubba. He had gotten rid of Miz Demetrice. The angels very nearly wept.

Chapter Sixteen

Bubba and the Epiphany

Saturday

Bubba Snoddy was one tired, smelly, sorry-looking individual. He had a black eye that had evolved into a sickening purplish-green color and a bruised cheek that was just turning brownish-yellow-black. A knot the size of a tennis ball showed prominently on his forehead. There was a matching knot on the back of his head that made his normally well-groomed hair look like it was pushed up from having slept on it while it was wet. Both bumps made it impossible to wear his Stetson the way any God-fearing Texan was supposed to wear it. Still hacking out smoke-induced phlegm from exposure to the fire at the caretaker's house, his voice sounded like he was a lifelong whiskey and cigar man. He smelled like he'd been the chef at an all-day barbeque and rubbed the ashes all over his body, which surely didn't smell right to any individual with any kind of normal sense of olfactory modality. Finally, he hadn't slept as much as a large growing boy ought to sleep and this consequently resulted in his present state of crotchetiness.

Fellow Pegramville residents might liken that to Bubba possessing the normal Snoddy genes. That would be normal for Snoddys, to be precise. Genes much like both his mother and his father possessed. These were genes for which his forebears had been well-known.

After making sure that his mother, Miz Demetrice, claiming duress the entire time, boarded the seven AM Amtrak train to Dallas, Texas, Bubba was not feeling the least bit sociable. Several people tried to say their howdies to the man at the station but were dissuaded either by the grim look on his face, the bruises on his person, or the smell of him in general. A few were firmly deterred by all of the above.

"My God," said Bryan McGee, who was still waiting on his truck to be repaired at Bufford's Gas and Grocery and didn't think much of George Bufford for his extra-marital activities with Rosa Granado, even if she was a hot little tamale. Bryan was there at the Amtrak to pick up his sister-in-law, who was traveling up from Lake Charles, Louisiana and was specifically coming to pester Bryan into an early grave, while his wife, her sister, had her gallbladder removed. But now, while his sister-in-law, Henrietta, was collecting her luggage and badgering some poor bastard of a porter, Bryan was staring with startled big brown eyes at Bubba Snoddy.

Bryan had heard the stories and had even spoken to George Bufford, himself via cellular phone about his disabled Ford truck, yet sitting in Bufford's garage, while old George was off carousing with hot Rosa in the Bahamas. All that aside, it didn't prepare him for what Bubba looked like of late. He seemed as though he should be in a hospital, with all that battering. It looked like someone had dropped the A-bomb on that poor boy.

Meanwhile, everyone with a mouth in Pegramville was talking about Bubba and the murders of Melissa Dearman and Neal Ledbetter. Now there had been some mighty fishy goings-on over at the Snoddy

Mansion. While Bryan was waiting on Henrietta to disembark from the train, Stella Lackey told him that a fire had consumed the Snoddy place right down to the foundation. Furthermore, she said that Bubba Snoddy was running around stark-naked, yelling things about the invasion of communist Cuban dissidents. Or maybe it had been communist Korean dissidents. Stella wasn't rightly sure, because she hadn't sleep too well since Newt Durley had knocked her telephone pole down in an abhorrent spree of reckless and dangerous drunken driving. Consequently, she hadn't had phone service with which to call the police because the telephone company contained, in her opinion, a bunch of sorry money-grubbing, sons of bitches.

"Which has what to do with Bubba Snoddy?" Bryan asked when Stella said that.

"Nothing, but it just means I cain't recollect everything of late. So it was either communist Cubans or communist Koreans. One or t'other," Stella said, adjusting her false teeth in her mouth with a total lack of personable etiquette. She was getting to be in her eighties and didn't justifiably care what most other folks thought of her behavior. The only reason she was at the Amtrak station was to pick up her son, Charles, who was coming in from New Orleans to talk her into moving into a retirement home. Stella cackled to herself at that and moved away from Bryan, who stared at the older woman as if she was becoming senile right in front of his eyes.

Bubba, on the other hand, was aware of people staring and a few trying to greet him, but he was too tired and angry to be much of a gentleman. He did, however, stop to help an older woman he didn't know by putting her bags in the back of her minivan. The older woman, who wasn't from Pegramville, said, "Thank you kindly, sir." And drove away, leaving him to feel maybe a little better.

After all, would a murderer stop to help a lady with her luggage? He didn't think so.

Bubba returned to his truck and his faithful dog, Precious. Precious sat in the passenger seat as far as she could get away from her master. He hadn't been very nice to her. Not only that but he smelled very interesting and he wasn't inclined to let her stick her wet nose anywhere she pleased which that put her out tremendously. Then there was that one human's presence in her seat. The one called 'Miz Adelia' was often directed by the one called 'Mama' to give Precious baths, which she didn't like, and sprayed perfume on her, which was even worse than baths. The worst insult of all was that that human talked to her as if she were merely a dog. Things like, 'Oo-ums-good-puppy-wuppy-uppy.' It was time to show her master the extent of her disdain. As soon as he wasn't looking she fully intended to pee on something that belonged to him.

Unfortunately, Bubba did not notice her dogly disdain. He wanted a strong cup of coffee, some decent breakfast to stop the empty ache in his stomach, and the sight of a beautiful woman to make it all go away. Since he couldn't feast his eyes on Deputy Willodean Gray, he would feast his eyes on the next best thing, Lurlene Grady. He stopped by her apartment, and one of her neighbors told him that she was filling in down at the café for someone who had called in sick. Thus, he went by the Pegram Café and discovered it was chock full of more gawking, gaping, nosy people.

Bubba entered the small café, and the room instantly silenced. He looked around, keeping a blank look on his face as if he didn't notice everyone suddenly being quiet. He recognized several people there. Noey Wheatfall was looking through the kitchen window at Bubba, a dark lock of hair hanging in disarray over one eye with an expression of interested curiosity on his face. Lloyd Goshorn and Foot Johnson were sitting together at a table with full plates of food before them. Both had paused mid-bite to look at the spectacle of Bubba Snoddy entering a public place. Foot had his mouth wide open, showing the large bite of scrambled eggs covered with ketchup therein. Mayor John Leroy, Jr. sat at a booth with Judge Stenson Posey, and both were goggling at Bubba like two small children. Bryan McGee seemed to have transcended the laws of physics by beating him here from the train station, to include dumping his sister-in-law at his house on the way. Even librarian Nadine Clack sat at the counter with a cup of tea in her hands, and her head arched around to look at what everyone else was looking at.

It was almost impossible but Bubba managed not to bark, "Just what in the hell do you people think you're looking at?" He settled on the certified Snoddy glare, making sure that no one in sight was spared and threaded his way through the tables to the counter. There were two empty stools on the end. He selected the one on the farthest side away from the next person in order to put off conversation from eager beavers.

After he sat down, Lurlene hurried in with a stack full of plates running down the length of both of her arms. She was rushed, a little sweaty, and appeared to be working hard this morning serving the breakfast crowd. Even the too-tired Bubba noticed that the waitress looked to be plumb worn out, as if she been out a little too late the night before. She hesitated when she saw Bubba but smiled at him. It was, perhaps, the first smile he'd seen out of a person this day, and like the woman he'd helped at the Amtrak station, it made him feel a little less like a monster ambling around the town, grunting menacingly, and looking to eat the next hapless human being who stumbled in front of him.

General conversation resumed behind him, and Bubba didn't look around to see what, or who, they were talking about. He really didn't need to know because he already knew. He could feel eyes burning holes in his back. A whole lot of holes in his back. And it didn't help that Noey was periodically looking through the kitchen window every so often as if Bubba were going to lose his mind in Noey's very café, which would be followed up with a mass murder on the spot.

Bubba knew what it was. One murder might be justified. After all, the woman had cheated on him in their very own bed. What kind of Texan would stand for that? It might have been a fit of rage, wrong all the same, but comprehendible. But the other murder, although to a disliked individual such as Neal Ledbetter, was a murder spree, and here was the prime suspect in their midst. Wanting to eat with them, wanting to act normally, and wanting to be treated normally. Well, that was stretching what was commonly and socially acceptable. One didn't associate with persons such as that.

Bubba had just become persona non Pegramville-grata.

Lurlene stopped in front of Bubba with a coffee pot in her hand and a cup in the other. "Here you go darlin'," she said, pouring coffee in the cup and sliding it in front of him. "You shore look like you need this. I heard about the fire. But I didn't want to get all in the way of the firemen. They did say that no one was hurt so I wasn't too worried about you. My Lord, I was up half the night when I heard."

Bubba drank in the coffee and also in the appearance of Lurlene. Her blonde hair curled nicely around her head. She had pinned it up at the base of her head, but ringlets had escaped and draped themselves around her neck. Her face was flushed as if she had been running, but she looked as attractive as ever in the tight, little uniform that all the Pegram Café waitresses wore, showing off all the right curves in the good spots. And here, she was concerned about his welfare, unlike the rest of the town.

She said something while he was lost in his thoughts, then she repeated, "You want something to eat?"

"The special's okay," he answered. Maybe it was the way she was looking at him, but he suddenly noticed that Lurlene looked oddly familiar. She looked like someone he'd seen recently. She looked like a picture he had been looking at in the not-too-recent past. Her doe eyes scrutinized him in a manner that said she was real interested in him at the moment. Not in the way a gal looks at a man she's been dating but in a way that he couldn't quite get. If he had to put a word to mouth, he would have said, "That would be a predatory look, I reckon."

"Eggs scrambled?"

"Yeah." No romancing or wry repartee this morning because not one single fancy word came to Bubba's thoughts. It was like having a big black hole on the top of his head. There was that odd deja vu and his extreme tiredness holding him back.

Lurlene hesitated again and then smiled at him, showing her white teeth. "We should get together tonight," she whispered. "Just you and me, big boy, hmm?" She hurried off before he could say anything.

Bubba's eyes were as big as saucers. He nodded slowly. Up and down. Up and down. He knew exactly what she was talking about, and even though he was as tired as a man can get without falling flat on his face, there was a little surge of energy. *There ya go. Someone does care about me. And I might even get lucky.* Except a sudden mental image of Lurlene appeared in his mind. Lurlene and Willodean and a whole mess of chocolate Jell-O pudding. Their hair was blowing in an imaginary wind. Lurlene took a moment to look back at Bubba, and in that moment, she looked exactly like a playboy model poising for a photographer. She looked just like...

He was dimly aware that conversation had halted again when Lurlene had swung by to pour the coffee, take his order, and proposition him. Bubba settled his face into a neutral expression and glanced over his shoulder. Everyone in the café, bar none, was gazing at Bubba with the oddest expressions on their faces. It was as if they didn't know exactly what to make of him. He could have been a Martian who had wandered into the Pegram Café to ask directions to Venus, and his flying saucer was parked outside with a dog sticking her head out the window.

Bubba turned back to his coffee and tried to think. He was all out of plans. He was all out of suspects. Even his own mother, for whom he would still take the blame, hadn't killed his ex-fiancée and the pesky real estate agent. Or, he reconsidered, she hadn't killed Melissa, he was sure of that. Neal Ledbetter was still up for grabs. He frowned to himself. Of course, Miz Demetrice hadn't murdered Neal either. He knew that.

So he was back to the eternal question or actually two eternal questions. Who had killed Melissa? Who had shot Neal in the middle of his forehead? Neal most of all, didn't make much sense. He was just that, a nettlesome real estate agent. He had tried to bribe Judge Posey once. He had tried to get Mayor Leroy to influence the city council about re-zoning several pieces of land around Pegramville, a dim-witted scheme that had failed miserably. He had invited himself into the mansion until Miz Demetrice pulled out her Browning shotgun. He had planted that equipment in the house with the express purpose of scaring the Snoddys off. All of which showed what a foolish man Neal had been. Since he had been a fool, he thought that other people were just as foolish. Only he would have pranced around a mansion in a sheet, moaning and howling. Only he would have placed wailing, groaning speakers that could easily be traced back to him.

Therefore, if Neal had been such a great big fool as all that, didn't it stand to reason that his accomplice finally figured out that his foolishness was a huge liability in the plan? So Neal was guaranteed the status of worm food by the nature of his own feebleminded actions. Or perhaps, that there had been a second plan after all, not to split the booty three ways but only two.

234

And if that was the case then it was likely that another body would turn up soon, because someone probably wouldn't want to share the loot.

Bubba finished his coffee and didn't even notice that Lurlene filled it up again. His eyes were staring off into the distance as if lost in another world. It wasn't until she served him a platter with eggs, bacon, sausages, and hash browns heaped on it, that he abruptly came back to the present. And it wasn't until he reached for the Tabasco sauce that he saw something that he had missed before, because he was simply so fatigued, because it was taking every single bit of energy that he had to simply sit there at the counter and eat.

There was a coat rack almost in front of him, behind the counter, where the employees put their coats and purses. He stared at a garment hanging on it for the longest time. It hung from one arm of the rack in his direct line of sight. He knew what it was. He recognized it for what it represented, and the puzzle fit itself together. But his mind was so exhausted, he wasn't sure if he weren't imagining things after all. Every bit of it made sense, a sick kind of twisted sense, but sense all the same.

"Hey," Bubba said, having an epiphany.

Then some other damn thing happened.

Chapter Seventeen

Bubba has an Epiphany and Goes to Jail...Again

Saturday once more

Bubba was aware that the conversation in the Pegram Café died out again as he stared at that last thing that had niggled him so. It petered slowly off as if the customers gradually realized that something else was happening. He didn't know it, but they had watched Sheriff John Headrick pull up to the café in his county car, get out, and walk slowly around Bubba's truck. They saw him pet Precious as she stuck her head out the open window. She slobbered as he scratched her under her jowls. They also saw Sheriff John reach in the back of the Chevy truck and pull out a hunting rifle.

Sheriff John held the rifle for a long time, sniffed the barrel end, and then looked inside the café with serious, searching eyes. The occupants of the café hushed as if with a magic wand. Sheriff John carefully put the rifle in his car and entered the restaurant. As he stood in the door, his eyes immediately sought out Bubba sitting at the counter. The Sheriff moved forward quietly and stopped just behind Bubba.

"Hey, Bubba," said Sheriff John.

Bubba took a drink of coffee. It dawned on him that no one was moving around him. Everyone was standing shock-still. Lurlene was watching from the swinging kitchen doors with large brown eyes and a little 'O' of surprise. Noey Wheatfall stared at Bubba with a most intent expression through the slot where he slowly slid the food out for Lurlene to pick up.

There didn't seem to be a lot of choice in it for Bubba. He looked over his shoulder at Sheriff John. "Hey, Sheriff." The sudden noise made several people jump.

Sheriff John didn't have a friendly look on his face. No, he was angry, by the way Bubba judged it. He looked all done in. "Let's take a walk outside, Bubba," said the older man. It wasn't a request.

Bubba gazed at his half-finished plate of food. The eggs were done just the way he liked them with the Tabasco flavoring them nicely. "You mind if I finish this?" He pointed with a fork. He himself wasn't in an ingratiating mood.

Sheriff John's eyes didn't move from Bubba. "Go ahead, Bubba. You might as well."

With that Bubba finished his breakfast. He poured a bunch of ketchup on the hash browns and scooped them up with his fork. He piled down the eggs. He ate every bit of the sausage and the bacon. When he was done, he finished his coffee, and pulled out his wallet. Out of the corner of his eye he saw the Sheriff jerk just a bit, so he slowed down to show him that it was merely his wallet.

Bubba left ten and five dollar-bills for Lurlene because he thought tipping should always be good for good service and there hadn't been anything wrong with the service. And in all of that time, no one even moved, not even to eat their rapidly cooling meals, or drink their lukewarm coffees. They watched Sheriff John watching Bubba as if they expected an old time Western shoot out.

Bubba slid the wallet in his back pocket of his jeans. He said to Sheriff John, "You want to put those handcuffs on me, Sheriff John?"

"I do believe so," that man answered. He fished them out and put them on Bubba's wrists as the other man presented them to him. Sheriff John repeated his Miranda rights to Bubba, in much the same manner as he had on at least on two other occasions in the past two weeks.

"Good breakfast," Bubba called to Noey Wheatfall.

Noey said uncertainly, "Uh-thanks, Bubba."

"See you later, Miss Lurlene," Bubba called to the waitress.

Lurlene waved at them albeit a little weakly.

Foot Johnson and Lloyd Goshorn were sitting at the table next to the door. Both men turned to look at Bubba as Sheriff John guided him out the door. Four eyes were as big as the white plates Noey used in the restaurant.

"Boo!" cried Bubba, leaning toward Foot Johnson. He had a strong recollection of the Foot being an out and out bully when Bubba had been in elementary school. As a matter of fact, Foot had often had his foot in some poor younger child's butt, which was the reason he was thusly called. Foot jumped about a foot, too.

Bubba smiled. So did Lloyd Goshorn, and behind them, Judge Posey chuckled loudly. Foot Johnson merely turned a bright shade of red and muttered something unintelligible under his breath.

Sheriff John said, "Knock that off, Bubba."

Once they were outside, Bubba said, "Listen, my dog is in my truck."

Sheriff John paused but didn't seem impressed. "So what's your point?"

"I cain't just leave her there." Bubba pointed awkwardly with his handcuffed wrists. "And you cain't just leave her there."

Sheriff John was silent for a bit. He would have asked if Miz Demetrice could come and get the damned dog, but he'd heard the news about her recent trip. Instead, Sheriff John shuffled his feet like a little kid. After a minute, he cursed, "All right, Goddammit. I'll get the damned dog."

A few minutes later Tee Gearheart said, "No dogs in the jail, Sheriff."

"Don't you start with me, Tee Gearheart," warned Sheriff John, removing the cuffs from his prisoner. "Just process Bubba, dammit."

"Hey, Bubba," greeted Tee. "We ought to name a cell after you. The Bubba Snoddy Suite. How'd you like that?"

Bubba shrugged. "What I'd like is to get some sleep."

"Heard about your fire," said Tee. "Empty your pockets right here."

Bubba emptied his pockets, and looked at the contents, wallet, soot, dental floss, wadded up dollar bill, more soot, and one green button. He removed his belt and placed it on the counter, as well. "Here you go."

"You want to talk about that deer rifle in the back of your truck, Bubba?" Sheriff John asked, watching him with steely eyes.

"I don't own a deer rifle," answered Bubba. He was hoping that Miz Demetrice didn't own a deer rifle. Of course, he hadn't known about all those other guns

239

she had around the house either. Bubba had used a deer rifle many times as a teenager with both of his grandfathers but had never taken to the sport. Fishing was more to his liking. No one got in arms over a man hauling in a batch of trout. He decided that maybe Miz Demetrice did own a deer rifle and that very quickly, Bubba was going to be in even more big trouble that he had been before.

"It's been fired recently," Sheriff John mentioned.

"Sign here," said Tee. He pushed a form and a pen across to Bubba. Bubba signed it.

Tee came around the big desk and guided Bubba away from the Sheriff. Bubba said to Sheriff John, "Don't suppose you believe me."

"It was in the back of your truck," Sheriff John called after them.

"It won't have my fingerprints on it," replied Bubba wearily. "You won't find any record of me buying a rifle. And besides you know where I was when Neal Ledbetter was shot."

Sheriff John knew very well. But what Bubba didn't know, was that the bullet they had dug out of the Donut Shop's wall was a thirty ought six caliber slug. And it had traveled through two other stores after passing through Neal's skull. Fortunately for Sheriff John and unfortunately for Bubba, it wasn't torn up a whole bunch, and Sheriff John knew that ballistics could easily match it to the weapon that fired it. Such as the Winchester hunting rifle in the back of Bubba's truck. Then there was the fact that while Neal's watch said a certain time, Doc Goodjoint could not narrow the time down to more than plus or minus a few hours of one PM. Bubba might have very well done it before he went into the Grand Jury, making him one of the

240

most cold-blooded killers that Sheriff John had ever run into in his entire career. He walked out of the jail shaking his head sadly.

Bubba watched Sheriff John leave and waited for the exterior jail door to shut before he said to Tee, "Say, Tee. I sure hope your wife's pregnancy is going all right. Poppiann's a real fine woman, and you all will make fine parents."

"Thank you," Tee said, a note of wariness creeping into his voice, as if his ESBP was kicking in with a vengeance. (Extra Sensory Bubba Perception or knowing when another damn shoe was about to drop) Bubba was one of those people Tee liked to have in the jail. For one reason, he didn't make trouble. For another reason, if there had been trouble and Bubba was in the jail, too, Bubba would make sure the trouble ended. Bubba was a good old boy from a good old Pegramville family, but Tee figured that Bubba was about to become trouble. It would be the worst kind of trouble, too. Not the kind that Tee could pound down with a metal sap and a firm word, but the kind that he had always feared. The logical kind. Oh, yes, the moral kind. The kind if one didn't do, then one would surely go straight to hell to roast marshmallows with all the other cursed souls.

"Gosh darn it," Tee muttered under his breath, scraping his large feet over the cement floor like a little elementary school child caught in the midst of a dismal dilemma. There didn't seem to be much else to do. Bubba wasn't actually in the jail cell yet. So Tee let him go and said, "What? Bubba, what already?"

"You think I'm guilty?"

241

Mike Holmgreen looked interestedly out from between his set of bars. "I don't think you're guilty, Bubba," he said.

"Thank you, Mike," Bubba said sincerely. "Tee?"

"It don't matter which way I think, Bubba," Tee said earnestly. "I'm the jailor. My job is to keep those in the jail locked up, safe, well-fed, and ready to go when they need to go. It's my duty. I swore an oath."

"What oath?" Bubba asked curiously.

" 'The City of Pegramville Oath for Allegiance, Duty, and Honor.' It's in the *City Charter*," Tee said. "You should read it sometime."

"I have read it," Bubba said right back. He had. It had been very boring. Even for him. And he still didn't remember anything about a city oath. But whatever.

"You remember when you were in high school, Tee," Bubba started slowly and carefully.

Tee's face darkened. "I knew you were going to bring that up. I just knew it."

"What?" Mike said. "What happened in high school?"

"Never you mind, Mike Holmgreen," Tee all but snarled.

"One dark night at prom there was a mascot minding its own bidness. A mascot from a rival high school, mind you," Bubba said innocently. "And someone kidnapped the mascot."

"Bubba," Tee said warningly.

Mike was a-goggle.

Bubba looked at Mike as if he were telling a story. "We were real young." He considered. "About your age. Except we didn't get caught."

"I didn't mean no harm to that goat," Tee said stridently. "It charged me and had its teeth on my..."

he stopped and looked at Mike's saucer-like eyes. "On my...uh...oh, heckfire. You know a goat can bite like a mean sonuva...beach ball," he finished lamely. Then he put in fiercely, "Do you know how lucky Poppiann and I are to be having a child after that?"

"Hey, that goat was fine after we took him to the vet," Bubba said. Then he added meaningfully, "A Snoddy family friend who happened to also be a veterinarian and who could keep his mouth shut..."

Tee glowered at Bubba and then growled at Mike, "You tell anyone about this and you'll be needing a vet, boy."

Mike didn't say anything.

"What do you want, Bubba?" Tee asked with calamitous reservation.

"Let me walk out. I'll go figure this thing out. Then I'll come back as soon as I can." Bubba smiled his most winningest smile. "I swear on my Mama's grave."

Tee thought about it. "No, I don't think so, and your mama ain't dead yet."

"Tee," Bubba started.

"I'll go with you," Tee said firmly. That way Bubba couldn't get into as much trouble. Hell, Tee knew Bubba wasn't a killer. So did half the town. But someone was killing folks. "So will the kid. He ain't got nothing better to do."

Precious suddenly felt left out of the conversation and woofed as if in agreement.

"But we're taking the minivan," Tee added. "And we need to be back before six PM else we're all in a heap o' trouble." He rubbed a hand over his perspiring forehead. "God, I have to call my wife."

Ten minutes later Tee was driving a minivan with Bubba, Mike, and Precious as passengers. Bubba said, "We're going to Bufford's."

"Bufford's?" Tee repeated. "What the heck for?"

"I need to talk to Melvin Wetmore about a job."

Bubba finally had figured out that coincidences did happen. Sometimes some lucky bastard hit all six numbers in the Lotto and walked off with tens of millions of bucks. Sometimes a fella got struck by lightning. Every once in a while that fella that got struck by lightning got struck again playing golf or some such silliness. But the literal odds were against it. So if Bubba happened to coincidently be by himself in Bufford's Gas and Grocery on that inauspicious Thursday night, then he'd take off his boots, deep-fry them in peanut oil, and eat them. With ketchup.

Chapter Eighteen

Bubba Has to Look-Up the Word "Epiphany" in the Dictionary and Also Talk to Some Folks

Saturday

Melvin Wetmore had eventually fixed Mr. Smith's transmission and, with Bubba's reminder, remembered to put the seal in. He had also figured out what was wrong with the Chevy Camaro. (It was a not uncommon ignition problem due to rodents nesting inside the infrequently driven car which had been parked in a barn for the last three years because of a long-lasting debate over marital assets on the part of the owner and the owner's wife. The owner finally got the title for the Camaro and discovered, for some reason, that it wouldn't start.) But Bryan McGee's Ford truck was a headache and a half. Normally Melvin would be snuggling a cute blonde in his arms on a Saturday morning, but Bryan had called George Bufford in whatever island paradise he was adulterizing in, to complain about the lack of mechanicking being accomplished on the truck. Then George had called Melvin to telephonically chew on Melvin's buttocks.

So on this Saturday, Melvin was looking at the engine of the truck, tapping his fingers along the radiator, wondering if it were too late in his life to consider a career change. Being an astronaut was probably out, but he thought he could definitely try the amazing and fun career of rodeo clown. He was picturing the clown make-up on his face when a blue minivan pulled up outside the open bay doors. The minivan was brand sparkling new and obviously not in need of Melvin's services. The driver was Tee Gearheart. The passengers were Bubba Snoddy, Mike Holmgreen, and Precious the dog, who was sitting in the child's carrier strapped to the rear passenger seat.

Melvin brightened. Bubba was a genius when it came to rooting out a problem with a vehicle. And here Bubba was to save the day or to save Melvin from his true calling.

All three men got out of the minivan. Precious barked annoyedly in the back of the minivan because they quickly closed her in with two windows cracked. Bubba had handcuffs on. Mike was sniffing the outside air like a dog that hadn't been out of the kennel for a long, long time. Tee was looking grimly determined. Melvin, who didn't think of himself as looking anything in particular, got a rag to wipe off nonexistent grease from his hands while he waited for the three to approach.

"Say, Melvin," Tee said. He stepped up next to Melvin and towered over the other man.

"Say, Tee," Melvin said back. He adjusted his glasses and glanced warily at Bubba. "Bubba. You outta jail already?"

Bubba raised his handcuffed wrists. "Not exactly. You know Mike Holmgreen?"

"Hey, Mike," Melvin said. "Pegramville's own little arsonist. Why ain't you got cuffs on, too?"

Mike grinned. "I'm not a flight risk."

"Melvin," Bubba said peremptorily, "you said you got offered a job at the Walmart up the way."

246

"Yeah," Melvin said, shrugging. "You want to take a look at Mr. McGee's truck, Bubba. I ain't got a clue why it's making that clanking sound. The last time I started it, it sounded like it was the bathroom at the Pegramville Café after the chili special."

Bubba sighed. "Tell us about the job offer, Melvin."

Melvin pursed his lips. It didn't matter to him. "Somebody up to no damn good called me up, offered me a job, said I needed to start Thursday night. You know, the same night you done went and kilt yer fee-on-say."

Tee frowned.

"You tell them you could start on Thursday night?" Bubba asked quietly.

Melvin thought about it. "No, as a matter of fact, she was real insistent about me starting Thursday night. I wanted to wait until Monday, and the lady on the phone said, 'No sir, it's Thursday night, or not at all.' Offered me a big raise, too." His shoulders slumped. "Don't know why someone would want to play such a silly trick on me. I ain't done nothing to no one."

"A woman called you," Bubba repeated. "You remember the name she gave you, or did she sound like she was from around here?"

Melvin's eyes crossed even more than they were naturally. "I don't think she said what her name was, but I think she was a Yankee. Sounded like one. Dint have no inflection in her voice. Trying to sound like one, you know, like folks who bin down in Texas a few years." Then he grinned. "She sounded like she was a blonde though. Wanted to get a look at her."

Bubba looked at Tee. Tee looked at Bubba. Mike looked at the poster on the mobile tool box that

247

featured Miss December of 2008. She was wearing a Santa hat and not much else.

"You sure about this, Melvin," Tee said in his gravelly voice. "That woman's voice couldn't have been say, Miz Demetrice or maybe Miz Adelia Cedarbloom?"

"I have done heard Miz Demetrice afore," Melvin said darkly. "She and Miz Adelia both have called here for Bubba. 'Tweren't neither of them. Of that, I'm sure."

"Miz Demetrice couldn't sound like a Yankee if you paid her," Bubba muttered.

"Okay, then. What happened to the job?" Tee asked.

"I went up there," Melvin said. "Weren't no job. Weren't no blonde human resources manager. Thought those people were going to die laughing at me. That fella in charge of that department was not only a man, but he wasn't blonde, and he sure as hell wasn't cute. I wasn't amused." He adjusted his glasses again. "Somebody done pulled a fast one on me. I'm inclined to wrap a monkey wrench round their head ifin I find out who."

"Uh-huh," Tee said. "You think maybe someone did that to get you out of the way on Thursday night?"

Melvin cogitated intently or as intently as Melvin could cogitate. "Why in the hell would someone want to do something like that?" He glanced at Bubba who was gazing meaningfully at Melvin. "Oh." Melvin took another prolonged moment to concentrate. "I reckon that could have been the way of it. But that would mean that Bubba dint kill no one and someone set him up."

Mike continued to stare absorbedly at the Miss December poster.

Tee nodded. "You need to speak to the po-lice, Melvin. You need to tell Sheriff John about this. Ain't no reason for Bubba to set himself up like that."

Melvin shrugged dejectedly. "I reckon I should. But hey, Bubba, you sure you don't want to take a look at Mr. McGee's engine? The valves are good. It ain't got nothing wrong with it, as far as I can tell."

Bubba rolled his eyes. "Change out the gas and let it run a half hour. Make sure you put premium in it and tell Bryan not to be so damn cheap when he's buying gasoline. As a matter of fact, tell him to stop buying from the Mayor's brother. Think Henry Leroy gets his gasoline from sucking it out of old farm tanks."

"Ah," Melvin uttered, feeling a ray of hope within him. "Bad gasoline. That could be it."

"Come on," Bubba said to Tee. "I want you to see something."

They left Melvin excitedly rubbing his hands together as he contemplated his next mechanical action. Tee took a rapt Mike by his shoulder and led him out of the garage bays. "Boy, they don't look like that in real life."

Mike said, "Oh, don't say that. I gotta have some dreams."

"Trust me."

Bubba opened the door to Bufford's Gas and Grocery, and there stood Leelah Wagonner who was polishing off the counter and straightening up the tray of scratch-off lottery tickets. The door tinkled as they entered, and she turned to look. Her eyes got big and round as she saw Tee, Bubba, and Mike. But when her

249

eyes dropped to Bubba's handcuffed wrists she said, "Oh, Bubba."

"Miz Wagonner," Bubba said without ado. "I hope your husband is doing well at the manure factory and your two children haven't being playing with mud pies and tennis shoes lately."

"SpaghettiO's," Leelah said dismally. "They poured SpaghettiO's in the VHS part of the DVD/VHS player. Good thing VHS tapes are as dead as the dodo. What are you doing out of jail, Bubba?"

"I have to prove that I'm an innocent man, Miz Wagonner." Bubba pointed at the surveillance cameras. "Did you know the cameras are dummies?"

Leelah's eyes flickered to the camera. "Well, yeah. You know about it. It's a big joke. George Bufford is a cheap bastard. A body could get robbed and killed and...oh, sorry Bubba. Well, there wouldn't be a soul to know about it, and...oh, I'm really sorry, Bubba."

"It's all right," he said gruffly.

Tee and Mike didn't know what to say. Finally Tee said, "What's your point, Bubba?"

Bubba stepped over to the camera and yanked out the wires that fed into the false unit.

"It's been cut. Someone came into the store and cut the leads, thinking the cameras were real." Bubba dropped the wires. "I bet every one of them has been cut."

Tee and Mike ascertained that all three fake security cameras had their leads cut.

Returning to the front counter, Tee put his hands in his Sam Brown belt and thought about it. "Well, ifin a person thought they were real, and they didn't want a record of them being in the store when in fact they were out murdering some poor woman, they might have cut them themselves."

"Bubba knew about the cameras being fake," Leelah protested. "We all did. If we got robbed, there's nothing to have a record of it and we all know how often a 24-hour place like this gets robbed. I've been robbed three times in three years and," she waved a hand at the fake device, "that's George's concession."

Mike perked up. "So, if someone were framing Bubba, and knew he would be alone here at Bufford's and didn't want him to have any proof of it, they might come in, wait until they had a free moment, and snip the wires. None of the cameras point at each other so there wouldn't be a record of it, even if there were a real camera. Just someone walking up and then blackness."

"That don't matter," Tee said. "Wasn't real. Are you sure Bubba knew about the cameras being fake, Miz Wagonner?"

"Sure," Leelah said. "All of us knew. It was a big old joke."

"But how would someone know that a customer wouldn't come in?" Mike said. "Or Bubba could have called someone to come in and take over the register."

"Thursday nights aren't busy," Leelah said. "Hours can go by without seeing a soul."

"Which brings us to witness number two." Bubba nodded. "I need Mary Bradley's address. Mark Evans, too. We need to have a few words with both of them."

The surprised expression on Leelah's face was comical. "Well, yeah, but Bubba, you're not going to...hurt...anyone are you?"

251

Bubba tilted his head and looked sternly at Leelah. "When have I ever done anything to make you think I was going to hurt anyone?"

Leelah ticked off items on her hand. "There was the time you threatened to string Foot Johnson by his...by his...by a bodily part ifin he didn't stop taking his Caddy down the back roads and messing up all the work you did on his suspension. Then there was the time that you told old man Witherspoon that he would be lucky if a surgeon could remove your foot from his ass on account of him pouring diesel into his gas engine and..."

Bubba interrupted. "Okay, but I didn't really do any of those things, did I?"

"Well, no, Bubba. I already told you I thought you were innocent." Leelah glanced over Tee and Mike's shoulders at the door. "But I'm not sure if she does.

All three men turned in unison to look at the purely petite and beauteous figure of one Willodean Gray, Pegram County Sheriff's Department Deputy. She had pulled in behind Tee's minivan, spent a few minutes speaking with Melvin Wetmore, and walked noiselessly into Bufford's with a determined look on her lovely face. It was the kind of look that said she wasn't going to take any kind of bull hockey. Or any other kind of hockey for that matter.

"What in hell are you all up to?" Willodean said with emphasis on the word, 'hell.' "I mean, what in the red blazes of the deepest nether regions are you doing, Tee Gearheart? You let your prisoners out. You got your wife's minivan and a baying Basset hound parked in the baby seat. You got a possible murderer with handcuffs on in the front and you got an arsonist without any kind of handcuffs just walking around.

252

Then you're escorting them around like you're Crockett and he's Tubbs. I don't know who in the heck that makes Mike, but Jesus Christ, Tee, you really ought to know better."

And, as Willodean's appearance often did, all three men goggled mutely at her, lost in the good looks of the deputy. Finally, Tee said, "Well, hey, Deputy Gray. We were just going out for burritos."

Chapter Nineteen

Bubba and More Questions

Still Saturday

"They're looking for clues," Leelah Wagonner said proudly. She glanced at Deputy Willodean Gray, saw that she was cute, sighed for her lost waistline, and told herself that life was good at the Wagonner house, no matter that Leelah would never be a size four again. Or a size six or probably even a size eight but that was really getting off the point. "Bubba's an innocent man."

Willodean stared at Leelah in a manner that only a licensed law enforcement official could accomplish. The stare stated emphatically, "What on God's green earth do you mean by that? Are you legally intoxicated? Have you been committing some kind of crime? How long do you think it will be before I get the truth out of you?" It was a patented stare that three generations of Grays had perfected over decades of law enforcement. It was a stare very similar to the Snoddy stare of doom.

Finally, Willodean turned to look at Tee Gearheart who winced and suddenly found the stained linoleum floor extremely interesting. Then she turned her authoritative gaze on Mike Holmgreen. Mike blushed and found a magazine nearby to examine. It didn't particularly matter that the magazine was called *Texas Country Gardener* or that he was holding it upside down. Finally, Willodean's daunting stare came to rest solely on Bubba.

Bubba didn't flinch, blush, or glance away. He liked looking at Willodean. She was the prettiest woman he'd ever seen, not only that, but she had a brain that she could actually use, plus she had a gun. Bubba wondered if she might be the kind of woman who liked to go fishing with a fella.

"Bubba," Willodean said. "I just talked to Melvin Wetmore."

Bubba nodded. A scene where Willodean and he were covered with chocolate Jell-O pudding popped into his head. Amazingly the two of them were covered with pudding and fishing for bass at the same time. *Hmm. It's purely amazing what a lack of sleep and being knocked unconscious will do to a man.*

"I guess you know what he told me about the night that Melissa Dearman was murdered," she said calmly.

"I guess Sheriff John didn't really care to find out why no one else was around that night," Bubba said, snapping back to the moment. There was a definite lack of chocolate Jell-O pudding. Dammit.

"I think he might very well say that you arranged it," Willodean said promptly. "That's what the D.A. is going to say. Then there wouldn't be anyone around to say whether you came, went, or stayed right here. After all, you've been planning it for years."

Bubba took a deep calming breath. A fella finally thinks of some circumstances that will take his butt out of a sling and here came someone to shoot him down. Not only was the shooter the beautiful Willodean, but she was most likely about to cut him off at the knees by dragging his hiney back to jail.

"Tell her about the wires on the cameras," Leelah said quickly. "Ain't no reason for Bubba to have done that. Uh-uh. He knew they weren't real. Hell, we had a pot on who was going to get robbed next and the amount of time before the po-lice gave up on catching the thief. On account of us not having real security cameras and George's die-hard stinginess."

"The security cameras are dummies," Willodean said, stating a fact.

"They are," Bubba answered. "Someone else didn't think so."

So Bubba patiently explained to Willodean while Mike let Precious out of the minivan for a dogly rest break and Leelah proceeded about her business in the store. Two curious customers later, Willodean was staring at the cameras and rubbing her jaw in an agitated manner. "I'm going to get fired," Willodean muttered. "I'm going to get fired and have to move back to Dallas and into my parent's house. Dad's going to say, 'I told you not to move down to bumpkinville, honey.' Mom's going to make so many chocolate chip cookies that my ass will explode. I'm going to have to beg for that patrol job back again on the south side of Dallas. Then I'm going to die when some seventeen-year-old robs a 7-Eleven because he wants Twinkies and doesn't have time to get his paycheck cashed from the fast food place he works at."

Bubba listened to Willodean's monologue with a great outpouring of sympathy. After all, Willodean didn't need to put herself out for Bubba. She barely knew him, even though he'd very much like to change that. But first there was the little matter of the multiple murder charges and, not to mention, making sure that Willodean didn't get fired in the process.

Ah, life can be such a challenge, Bubba considered. "So are we a go?"

"Dammit," Willodean grumbled miserably. "Where does Mary Bradley live?"

Leelah told Willodean happily.

Twenty minutes later, one county car with one deputy and one alleged felon drove up to the front of a house on Wagon Wheel Road. The county car was followed by a minivan with one jailor, one felon, who had pled his way into a very light sentence, and one Basset hound who was perturbed that she hadn't been allowed to ride with her very favorite human in the whole world.

Like all of the houses on Wagon Wheel Road, the one at which they'd stopped was one story, built in the 1950s, had a red brick exterior, and a car port big enough for the three rusting refrigerators and an automobile engine of unknown origin. There was also a decrepit Mercury Villager parked in the meager driveway indicating that at least one person was in residence.

Bubba got out of the county car and walked around to open the door for Willodean. Willodean was not amused and used her own unhandcuffed wrists and hands to open the door for herself. She put her baton back into her belt, adjusted her shirt, and said, "Let me do the talking, Bubba."

The minivan parked behind the county car and Tee clambered out, followed by Mike, and Precious, who wasn't about to let an opportunity pass her by again.

Consequently, there were four adults and one dog waiting at the front door when Mary Bradley answered the bell. Mary was in her forties with short blonde hair and bright blue eyes. She wasn't trim and she wasn't fat. She wore tight jeans and a t-shirt that proclaimed, 'I'm still hot. It just comes in flashes.'

Mike started to ask what the t-shirt meant when Tee lightly slapped the eighteen year old on the back of the head.

Mary stared at her visitors and finally said, "Okay, then. Bubba, I didn't know I was having a party today."

Willodean grimaced and said, "I'm Deputy Gray from the Pegram County Sheriff's Department and you would be Mary Bradley."

"Someone didn't die, did they?" Mary asked calmly. "Unless it was my weird Uncle Felix. That man's got screws loose that you couldn't find with the most powerful magnet in the world. But he does have some money and no real children." She considered and added, "That we know about."

"No. No one died. At least not in your family. You are Mary Bradley?"

Mary had an expression on her face that said, "Heck, yes, I'll play this game." "Yes."

"Good. You remember a week ago Thursday?" Willodean said quickly. Bubba was getting antsy, and she stepped on his toe to give him something to really think about.

Bubba looked down at her petite foot in its brown work boot and wondered if a fly had landed on his boot. But he did give Willodean points for accurately gauging his frame of mind.

"You mean the day Bubba went out and..." Mary stopped and looked at Bubba.

"Allegedly," Mike put in.

"Right," Mary said. "You're that kid who tried to burn down the school." Then she looked at Tee and saw the patch on the shoulder of his uniform. "And I know your wife from our knitting circle. How's the pregnancy going?"

Tee smiled genially. "Poppiann's real good. Snores a lot but that's because she has to sleep on her back, and..." he stopped as Willodean turned and landed that terrible gaze upon him again.

"Last Thursday," Willodean said slowly. "What was going on?"

"Well, I took my mother to Pokerama. She said she saw you there, Deputy," Mary said amusedly. "Then I watched a DVD with my son. *Young Frankenstein*. You know that old Mel Brooks film. God, that's my favorite. We burned the popcorn." She giggled to herself. "Had to leave all the windows open for hours to get the smell out."

Bubba bit his lower lip. "You were home all night," he said firmly, not asking a question.

"Yeah, Bubba. I heard Mark Evans quit, but I don't know why I didn't get called to work." She smiled. "I need all the hours I can get. Alimony only goes so far, you know."

Frowning, Bubba started to say that he had called Mary. She hadn't answered. He remembered very well because he knew that he hadn't wanted to run the cash register in the store. Hell, he didn't even know how before that night. As a matter of fact, the burn on his arm from the thrice-cursed hot dog machine was still healing.

"But h-ey," Mary said with sudden clarity before Bubba could get into the first sentence. "That must have been the night my phone went dead."

"Your phone went dead," Willodean repeated.

"Sure. I don't know exactly when, but I had to call the phone company on Friday because I didn't have any service. I went next door to the neighbors on both sides, and they had service. I even checked to make sure the phone was plugged in correctly." Mary shrugged. "The service guy came out on Monday." She made a disgusted noise. "Said someone played a joke on me."

"Let me guess," Bubba said. He made a cutting motion with the index and middle fingers of his right hand. "Clipped your phone lines."

"Right around the side of the house," Mary confirmed. "Right where they go into the house. Kids I reckon." She looked pointedly at Mike, who rapidly looked up at the sky.

"And this happened on Thursday," Willodean said.

Mary's face wrinkled in concentration. "I think so. I didn't have to call anyone until Friday, and I remember getting a call from a cousin on Wednesday. So on Thursday, I dropped Mama off you know where and then stopped off to get some KFC. My son got the DVD from Blockbuster's and that was the whole kit and caboodle."

"It didn't matter if she knew about the phone wires being cut or not," Bubba said slowly. "As long as no one could call this number from work and get an answer."

"Holy crap," Mike said. "Oh, sorry. I meant holy carp. But someone really was trying to set Bubba up. They knew he would call Mary so they cut her wires."

"But how did they know Mark Evans was going to quit that night?" Tee said.

Mary looked at the four people and one dog, who were all looking at each other. "Good question. You going to see Mark next?"

Bubba sighed. "None other. You know, Mr. Evans said some very nasty things about my mother."

Willodean sighed in response. "A lot of people say some nasty things about your mother."

Mike chirped in. "I don't."

"That's nice, Mike."

Then Precious woofed to put her two cents in and then proceeded to chase her tail for a solid minute. Mary took the brief respite to ask Bubba, "Is it true what they say about the Snoddy Mansion, Bubba? There's a sh-" she glanced meaningfully at Mike, "a bunch of buried you know what out there?"

Bubba glared meaningfully at Mary, who got the message and shut up.

Mary watched the two vehicles drive away and wondered what the Jolly Green Giant was going on. Then she went to call her mother and tell her all the gossip. Ten minutes later someone else knocked on the door and asked Mary where Bubba Snoddy had gotten to, and Mary answered truthfully.

Willodean drove her county car to Mark Evan's address and silently smoldered. Bubba didn't say anything, but she could feel his presence beside her like a very large, very solid rock. A rock that smelled of musk and dog. A rock that had a whole lot of bruises, and cuts, and bumps on it. Quite probably a rock that had been set up as a patsy to take a fall.

"Why?" she said finally.

"Why," Bubba repeated.

"Why set you up?"

"To get the Snoddy Mansion and all the Snoddy lands that go with it," Bubba answered. "All proper and legal."

Willodean had seen the Snoddy Mansion. It was a ghost of what a Southern plantation house was in its heyday. The paint was peeling. A couple of the

261

columns were listing like the Leaning Tower of Pisa. The grass was overgrown, and the Spanish moss had taken over the live oaks down the driveway. In addition, the caretaker's house was ruined by the fire so recently set to it. To be even more precise, half the land was reputedly swamp and useless for anything except catching mosquitoes. "No offense Bubba, but I don't get it. It's a dump."

"Yeah," he said slowly. "Pretty much. It's going to fall into the ground soon, and it's going to be the Snoddy Hole. As soon as we find Mark Evans, I'll tell you why someone wants the damn place. And it ain't because they wanted it to be a Walmart Supercenter."

However, finding Mark proved elusive. His one room apartment was empty. The neighbor said that Mark was probably at the community college. The registrar at the community college said Mark was in Psychology 101. The Psychology 101 professor said Mark was absent because he needed some extra cash serving warrants, and writs, and such.

Bubba could tell Willodean was getting tired of it all. He could even see by the look in her eyes that she had visions of being very publicly fired dancing merrily about in her head.

"Serving papers on folks?" Tee said to the Psychology 101 professor. All the students gazed on interestedly. It wasn't every day that a pretty sheriff's deputy, a large man with more bumps than a Motocross track, a large jailor, a teenager who looked like he was having the time of his life, and a Basset hound wandered into their classroom looking for one of their own.

One of the students raised a hand. Tee glanced at the young woman wearing a Jim Morrison t-shirt and said, "Yes, Ma'am?"

"Mark works for Minnieweather Process Serving," she said proudly, sticking her chest out. She was a pretty young woman with blonde dreadlocks and bright blue eyes. Mike stared at her chest until Tee slapped him on the back of his head again. The dreadlocked blonde went on blithely, "Some of us do stuff for Minnieweather sometimes. Extra cash." She smiled knowingly. "No one expects to get served divorce papers from me."

"I wouldn't expect to get divorce papers from you," Bubba acknowledged wryly. "But first I'd have to be married."

The blonde with the dreads handed a business card to Willodean. "I've heard of this guy," Willodean said moodily. "He serves papers on anyone. And I do mean, *anyone.*"

Twenty minutes later the troop was standing inside a miniscule office looking at a man who could have been Colonel Sanders's long-lost twin brother right down to the white suit, black bow tie, and snowy goatee.

The sign on his desk proclaimed him to be Edward Minnieweather, owner and proprietor of Minnieweather Process Servers. Edward appeared mildly surprised to have this many people in his office, all at the same time, and one with hand cuffs still attached to his wrists.

Bubba was getting tired of running around town. He said simply, "Mark Evans."

Edward blinked.

Bubba said, "Where. Is. Mark. Evans."

263

Willodean sighed.

Tee glanced at his watch.

Mike farted and pretended that Precious did it.

Precious tried to get as far away from Mike as she could. It was very difficult considering that it was a very small office.

"Hospital," Edward said.

Everyone's attention focused solely on Edward Minnieweather.

"He was serving papers on Dan Gollihugh," Edward explained, as if that was enough.

For Bubba it was. Daniel Lewis Gollihugh was the biggest (7 feet tall), baddest (four felony arrests, two convictions, one dismissal, and one that was pending), most obnoxious (one of the arrests was for peeing on a police car while the police officer was in the car) individual in all of Pegram County. He went through wives like candy and was working on wife number six. Additionally, he didn't care for authority (as significantly evidenced by his aggravated urination on an official vehicle). Finally, he had an infamous temper (upon learning of his latest wife's wish to divorce him, he had dumped a load of cow manure in the back of her Ford Mustang convertible and slugged the mailman just because the unfortunate person happened to be delivering mail at the wrong time).

Every police officer in Pegram County knew about Dan Gollihugh. One didn't go to his farmhouse property without backup of at least ten other officers in full riot gear. One didn't go without having pepper spray, Tasers, and the heavy-duty bean bag gun. It was very likely that the police would use all three in the process of apprehending Dan. And lastly, one didn't go to his place on a Friday or Saturday night whilst Dan was likely to be drunk on homemade rotgut and ten times more agitated than usual.

"Mark Evans went to serve divorce papers on Dan last night around nine PM," Edward said by way of explanation.

"That poor, poor bastard," Tee said pityingly, referring to Mark Evans, not Dan Gollihugh.

Even Mike had heard of Dan. "What did Mark ever do to you?" he asked Edward derisively, as if Mike knew both Mark and Dan personally.

"I told the kid to wait until this morning," Edward said hastily. "Told him three times, but he said he had a psych class on Saturdays he didn't like to miss. Something about the cute blonde with dreadlocks who does work for me sometimes."

"Yeah, she's awful cute," Mike murmured, thinking of her Jim Morrison t-shirt.

Willodean and Bubba were still staring at Edward. Bubba said, "You sent Mark Evans to serve divorce papers to Dan Gollihugh, and Mark is now in the hospital because Dan made mincemeat out of him. Would that be about right, fella?"

Willodean nodded firmly in agreement of Bubba's question.

Edward nodded slowly. "Yes."

Bubba unhurriedly scanned the room. In the back of his mind he was looking for the eleven herbs and spices that made up Colonel Sanders's secret chicken recipe. It wasn't there. Truthfully, he was running out of ideas and patience. Melvin Wetmore and Mary Bradley's statements were enough to cast a shadow of doubt upon Bubba's guilt. As a matter of fact, Willodean was looking upon him with an expression akin to pity.

Pity. Bubba frowned. He didn't want pity from Willodean. And he needed a whole lot more than a little doubt to clear his name. Sheriff John wasn't going to go for it. As a matter of fact, Bubba would be elevated to the level of master criminal for such inventive planning.

"Can he...uh...talk?" Mike said. "Whatshisname? Mark?"

Edward shook his head. "Dunno. Cracked ribs. One broken tibia. A fractured collarbone. A shattered patella. Three missing teeth. Three fingers sprained. Believe Dan stomped on his hand at one point in time. And...well, finally, Dan decided to put poor Mark back into his car." Colonel Sanders's long-missing twin brother grimaced in compassion. "Via his head through the front windshield. I went to visit him this morning and he's on one of those machines that injects morphine directly into the veins. Mark didn't flicker a single eyelid while I was there."

Bubba let out a breath that was the last vestige of hope of his future freedom. If Mark Evans were conscious, he might be able to tell them who had tipped him off about getting fired from Bufford's. Mark had said something about it when he had served Bubba his grand jury notice. Bubba hadn't been at the top of his game that day and it had slipped past him. But it wasn't slipping past him now.

They had to try, however. All of them loaded up, drove to Pegram County General Hospital, where a nurse screamed at them about the hygiene of animals, until Willodean said that Precious was a seeing-eye dog and Mike pretended that he was blind, stumbling crookedly into a wall, a coke machine, and a little old lady in a wheelchair, until the determined nurse

266

relented. They badgered another nurse into taking them into the critical care unit, where they ended up staring down at Mark Evans, who was thankfully (for him), unconscious.

Mark was a mass of bruises, casts, bandages, and tubes. Dan Gollihugh had wiped the proverbial floor with him and then squeezed him out to dry.

"I don't think he's coming to, any time soon," said the nurse not unkindly.

"Well crap," Mike said. "I mean, carp. You're going to have to wait until he wakes up."

Bubba didn't say anything. It could be days, weeks, or months before Mark woke up. Provided he woke up at all. *The pathetic, dumb son of a bitch.*

"Jesus Christ have mercy," said a new voice. "Do you know how hard it was to track you down, Bubba Snoddy? Do you have any idea how many places you've been today since skipping out of the jail? Do you know how much gossip is circulating in this cesspool that we call home?"

Everyone in the crowded hospital room turned to look at the latest addition. It was Miz Demetrice, and boy-howdy, was she ticked off.

Chapter Twenty

Bubba Goes to Jail...Again...But Not Before a Little Trip
to the Local Bordello

Saturday

There Miz Demetrice Snoddy stood in all her livid
glory. She was wearing the same charcoal gray suit
she had on when she'd reluctantly stepped on board
the Amtrak train, with not inconsiderable assistance
from her son, Bubba Snoddy. She was missing her bag
and her hair was mussed as if she had been driving in a
convertible with the top down. The teeth-gnashing
expression on her face spoke of the future hell that lay
in Bubba's life concerning his recent betrayal. There
was a silent, tall man standing behind her fretfully
shuffling his feet.

Miz Demetrice glanced angrily at the rest of the
group and then at Precious who hid behind Tee
Gearheart. Lastly, she looked briefly at Mark Evans
who was lying supremely unconscious in the hospital
bed. She brought her glare back to Bubba and then
instantly went back to Mark. "What in the name of
holy peaches and cream happened to him?" She took a
step forward. "Is that that young man who served you
your papers the other day, Bubba? Did you beat him
up? My Lord, the young man looks like Elgin the time I
tried to run him down with the bush hog. The mean
bastard was more resilient than I figured. Of course,
that didn't stop me from drowning him later." •

Willodean blinked slowly.

"Ma, Pa died of a heart attack," Bubba said patiently. "And I didn't touch Mark Evans. Dan Gollihugh got to him first."

"Dan Gollihugh," Miz Demetrice repeated. Then with abrupt comprehension, she added, "Oh. Oh, that's not good."

The critical care nurse, who had been in a state of shock, suddenly came to her senses and declared authoritatively, "Everyone's going to have to clear out of here. Especially the dog."

Before anyone could tell the nurse that Precious was a seeing-eye dog or Mike could stumble into a wall or piece of equipment, Precious went to nip the nurse's ankle. Bubba caught Precious by the collar before any damage could be accomplished. However, the group obediently piled out of the room, leaving Mark alone and blissfully unaware of the glorious melodrama that was occurring all around him.

Bubba let go of Precious and pointed at the tall man who had followed Miz Demetrice into the hospital. "Who the heck is that, Ma?"

"Oh, that's Joe Bruce," she answered reasonably. "He gave me a ride back when the Amtrak stopped in Waxahachie. Right friendly fella. Told him all about the goings on around here and he thought he'd take a gander."

"Hey," Joe Bruce said. He was in his fifties, well over six feet tall, and had inquisitive gray eyes. Bubba sized him up and decided he was harmless. Miz Demetrice had probably told him about the Snoddy Mansion and the Snoddy estates, and Joe Bruce thought he was going to hook a live one. If that was truly the case, then Bubba would quickly and unequivocally dissuade Joe Bruce.

"Now what?" Willodean said. Tee nodded in agreement of the question.

Mike Holmgreen said, "You talked to Melvin. He corroborated your story. So did Mary Bradley. Probably Mark Evans would too, ifin he were awake. If that isn't enough to suggest Bubba is innocent, then I reckon you need to find that guy that filmed all those cops beating up that guy in L.A. and ask him who his lawyer was."

Tee lightly smacked Mike on the back of his head. "Son, do you even know what corroborate means?"

Miz Demetrice was mentally chewing on the information she had received. "Bubba, why are you wearing handcuffs? And all these people are saying that someone set it up so you would be the only one at Bufford's that night. So you'd be the one everyone thought was guilty?"

"Someone cut the security camera wires at Bufford's," Bubba said.

"But Sheriff John said they were fake," Miz Demetrice said indignantly.

"They are," Mike said.

Miz Demetrice eyed Mike suspiciously until she figured out who he was. "Don't you have some school to burn down?"

"Don't mind her," Bubba said kindly. "She's just mad because someone dropped a house on her sister."

Miz Demetrice and Tee gasped in unison. Bubba added, "I know you're angry, Ma, but take it out on me, not the kid."

Willodean gritted her teeth and thought about going home to her quiet and cozy place, listening to Nina Simone sing the sultry blues, and drinking some chamomile tea after she was summarily dismissed for

270

gross dereliction of duty. Finally, she ungritted her teeth and said, "Bubba, what next? I'm out of ideas and what I should do is run the three of you," she was including Mike, Tee, and Bubba in that count, "back to the jail."

Miz Demetrice quickly got into the swing of things. The beautiful deputy, the oversized jailor, and the absconding arsonist were all on Bubba's side. It was a whole lot better than nothing. "What have we got?" she asked. "I mean, what's the evidence that proves Bubba's been set up?"

"Everyone was systematically lured away from Bufford's that night," Bubba said. "Leaving me."

"Someone cut the security camera wires, not knowing that they're fake," Mike added.

"Someone called ex-fiancée up and got her to gallivant down to Texas on account of Bubba," Tee said.

Joe Bruce said, "And they called Melissa Dearman from the Snoddy Mansion."

"And that same someone killed Neal Ledbetter and planted the rifle in the back of Bubba's truck," Willodean mused. "But they wiped all the prints off the weapon, which doesn't seem like something Bubba would do if he were putting the gun back into his own truck." Then she turned and looked intently at Bubba. "So what does Melissa Dearman have to do with someone getting their hands on the Snoddy properties?"

"Her? Not a damn thing," Bubba muttered irately. "She just happened to be a woman that, if she were murdered, I could be easily framed for her death. She would have been easier to get to come to Pegramville than her husband would have been, as he was in Italy.

271

Once Melissa was dead and I was suitably framed, I suspect Miz Demetrice would have been forced to sell off the Snoddy Mansion and the Snoddy lands to pay for a decent lawyer. Neal Ledbetter would have swooped in with a take-it-or-leave-it offer, betting that Miz Demetrice would have been so demoralized by the whole sorry affair that she would have taken it immediately." He glanced at his mother. "Neal definitely would have been underestimating Mama." It wasn't a compliment and he didn't mean it to be.

Miz Demetrice glared.

"Then Neal would have gotten the property to be the next Walmart Supercenter, and his collaborators in crime would have all the time in the world to find what they were looking for." Bubba went on, ignoring his mother.

"Oh, for the love of St. Peter," Willodean cursed. "What the hell were they looking for?"

"Confederate gold," Bubba said slowly. "A whole wagon load of it. Stolen from the Confederacy in 1864. That's what that article in People Magazine was all about. Lost treasure. That's why there are about a million holes in the ground on the Snoddy properties. That's why someone broke into the library and stole Colonel Snoddy's private papers. Gold. Gold. And a little more gold."

Miz Demetrice groaned. "Damned frumpy Miz Clack should have called and told me about the stolen papers. Uptight librarian."

The expression on Willodean's face was as priceless as the smile on the Mona Lisa. It declared with great skepticism that she didn't believe it. The Snoddy stolen Confederate gold story was a big fat crock, and a tall tale, and the smelliest horse poop she'd ever smelled.

Tee nodded and added, "Folks have been running out to the Snoddy place for the last hundred years to dig a hole here or there. The fact that ain't no one found it don't seem to be stopping people."

Joe Bruce said with an avaricious note, "How much gold is in a wagon load?"

Miz Demetrice rolled her eyes. "Hundreds of pounds. Do you need a calculator, dear?" She stopped to gather her thoughts and then added, "Before I murdered Elgin by putting a rattlesnake in his bed, he used to go out and frequently dig holes, especially when he was drunk. He never found anything either. And Elgin knew about the truth of the matter. Couldn't help himself."

"Okay, I'll buy lost Confederate gold as a reason," Willodean said reluctantly. "But how about who?"

"Do we have time for one more trip?" Bubba asked with a devilish glint in his eye. "You won't regret it."

Twenty minutes later they were standing in a lavishly decorated living room. Red velvet abounded. Satin glimmered in the light of real Tiffany stained-glassed lamps. A lead crystal chandelier stridently glittered its proclamation that gaudy but dazzling garnishment was not dead. When someone said that a room was decorated like early American whorehouse, they were talking about this room, right down to the actual-sized portrait of a naked woman leaning over a red velvet chair.

Bubba, Willodean, Miz Demetrice, Mike, Tee, Joe Bruce, and Precious were all staring up at the portrait of Miss Annalee Hyatt, savior of Pegramville from the Union.

Doris Cambliss had let them in without aplomb and hadn't even commented when Bubba had told her what they needed to look at. "What took you so long?" she asked knowingly. Bubba blinked with trifling confusion.

"Wow," Mike said, his eyes locked on the portrait.

"Shut your mouth before you drool on the carpet," Tee instructed. He'd seen the portrait before but he didn't want to admit it where it might get back to Poppiann in her delicate and highly volatile state. That was Tee's major A-number-One rule lately: Thou shall not upset a pregnant woman. He intended on following that rule diligently.

Joe Bruce said, "Good Golly, Miss Molly."

"Miss Annalee," Bubba corrected lightly.

"You know," Miz Demetrice said quietly, "I always wanted to see what this portrait looked like. Elgin, before I shot him dead with a muzzle-loader, used to visit the Red Door Inn frequently." She folded her arms across her chest and carefully scrutinized the portrait. Then she tilted her head to one side. Unconsciously, Bubba, Tee, and Mike did the same thing.

"Does that look like...?"

"She seems like she reminds me of..."

"She's the spitting image," Miz Demetrice said firmly. "I cain't believe you fools never noticed it before."

"A portrait doesn't prove anything," Willodean said cautiously. "It could be a coincidence."

"Mama," Bubba said, "do you remember where Miss Annalee Hyatt's daughter hailed from when she came to visit Pegramville?"

"I believe Mother Snoddy," she said, referring to Bubba's paternal grandmother, "said she was from someplace in the West. The Northwest, if I recollect correctly."

"That might be someplace like Oregon or Washington," Bubba said musingly.

"Yep," Tee said. "Poppiann wants to visit Mount St. Helens one day, so she can see it pop." He grimaced. "Don't know what's got her thinking that way. Anyway, they call that whole section the Northwest."

"Wow," Mike said again.

"You know, Washington," Miz Demetrice said calculatingly. "The state."

"But why now? Why not Miss Annalee's daughter or her grandchildren? Why now?" Tee asked quietly.

"Something happened," Bubba said. "Like someone looked through an old chest. Someone read some old diaries. Something. Maybe they were doing some genealogy and dug up something in some old letter their mother had stuck in the middle of a family bible. They came across that old *People* article and suddenly discovered a love for old papers."

Willodean sighed hard. "Will someone please explain what in the name of Jehoshaphat you are all talking about?"

Bubba said firmly, "We've got to go one more place."

"Do we have to leave?" Mike asked plaintively, his eyes glued to the portrait.

"Yes," Tee said. "Your mother's going to kill me. So's your grandmother, when she finds out about this. So's my boss. Maybe Poppiann, too."

"It's real close to the jail," Bubba said convincingly, correctly gauging Willodean's rising level of reluctance.

Willodean looked pointedly at her watch. "One more place. No more people, dogs, rats, bats, or naked ladies allowed."

They arrived at the Pegramville Café en masse. It was an odd assortment of people, an animal, and vehicles. Miz Demetrice drove with Joe Bob in his late 70s Porsche convertible. The car was as ragged and questionable as he was. Tee drove Precious and Mike in the minivan. Bubba got back into the county car with Willodean. Doris cheerfully followed in her Cadillac having decided she couldn't miss the denouement.

They all clambered out of various and sundry cars and stood in an awkward circle. Then Sheriff John showed up and very publicly re-arrested Bubba Snoddy. He led Bubba away to his county car, saying loudly, "We've got all the evidence we need to put you away until they stick the needle in you. You ain't gonna see the daylight ever again!"

Miz Demetrice and Precious both wailed in unison. Then Miz Demetrice yelled theatrically, "I cain't take this no more! I'm going to Dallas to stay with my sister! Come on, Joe Bruce!"

Joe Bruce shrugged regretfully.

Chapter Twenty-One

What the Heck Happens to Bubba?

Saturday (still, but later in the day, much later, in fact, it was almost Sunday, but not quite)

Well after the sun had set and under cover of darkness a lone old, rusting Pontiac Grand Am drove down the road in front of the Snoddy Mansion. Its headlights were off, and it carefully maneuvered down the shadowed lane. It slowed down as it went past the crookedly hanging front gate with its three-foot-sized 'S' on either side. The Grand Am cruised down to Roscoe Stinedurf's driveway, turned around, and cruised back. Finally, it drove off into the night going back the direction of town.

Fifteen minutes after that, the very same Grand Am car returned and sat in front of the gates for a long time with its lights still turned off. Ultimately, a decision was made, and the car went through the open gate, progressed down the Snoddy driveway, and parked around the side of the house, where it would not be visible from the road. Two people got out, careful not to allow the interior light of the car to go on, as they opened the car doors.

One said, "Are you sure about this?"

The other said, "Of course I'm sure. Bubba's in jail but for good. Everyone and their sister's cat heard Sheriff John say they wouldn't be letting him out this time. His mother is off to Dallas. And the housekeeper doesn't live in. You know that."

"Well, we've looked all over the house before and dint find nothing."

"We didn't have much time before." The other was irritated and allowed it to show. "I told you I have access to papers about the damned house. There was that hidden door, wasn't I right about that?"

"Well, yes," replied the first one.

"My great-great-grandmother was Miss Annalee Hyatt's illegitimate daughter, and her son was illegitimate, too. That's how I ended up with the same name," said the other. "Anyway, Great Granny kept all kinds of diaries about what her mother used to talk about. She said there was a wagon full of gold stolen from the Union soldiers in 1864 that was never recovered. I did all of the research. It was never recovered. And since the Snoddys don't seem as though they're living high on the hog, it stands to reason that it's still here someplace."

"I know all that," snapped the first one. "But we could simply wait until Bubba's convicted and the mother is forced to sell the property to pay the lawyers. Then Neal Ledbetter was going to make the place a Walmart. That was the plan."

"A Walmart *Supercenter* and I don't want to wait," said the other. "We've waited long enough. I've spent too much time waiting around. Get the shovels and the metal detector."

"They're in the trunk."

"Get them then."

"I got a problem with all this," said the first one.

"Yeah?"

"What's to stop you from doing the same thing to me as you did to Neal Ledbetter?" asked the first one.

278

"Darlin', I would never do that to you. You know how stupid Neal was being. I cannot believe that he planted some piece of electronic crap in the house to scare off Miz Demetrice. Something he bought at Radio Shack. He was so proud of it he told me all about it." The other sighed. "He would have folded on us. Do you want to go to jail for murdering that Dearman woman?"

"I didn't murder her," protested the first one. "You snuck off from Grubbo's, came here, shot her, and then went back to the tavern."

The other snorted. "So I pulled the trigger. It doesn't matter. You were there. You helped with all of the planning. You're as guilty as anyone. Just ask a cop. And don't forget about setting fire to Bubba's house."

There was the sound of keys rattling, metal scraping on metal, and the first said, "Here's the dammit shovels."

"Okay then," the second one said. "Fifty paces due south from the southwest corner of the mansion is an old oak stump."

"What the hell is this? You never said anything about an old oak stump before," the first one said angrily.

"Sweetums," the second one replied plaintively, "we needed to see what the Snoddys had inside before we started digging around their place, and besides, I said we had to eliminate all the places the treasure could be located first. Besides Miss Annalee said the Colonel told her about twenty places that he had buried the gold. We've been saving the places closest to the mansion because we couldn't hide the holes there. Right?"

"Well, okay," the first one grumbled.

They stumbled to the southwest corner of the mansion, consulted a glow in the dark compass, and counted fifty paces. "There's no frigging stump," the first one complained immediately.

"It was written right after the Civil War, baby," the second one explained. "The stump probably rotted away a hundred years ago. Use the metal detector."

There was a series of long beeps and whistles. Then there was a very loud whine. "Omigod," said the first one elatedly. "Something's here. Something really, really big."

"I knew it," the second one said confidently.

Then they started to dig, using one flashlight and occasionally consulting the metal detector. While they dug, Bubba Snoddy thought about the recent turn of events. He sat hidden in the shadows about fifty feet away from the pair of diggers, along with several other people and several sophisticated listening and recording devices. He would have never believed that it could have been that easy, but it was. The entire time Sheriff John had had his doubts about Bubba's guilt. So had Deputy Willodean Gray. Willodean had discovered the unhealed dog-bite wounds on Neal Ledbetter's left leg and knew that he had been the 'ghost' haunting the Snoddy Mansion. Although that might very well have been a reason for Bubba to murder Neal, it was also something that put a hole in the whole Bubba/murderer theory. What kind of man wipes a weapon clean and then hides it in a woodpile? What kind of murderer wipes a rifle clean and puts it in the back of his truck where anyone could see it? They didn't know right off the bat, but it wasn't Bubba.

The first thing that Sheriff John had said when he'd gotten Bubba in the jail cell was, "What about Melvin Wetmore, Mark Evans, and Mary Bradley, Bubba?"

Willodean answered. "Melvin Wetmore got hired for a job at the Walmart up the road. Someone called him up and said to show up on Thursday evening. When Melvin showed up, it turned out there wasn't really a job." Willodean smiled at Bubba and Bubba felt his heart drop. "Melvin was real put out. Said someone had played a mean trick on him."

"And Mark Evans?" Sheriff John said.

"Mark Evans quit on Thursday night, the same Thursday night. Turns out some anonymous soul called him up and told him that George Bufford was about to falsely accuse him of theft to get some insurance money or something of the like. Mark woke up in the hospital about an hour ago." Willodean had winked at Bubba. Or at least he had tiredly thought she did. It could have been a speck of dirt caught in her beautiful green eye. He surely hoped not. "So he called up to quit and that got Bubba all by his lonesome."

Bubba had stopped himself from scratching at his pits, remembering just in time that was something he didn't want to do in front of Willodean. "It didn't seem rightly important," he'd said, looking down at the offending hand and then putting it down quickly.

"Finally, there's Mary Bradley," Willodean had said quietly. "She wasn't at Bufford's Gas and Groceries that night. Care to tell the Sheriff what she does for a living, Bubba?"

"Mostly she lives off her ex-husband's alimony, and sometimes she's the relief cashier at Bufford's, when she's not taking her mother to places to play...um...games," Bubba had said solemnly. "She didn't answer her phone on Thursday night. Or at least that's what I thought happened."

Willodean had nodded. "Turns out her phone lines went down that night. The telephone company came by and told her some kids must have been fooling around with the wires just outside her house." She'd made a scissoring motion with her hand consciously imitating Bubba when he had done the same motion with Mary Bradley. "All cut."

Sheriff John's lips had made an 'O' of surprise.

"Finally," Willodean had announced, "there were those dummy security cameras at Bufford's. Turns out someone who didn't know that they weren't, cut their wires, too. All the employees knew about it, including Bubba, so why would he have bothered with that?"

All of which added up to a great big conspiracy to frame Bubba. Willodean had figured that out, but she and Sheriff John couldn't quite figure why this would have been the case.

On the other hand, Bubba had known. And he had told them. His evidence was scanty. First, there was the green button. It was retrieved from Tee Gearheart's possession and shown to the law enforcement officers. It was generally agreed upon that it wasn't a typical kind of button. Then Deputy Simms had said, "You know that button looks like the kind that are on Miss Lurlene's green sweater that she wears in the café when Noey Wheatfall turns up the air conditioning too high."

Bubba had stared at the officers. He told them where he found the button. He told them that he asked his mother about the button right in front of Lurlene, and she had kept her mouth firmly shut, even acted strange about it. Then there had been all the questions she had asked Bubba about the Snoddy family history over the entire time they had dated. There had also been her interest in the Civil War period.

"Which has to do with what?" Sheriff John had asked. "That's all circumstantial, Bubba."

"Do you remember the *People* article?"

Sheriff John had remembered. He was the one who had had to deal with trespassers looking for buried treasure on the Snoddy properties for untold years. And Miz Demetrice had shot two of them with salt rock.

But Bubba had explained for the deputies and especially for Willodean. "People wrote an article about ghosts and Civil War treasure. One of the houses featured was the Snoddy Mansion. My mother, Miz Demetrice, embellished some of the old stories because she was always looking for more revenues in the spring and fall openings. Her reasoning was that more people would visit the place just to see a haunted house. But it backfired on her because more treasure hunters came calling than anyone else. Digging holes on every inch of the property. Running all over the place at nights with flashlights and four-wheel drives. My own father even believed the stories. Went out and dug quite a few holes in the company of a pint of vodka."

"What was the story?" Deputy Simms had asked.

"My ancestor was Colonel Nathaniel Snoddy, who was a Confederate officer. He was involved in a group of soldiers who robbed anything with a Union flag on it. One of the things they robbed was a load of gold from a Union train in 1864. And that is well-documented. That actually happened. Where my mother varied from the truth was that she told that reporter that Colonel Snoddy's ghost still haunts the place looking for a wagon full of gold that had been his share. He hid it somewhere on the land but died before he could recover it. And since he didn't tell anyone else about it, his ghost still looks for it." Bubba had shaken his head sadly, as if commiserating for the ghost of his distant ancestor.

"So what really happened?" Sheriff John had asked.

Bubba snapped to the present and listened to the sounds of digging. It had become less frantic as they had dug deeper and deeper. Willodean poked Bubba in his side and whispered, "Why do we have to wait until they dig it up? It's going to take forever."

Smiling in the shadows, Bubba whispered back. "So they'll be good and tired when Sheriff John and you all arrest them." Sheriff John had been amenable to the idea. He didn't mind if everyone waited and got the legend off the books. Either there was gold under where the old oak stump had been located and it would be finished, or there wasn't and it would be finished.

An hour later, the sound of a shovel hitting metal made everyone sit up straight. The first voice said, "I found it. Holy Jesus God, I found it."

The other voice said, "Brush it off! Hurry, what is it? Coins? Bullion? Ingots?"

The furious efforts of frenzied digging started anew. There were a few frantic curses. Then they paused for the longest time. Finally, the first voice said in a heavily strained tone, "Is that what I think it is?"

"Motherfucking son of a bitch!" the second voice screamed furiously. "It's a...it's a goddamned..."

Bubba recalled the answer to Sheriff John's question of, "So what really happened?"

Here was what Bubba had said: "Colonel Nathaniel Snoddy was an inveterate philanderer who made his wife, Cornelia Adams Snoddy, a most miserable woman by sleeping with anything with...uh, breasts, beg pardon, Deputy Gray. But old Nate, he wasn't quite right in the head. He'd slept with one woman too many and had contracted syphilis, which had apparently gone into his brain. He brought back a wagon full of something in 1865, telling everyone it was gold, but the truth was that he was crazy by that time, and he brought back a load of rusted-out iron. He spent some time burying it some damn place and then died of syphilis." Bubba had shaken his head sadly. "As far as I know old Nate never haunted the Snoddy Mansion. More likely he would have haunted the Red Door Inn. Miss Annalee Hyatt was one of his favorite prostitutes, and it's said that she gave him the syphilis which killed him. Supposedly, she gave it to the Union colonel who was so enamored of her, too. A little historical irony."

"So someone's looking for the so-called gold?" Sheriff John had asked incredulously.

"Not just anyone, but you should have a look at Miss Annalee's portrait in the Red Door Inn. I'm sure Miz Cambliss will show it to you. It looks just like Miss Lurlene." Bubba had hesitated, a little ashamed of himself. "Or at least her face does. I'm not rightly sure about the rest. I don't think that Lurlene Grady is her real name."

"It's not," Sheriff John had said. "And although this sounds like something out of a dime novel. It fills in some of the details. You see, Bubba, we have records of phone calls made to and from the Dearman residence. We figured that we could catch you in a lie about having contacted Melissa Dearman." Bubba had already known that, but he didn't let on with Sheriff John about where the information had come from.

And Bubba had already knew that he hadn't called Melissa. Sheriff John had went on, "We only found the one call from your house to Melissa Dearman's, and we also found five calls from Lurlene Grady to Melissa Dearman." He had stared at Bubba's face. "At first I thought you'd called from her place, but she confirmed you ain't never been there. So did the landlord. Said two other fellas had been though. One who seems like it might have been Neal Ledbetter. So we got Miss Lurlene's phone records, and she's made all kinds of calls to Neal Ledbetter. The same with Neal's phone records, fifteen calls in the last week to Miss Lurlene and seven to the Pegram Café. There was a fingerprint on the cartridge in the .45. Clear as day. It belongs to a Miss Donna Hyatt of Spokane, Washington. A woman with a record of fraud and larceny a mile long. We got her driver's license picture about two hours after I arrested you. Miss Donna Hyatt and Miss Lurlene Grady is one and the same woman."

There was a certain amount of shock involved. Up until the time when the murderers so casually confessed to the planning and murdering of a completely innocent woman, Bubba had assumed the best of the worst scenario, that Melissa had come to see him to apologize for past deeds and simply been in the wrong place at the wrong time. But the truth was far more insidious. The theory was that she had been lured by Lurlene in order to frame Bubba for murder. The story about Bubba and his ex-fiancée was well-known in the community. It was only a matter of finding the details. Then there was the simple process of stealing a gun from Miz Demetrice's house. That was another well-known fact in the community; Miz Demetrice liked to keep guns around her house. The gun was used in the murder, wiped clean, and then hidden in Bubba's woodpile, where the police would almost certainly find it, which they had with the help of an anonymous phone call.

It was true that all of this evidence was circumstantial, but they had a partial confession on tape, as they had all listened to the conversation between Lurlene Grady and Noey Wheatfall, her erstwhile companion in crime. Bubba had seen the three conspirators together at the strip mall on Farmer's Road himself.

Lurlene was really Donna Hyatt, of Spokane, Washington. She hadn't really been born in Georgia after all. She had in her possession diaries from her ancestors narrating the treasure story or at least the popular version. She also had Colonel Snoddy's stolen papers from the library. Half the town of Pegramville had seen Colonel Snoddy drive into the town with a covered wagon, which he had guarded ruthlessly. She happened upon the People article years after it had been written and figured she had as good a chance to find the gold as anyone. She even did some research on the Snoddy family, figuring that they hadn't found the gold either, and then moved down South, with a new name, and a new accent that sometimes went away. She had slowly gotten Noey into the act, followed by Neal Ledbetter, who had stumbled on them, when they were looking for the gold one evening. They had figured that all three could get what they wanted by simply removing Bubba and Miz Demetrice from the property. So they would frame Bubba for the murder of his ex-fiancée, and Miz Demetrice would have to sell the place for money to defend her son. Neal would be waiting to buy the place up. They would get to search for the gold at their leisure, and Neal would get to make the place a Walmart Supercenter. Everyone would be happy except for perhaps Bubba and Miz Demetrice.

Except there was one little niggling detail; Bubba wasn't so easy to frame. And he found the button that Lurlene/Donna had lost the night she had shot Melissa in the back. A button from a sweater that she had been wearing that night that the murder occurred, that shouldn't be on Bubba's porch because Lurlene/Donna had never been on Bubba's porch, as far as Bubba knew. So there were the break-ins to recover the button, and then the fire, both of which failed. Then Bubba saw the cardigan hanging in the Pegram Café, and it all came to him in a sudden flash of knowledge. The sweater, Lurlene/Donna, the full-length portrait of Miss Annalee Hyatt, the missing Snoddy diaries from the library, the holes in the property, the missing forty-five. All of it.

Bubba couldn't even manage a hoarse laugh. It wasn't funny. Lurlene, AKA Donna Hyatt, had killed two people for a supposed wagon full of gold. There was sad, pitiful irony in all of that. It might very well been avoided, if she had just asked Bubba about the legend. His mother might still protect the Colonel's not-so-sainted memory, but Bubba would have told her the real story without reservations as he had to other people upon occasion.

The Snoddys hadn't had a pot to piss in after the Civil War. There was the mansion and the caretaker's place. There were only fixtures left in the house, with a lot of blank walls, where various artworks had been sold off to support them. All the Confederate money that had been left over had been burned in the fire place in 1869 because it had been a very cold winter, and the money had been worthless. The Snoddys lived on revenues from his grandfather's clothing sales business that had been sold to Sears in 1956. It wasn't much but it still supported Miz Demetrice nicely.

With the Sheriff and the deputies convinced of his innocence, Bubba pleaded with them to stake out the Snoddy Mansion. Lurlene/Donna and Noey had been present in the café when Bubba had been arrested the third and fourth times and had heard Miz Demetrice's declaration to return to Dallas via a beat-up Porsche convertible. They didn't have Neal to buy the place anymore so they would have to search at night when no one was around. This particular Saturday night was perfect for rooting out lost Yankee treasure.

To Bubba's surprise Sheriff John had agreed and even took Bubba along. They set up recording devices and an amplifier to listen to any conversation the two had. Sheriff John even had someone tail the pair from the café, where it became obvious that something was up because Noey Wheatfall closed the restaurant early on a Saturday night.

Bubba was amazed that after everything he had gone through, that it turned out to be so damned easy. Not only was it easy but the pair of murdering would-be thieves got to dig up a rotting 1946 Chevy truck. One of his great-uncles, who had supported the Republican candidate, Dwight E. Eisenhower, had

289

stolen it from the governor of Texas in 1952 because he was a damned Democrat. Stealing the truck and burying it in the backyard was about the only way he could think to teach the damned idiot governor a lesson. When the great uncle buried the truck he found the load of rusted-out pig iron and such, and the whole Snoddy clan had a big laugh about the so-called buried treasure. It was common knowledge that there had never been Confederate gold on Snoddy property. Not then and certainly not in the present.

But Lurlene, also known as Donna Hyatt, had loudly and clearly incriminated herself, and then gave up without incident, only pausing to snarl at Noey, "You better not say nothing to anyone." Any hint of a Southern accent had gone and apparently was gone forever.

Even Noey had been dumbfounded at the sudden appearance of a dozen police officers all around them. But the tape of the murder confession was strong evidence against them. Bubba didn't know it, but Sheriff John was planning on getting Noey alone to work out a deal with him. He thought that Noey would testify against Lurlene/Donna if he were promised a lighter deal in this whole mess.

Sheriff John stood beside his county car, watching the deputies secure the suspects, when Bubba stepped up beside him, Precious following at his heels. "Hey, Bubba," Sheriff John said.

"Hey," said Bubba. "You owe me an apology."

Sheriff John choked for a moment. "I don't think so."

"Cain't you even say you was wrong about me?"

"I notice that your accent goes country when you want it to," Sheriff John remarked, folding his massive arms across his chest.

Bubba mimicked the motion. "So does yours."

Sheriff John shrugged. "For your information, I've always had doubts about your guilt. So I wasn't necessarily wrong."

Bubba shrugged, too. He looked at Lurlene, no, it was Donna Hyatt. She was handcuffed and being held by one arm by Willodean Gray, listening as another deputy rattled off her rights to her. He knew that Sheriff John had ultimately been persuaded by Willodean herself, upon the issue of Bubba's innocence. She had done the digging that had come up with the information on the telephone records and the driver's license photo of Donna Hyatt of Spokane, Washington. "You mind if I say something to her?" Bubba asked, referring to Lurlene/Donna.

"You're not gonna hurt that woman?" Sheriff John asked, only half serious. Privately, he was glad that an arrest was made and that it wasn't Bubba who was going to be staying in jail. Bubba was a popular fella, and the townsfolk were looking at the sheriff like he was a mean, mean man of late. But not only that, it turned out that that young woman he'd hired was a fine detective and would probably do very well in the Pegram County Sheriff's Department in the future. And that was even if her methods weren't always above board.

"Won't touch her," vowed Bubba.

"Go ahead." Sheriff John waved him on.

Bubba approached Lurlene/Donna and gazed down into her face. It seemed a different face now, a face full of sly intent and even coldly homicidal

291

tendencies. There was not only that, but her features almost seemed a mirror image of the heroine, Miss Annalee. Why hadn't he seen it before? Maybe it was because he hadn't looked at Miss Annalee's portrait for years before that one night he'd dropped off the drunken Major Dearman.

Lurlene/Donna returned his scrutiny, saying nothing. He had intended to tell her that there wasn't any gold, that it had only been a pile of rusting junk, that she had murdered two people for no good reason, but clipped it short on his tongue. Instead, he said, "Miss Lur-uh-Donna, I don't think we should see each other anymore."

Donna's eyes opened up wide. After a long time, she said incredulously, "You're breaking up with me, Bubba?"

"I don't associate with people of your ilk," he said, with a regal air that would have reminded anyone instantly of Miz Demetrice had they been listening.

The other woman stared at Bubba as though she couldn't believe what she was hearing. Finally, she screamed, "BITE ME!"

Willodean happily restrained her prisoner and finally shoved her into the back of a police car with the assistance of another deputy. Bubba said cheerfully, "It's only been seven dates not including lunch with my mother. You're taking this too seriously."

Donna unleashed another string of profanities unfit for man or animal alike. But Willodean shut the county car door on her, and the words instantly became too muffled to understand.

Willodean turned to Bubba with a smile that seemed to light up her whole face. "So, big fella, what do you plan to do now?"

Bubba smiled slowly. "Do you happen to like chocolate Jell-O pudding? I seem to have a real hankering for it of late."

Epilogue

The Legend of Bubba

A few weeks later

"It turned out that Noey Wheatfall did roll over on his partner, the lovely Miss Donna Hyatt of Spokane, Washington. He spilled his guts. Then he spilled a little more," said Lloyd Goshorn, who was a consummate gossip. He stood at the bar of the Dew Drop Inn while a tourist from Dallas bought him all the whiskey he could drink. As a matter of official Pegramville history, Lloyd could drink quite a bit of whiskey before he dropped, and he had proven it on several occasions. "The Major went back to the military and buried his poor wife with full military honors. She had been in the service, too."

"And Bubba Snoddy?" the tourist asked, a man in his late thirties, with a paunch and a Dallas Cowboys cap perched jauntily on his head. He looked at Lloyd as if the other man were speaking the gospel.

"As clean as a brand new washing machine," Lloyd said with a smile. "As innocent as a newborn baby."

"So everything went back to normal?" the tourist's wife asked, sipping on a beer herself. She was a short, fat woman with long brown hair, and her blue eyes were fixed on Lloyd as well.

Lloyd Goshorn shook his head. "No. I didn't say that. Bubba got the girl, the beautiful Willodean Gray, the most beautiful Sheriff's deputy this side of the Mississippi River. They're planning on getting married next spring. They're going to have ten bride's maids, no, maybe twelve and the biggest wedding cake in the history of Texas. Bigger than a car even. They fell in love that very night. They found the gold in the potato cellar, mind you. When it was weighed, it was three hundred pounds of the purest gold on the market today. They dug it all up one night soon after, and sold it on the international market. They say it was worth over seven million dollars because the bricks was all stamped 'Property of the United States of America, 1860.' So they had to sell it in secret. Miz Demetrice Snoddy is fixing the Snoddy Mansion up like when it was brand, spanking new."

"Boy, that's something," the man commented with awe in his voice.

"Sure is," Lloyd replied, finishing off a shot of whiskey. "Another?"

"Bartender," called the man. "Another round here."

"But here's the funniest part," continued Lloyd as they waited for the bartender to bring them the drinks. "Colonel Nathaniel Snoddy is no longer haunting the Snoddy Mansion, rattling chains, and coming through the secret door in the living room."

"No?" breathed the wife.

"He's over at the bordello, only it ain't a bordello no more, the Red Door Inn," Lloyd was sincere. "It's a bed and breakfast with Miss Doris Cambliss running the place. That's where you can see the Colonel waiting for his one and only true love, Miss Annalee Hyatt, the savior of Pegramville from the rampaging, murdering Union troops. He waits for her in front of her portrait, a full-length one of the lady in all her wonderful glory, in the living room of the Red Door

Inn. Maybe when she comes to him, he won't haunt the place no more. So there he sits, waiting for her, all ghostly like, pale, and agleam, only seen in the latest hours of evening with an eerie greenish glow as if from the gas lights of the late 1800's. People have been seeing him for weeks. On nights like this one, with the moon shining through the lead glass windows, so you don't even need a light to walk through the house at midnight. The night as calm and silent as can be. You'll see."

"That's where we're staying," the husband whispered excitedly. The pair of them was wide-eyed, mesmerized with the intricate story of murder, mayhem, ghostly hauntings, and stolen Union gold. It would make a fantastic movie, but it was a great tall tale.

Lloyd nodded, smiling to himself. So what if he aggrandized the truth a little. He considered, *Well, a lot.* What were some colorful, trumped-up additions to a good story? What difference did it make if the story got longer and more embroidered each time he told it and got some whiskey in him?

Maybe that wasn't really the way it happened. But it was the way it should have. It should have.

The End

~

Look for more Bubba in Bubba and the 12 Deadly Days of Christmas.

Bubba Snoddy's got some problems. His family has descended for the Christmas holidays and not in a good way. His cousin wants to own the Snoddy Mansion, decrepit, falling-down columns, termites, wood rot and all and isn't above using manipulative behavior to achieve his ends. Miz Demetrice is up to nefarious and illegal activities while trying to entertain relatives. His cousin's ten-year-old son is the personification of a demon and has hobbies of looking at medical photographs, making stun guns from scratch, and causing havoc wherever he roams. The woman of Bubba's dreams, Deputy Willodean Gray, is still evading his romantic pursuits. Patients from the local mental institute are wandering over the town, ostensibly assisting with the Christmas Festival thanks to a program established by the mayor to cut costs. And Bubba has just found the dead body of a man dressed as Santa in the Christmas scene at City Hall. Oh, Pegramville, Texas is just the best place to be at Christmas if a fella has a bullet proof vest and a linebacker's helmet. All the folks think Bubba might have done did it...again, even though it was proven that he didn't done did it the first time, and Bubba has to move quickly in order to catch a murderer.

About the Author

C.L. Bevill has lived in Texas, Virginia, Arizona, and Oregon. She once was in the US Army and a graphic illustrator. She holds degrees in social psychology and counseling. She is the author of *Bubba and the Dead Woman*, *Bubba and the 12 Deadly Days of Christmas*, *Bayou Moon*, and *Shadow People*, among others. Presently she lives with her husband and her daughter and continues to constantly write. She can be reached at www.clbevill.com or you can read her blog at www.carwoo.blogspot.com

Other Novels by C.L. Bevill

~

Mysteries:

Bubba and the Dead Woman
Bubba and the 12 Deadly Days of Christmas
Bubba and the Missing Woman
Brownie and the Dame
Bubba and the Mysterious Murder Note

Bayou Moon

Paranormal Romance:

Veiled Eyes (Lake People)
Disembodied Bones (Lake People)
Arcanorum (Lake People)

The Moon Trilogy (Novellas):
Black Moon (The Moon Trilogy 1)
Amber Moon (The Moon Trilogy 2)
Silver Moon (The Moon Trilogy 3)

Cat Clan Novellas:
Harvest Moon
Blood Moon
Crescent Moon

Shadow People

Sea of Dreams

Suspense:

The Flight of the Scarlet Tanager

Black Comedy:
*The Life and Death of Bayou Billy
Missile Rats*

Chicklet:
Dial 'M' For Mascara